THE GOD WHO SERIES

Who Touches the Mountains

Deborah Raney

RANEY DAY PRESS

Other books coming soon in
The God Who series
by Deborah Raney

Who Touches the Mountains
Who Stirs Up the Sea
Who Names the Stars
Who Measures the Oceans

For Tarl, firstborn and constant delight of our lives.
For Michelle and Ryleigh,
precious and long-prayed-for additions to our family.
You have brought so much joy into our lives.
And for precious Baby Boy Raney—
we can't wait to meet you!

May the glory of the Lord endure forever; may the Lord rejoice in his works, who looks on the earth and it trembles, who touches the mountains and they smoke! I will sing to the Lord as long as I live; I will sing praise to my God while I have being. May my meditation be pleasing to him, for I rejoice in the Lord.

Psalm 104:31-34
English Standard Version

Author's Note

I was first introduced to the gorgeous Blue Ridge Mountains of North Carolina twenty years ago when I began teaching at the Blue Ridge Mountains Christian Writers Conference at Ridgecrest every spring. Later, I attended a writers retreat there called October in the Mountains. The area around Asheville and Ridgecrest became almost like a second home to my husband and me, and it wasn't long before I knew that someday I wanted to set a novel in this beautiful part of God's creation.

That "someday" finally came about three years ago when I started working on a proposal for what would become The God Who series. I knew that the delightful North Carolina towns of Black Mountain, Chimney Rock, and Montreat would be the prototypes for my fictional town of Willowtree. What I didn't know was that while I was working on the final chapters of this book, Hurricane Helene would devastate these little towns and the surrounding area, causing death and destruction beyond belief, including damage to the property of several personal friends in the path of the storm.

At first, I questioned whether it might be thoughtless to even go ahead and publish the book. I didn't want to appear to be capitalizing on such a tragedy. But then I realized that my story reflects and honors the resilience and fortitude of these people and their towns, and that donating a portion of the sales from this book could be one small way to help these communities rebuild.

While Zach, Liesl, Sadie, and the rest in the charming town of Willowtree, North Carolina are fictional, the real people who make up the communities affected by Hurricane Helene have proven to be beautiful examples of the hands and feet of Christ, serving one another and pulling together, even when all they have to give is themselves. As my friend, Michelle Cox, who calls this area home, put it so profoundly:

As I've watched the beautiful folks from the mountains of North Carolina (my people) these past few weeks, I've never been prouder. Neighbors helping neighbors—even though they've been impacted themselves.

Our area is decimated. Life is anything but normal, but I don't hear people complaining. I hear them saying, "I'm good. I'm blessed. No, give those supplies to someone who needs them more than I do."

Hurricane Helene destroyed the scenic loveliness of the North Carolina mountains, but the true beauty of our mountains lies in the people who live here—and they've never been lovelier.

I recognize the buildings peeking from the flood waters. I'm watching my memories of places I used to shop. Of roads I used to take to bypass traffic on our main busy roads. Of restaurants where we met family and friends for meals and laughter. Of places that have been familiar to me since I was a little girl. Places that are sentimental to me for a variety of reasons. I'm grateful for those memories, heartbroken for the devastation to our area, and thankful that while things can quickly change forever in our lives, Jesus will always be the same. And because of that, all is well."

Yes, my heart, too, aches for the devastating losses, but how thankful I am that God is still on the throne and He holds each one of these precious ones in His hands.

I hope you enjoy *Who Touches the Mountains,* and I pray that you know, personally, the God who touches the mountains, who names the stars, who measures the oceans, and who stirs up the sea. Since I met Him and gave my life to His son, Jesus Christ, I am forever changed for the good.

Chapter One

May

Stooping in front of the toilet, Zach Freylan lifted the dripping toilet brush and cocked his head, listening. The doorbell. He sighed. Leaving the brush resting in the bowl of blue suds, he stripped off the pink rubber gloves and draped them over the edge of the trash can. He'd be glad when school was out and Sadie could get back to cleaning three days a week.

He washed his hands, and on the way down two flights of stairs, dried them on his jeans.

The doorbell chimed again, twice in quick succession. Somebody was sure impatient.

"It's open!" he yelled. Guests who seemed incapable of reading instructions drove him insane. If people would so much as skim the e-mail he sent with every reservation, they would know to come on in, make themselves at home. And leave him alone!

In the entryway, he pushed aside the curtain on the window overlooking the front porch. A nondescript black sedan was parked in front. The man standing on the porch wore a suit and tie and carried no luggage.

Frowning, Zach opened the door. "May I help you?"

"Zachary Freylan?"

"Yes." Zach stepped onto the porch and pulled the door closed behind him.

"I'm Robert Langford with Marta Snelling's office."

"No." Zach shook his head and reached behind him for the doorknob, ready to make a quick retreat. "I have told Ms. Snelling repeatedly that I am not interested. If she doesn't quit—"

"Wait. Let me explain, Mr. Freylan." The man held up a hand. "We've recently found new evidence in the case. This may not involve seeking a judgment from the county as before, but instead from the individual who actually caused the accident. As you know, the statute of limitations—"

"Wait. What do you mean the individual? What evidence are you talking about?"

"An inspector found evidence at the scene of the accident— car parts that indicate there may have been another vehicle involved. Nothing conclusive yet, but we're working that angle."

"What? After two years, you're telling me another car caused the accident? Who?" His pulse raced. It had always bothered him that the wreck had been determined to be a one-vehicle accident. Jenny was a conscientious driver and although the roads had been wet with rain that night, it hadn't been freezing or treacherous. Jenny grew up here. She knew how to drive on these winding mountain roads in the rain.

"We don't know for sure yet, but a passenger-side mirror was found not far from the wreckage and it did not belong to your wife's car. Of course, it's possible it was from a previous accident or just tossed out as junk, but we're looking into it. It might be hard to prove conclusively. Like I started to say, the statute of limitations is fast approaching and if we miss that deadline, we—*you* forfeit the right to recover damages."

Recover damages? He shook his head. As if any amount of money could make up for the hell he'd been through these past two years. Had Marta Snelling been so desperate to turn his tragedy into a money-making proposition, so desperate to find somebody at fault, that she'd literally dug through the wreckage looking for evidence?

He wasn't going to let some ambulance chaser dredge up all the grief he'd worked to put behind him. He'd spent too much energy being angry with the weather, Jenny's car, with these curvy mountain roads—with the mountains themselves. The last thing he wanted was a flesh-and-blood person to pin his anger on. Roads and mountains didn't need forgiving. People did. And he did not want to be put to the test.

Chapter Two

Liesl Bachman checked her phone, then looked through the bug-splattered windshield at the clapboard house behind the scraggly hedge. 421 Rosebud Lane. The house number on hand-painted tiles confirmed she was at the right place, but what stared back at her bore little resemblance to the pictures in the app. If "overgrown English cottage" was the look The Inn at Rosebud Lane was going for, these proprietors were overachievers.

She let the engine idle and turned up the fan on the air conditioner trying in vain to dispel the cloying humidity. Checking her phone again, she sighed. Still no response. But then, these hosts had been slow to respond about everything since the day she'd first inquired about booking the place. She made a mental note to ding them for that when she reviewed the inn after checking out a few weeks from now. *If* she ever actually managed to get checked in.

She prided herself on being honest in her reviews, even though she hated to ding a nice host. But she was merely applying the Golden Rule. If other guests weren't honest, then what was the point of reviews, and how was she supposed to weed out the less-than-stellar establishments?

She scrolled her phone, checking for the code to get in. Ah, there it was:

Come on in and make yourself at home. Even if we're not currently on the premises, our door is always open. Please park on the east side of the house and use the front door. Your suite is at the top of the stairs. The small upper story is yours while you're our guest. Our main level also houses guests, so please observe quiet hours. Guests may also share our backyard space and kitchen (with some limitations...please see additional notes on fridge).

The directive was intended to make her feel welcome, but how *secure* could she feel in a place that wasn't locked when the hosts were away? At least the blurb used proper grammar and punctuation. Given how many of these inns did not, this listing redeemed those lost points with properly spelled contractions and appropriately placed commas.

A notification dinged and she tapped her phone. The fresh-faced couple smiling from the tiny icon appeared too young to be proprietors of a well-established inn, but then none of her hosts ever looked like their professional photos.

She studied her reflection in the mirror and brushed a wayward strand of light brown hair out of her eyes. She probably didn't look like her photo on the app either. It was the same one she used in her bio for the travel books and magazines she wrote for, and she'd learned the hard way that there were advantages to *not* looking like your professional photo. Her hair was in desperate need of highlights and six inches longer now than in the photo—the better to pile it atop her head when she was working. She never wore as much makeup as she had on in the headshot, but maybe she should remedy that—if she was really serious about what she'd told her brother last week—and at least put on some lipstick.

She pushed the thought aside and checked the app again. It was probably too late to book another place on such short notice, and she was used to less-than-glamorous accommodations, but she did need to be sure she could keep her camera and laptop safe when she left them behind at the inn.

An unexpected wave of sadness washed over her. The bloom was definitely off the rose as Grandma Bachman would have said. Where had the days gone when she'd felt such elation at arriving at her destination with a whole new city to explore, gorgeous scenery just waiting to be captured with her camera, and interesting people to befriend.

The job she'd loved so much in the beginning had gradually become more like drudgery. An assignment to complete so she could get the heck out of Dodge. And for what? So she could get back to her real life? This *was* her real life. And it was nothing to write home about, let alone to write about in some adventure magazine.

GRAVEL CRUNCHED on the driveway outside his office and Zach rose from his desk and crossed the room. Still rattled from the last visitor who'd knocked on his door, he parted the curtain to look out on the drive.

A white Honda Accord sat there, its engine idling while the woman behind the steering wheel scrolled on her phone. He couldn't see the license plate from this angle, but it was likely just his next guest. A travel writer from Iowa, according to her profile. Did she really think there was a month's-plus worth of things to write about in this little mountain town? Not that he was complaining about having the upstairs suite booked for a full five weeks. It would save him some major hours only having to clean once or twice a week instead of a full daily turnover.

He let the curtain fall and returned to his desk. The instructions on the inn's website *and* on the app were clear. She could let herself in when she was ready. Unless—like ninety percent of his guests—she didn't read the instructions that Jenny had worked so hard to make as precise as possible. He hadn't read them in a while himself. Maybe he needed to rework the paragraphs. Jenny had been more intent on sounding friendly and polite. Maybe what was needed was a firm list of bullet points:

• *Read these instructions, please! Everything you need to know is answered here.*

• *Any questions? See above.*

Jenny would have laughed at that. But she would *not* have accepted his edits.

The front door opened. "Hello? Anyone here?"

Swallowing back his rising irritation, he closed his laptop and went out to the hallway.

A pretty woman with honey-colored hair and an athletic build stood on the welcome mat.

"Hi." He offered a hand. "I'm Zach. Welcome."

"Thank you." She hitched a backpack up on her shoulder and shook his hand. Her friendly smile went a long way toward tamping down his annoyance. "I have a reservation... Bachman."

"You must be Liesl. Did I say that right? Rhymes with diesel?"

She tossed him a perfunctory smile. "Actually, it's Liesl...with an S sound. But yes, rhymes with diesel." She pronounced the word with an S.

"Hmmm... You must not be from around here."

She tilted her head. "Why do you say that?"

"Diesel with a S? It's a German word, you know. Diesel." He emphasized the Z with a bob of his head.

"Hmmm..."

Was she mocking him?

But she looked genuinely confused. "Well, for what it's worth, I have German roots going back about four generations, but I've never heard anyone in my family—or anywhere else, for that matter—pronounce *diezel*"—she put a hard emphasis on the Z—"*that* way." She put a hard emphasis on *that* too.

He tried a different tack. "How about Liesl, rhymes with... easel? That would be less confusing."

"You're kidding, right?" Her earrings bobbed and she studied him as if daring him to challenge her. "Easel is with a Z sound."

"Oh, you're right. Now I'm confused. So, it's Liesl with an S but not to rhyme with diesel?"

She waved a hand. "I don't have time to argue with you, but if you ever think of a different word—*any* word—that rhymes with my name, I'd love to know it. You know, so I could avoid another exchange like this."

He thought he caught a hint of teasing in her tone. "How about Cecil?"

"Who's Cecil—oh, you mean to rhyme." She rolled her eyes. "Cecil is a man's name. I mean, it *does* rhyme, but I'm afraid that would be equally confusing."

He shrugged and threw up his hands. "Then I've got nothing. Maybe it'd be easier to just change your name?"

She actually laughed. "Okay. You win. We'll go with Cecil."

"But it's a nice name...Liesl, I mean." he said quickly, emphasizing the S. "From *The Sound of Music*, right?"

"So my mom tells me. I'm the only other Liesl I know."

He wondered if she'd seriously never seen the classic movie, but decided not to push it. Instead, he glanced pointedly at her backpack. He'd already exchanged as many words with her as he usually did during the entirety of a long-term guest's stay. "Do you need help with your bags?"

"Oh, no thanks. I just have one small suitcase in the car. I can bring it in later."

"If you're sure." One small suitcase for a month-long stay? What sort of woman was this? But it wasn't his business. And he'd offered. "Well, as I'm sure you saw in the instructions, your attic room—" Hearing Jenny's voice clearly in his mind, he corrected himself. "Your attic *suite* is two flights up at the top of the stairs, and any additional information that wasn't on the website is in the notebook you'll find in the nightstand."

"Thank you. Any recommendations about where to find dinner?"

He gave her what he hoped was a long-suffering smile. "You'll find a whole list of restaurants in the notebook."

"Got it." She started up the stairs, then turned and looked down on him, pointing in the direction of the gravel drive. "Is my car okay parked there?"

"Um... It's fine for now. It'd be better if you move it when you come back after supper."

"Oh? Move it where?"

"You'll find all that informa—"

"Yeah, yeah...in the notebook. Okay."

"Or on the app or our website."

Not acknowledging him, she turned and hurried up the stairs, then disappeared around the corner.

He immediately felt a stab of guilt and recalled a conversation with Jenny shortly after they'd opened the inn. "Zach, be friendly! B&B people like to interact with their hosts. The personal touch —that's why they choose us over a hotel."

"I thought it was because we're cheaper."

"We're really not that much cheaper. Not after all the fees and taxes."

"Then maybe we should lower our prices."

"No, silly, then we couldn't make a living doing this."

He pulled his thoughts back to the present. Since he was stuck making a living from the inn, he'd better shape up and be as friendly as he could manage. But wasn't it a little rude to agree to stay in someone's home and then not even have the courtesy to read the directions? Ah, well. He had a month and a week to make it up to Liesl—*with-an-S*—from Iowa.

Jenny would have been proud.

Chapter Three

Liesl burrowed deeper into the covers and tugged the extra down pillow over her ear, but the birds chirping outside her window only upped their game. Finally giving up on trying to get back to sleep, she threw back the covers and squinted at her phone on the nightstand. Eight o'clock? That couldn't be right.

But the clock on the bathroom wall testified that it was. She'd apparently slept like the proverbial log. After splashing water on her face and running a brush through her hair, she took a quick inventory of this little suite that would be her home for the next five weeks. She'd noticed the bedroom could use a more thorough dusting, but at least the bathroom was pristine and smelled of pine-scented cleaner.

She drew back the curtains in the bedroom, fluffed the pillows, and pulled up the sheets, smoothing the comforter over the mattress. The old-fashioned quilt's sunny yellow and orange patches weren't exactly her taste, but looking around the room in the light of morning, *charming* was the word that came to mind.

An overstuffed chair in one corner was draped with a cozy throw, and in another, an oak library table with matching chair would serve nicely as a work desk. Of course, she planned to do most of her writing in the field, exploring Willowtree's downtown shops and restaurants and talking to tourists and locals about their favorite haunts.

So far, she was suspicious the little town wouldn't live up to its reputation as a top-ten North Carolina vacation spot, but then she hadn't even been here twenty-four hours, and it had been almost dark when she drove down Main Street on her way back from picking up a pizza last night. And it wasn't fair to let a semi-grumpy innkeeper color her opinion of the place. She prided herself on giving every assignment a fair shot. Willowtree, North Carolina would be no different.

She eyed the pizza box on the dresser. She could finish that for breakfast, but she couldn't go long without coffee. She'd read something about coffee being available in the kitchen's common area, but given that it was after eight and the inn had four other guest rooms, she probably shouldn't risk going down in her pajamas. She didn't remember seeing other cars in the driveway when she parked last night, but the other guests had no doubt been out enjoying Willowtree's nightlife.

She showered quickly, pulled on jeans and a sweater, piled her still-damp hair into a messy bun, and threaded dangly earrings through her earlobes. As an afterthought, she slicked on lip gloss before heading downstairs.

Near the front door, a young couple headed her way with coffee mugs in hand, talking in low tones.

"Oh, good." She raised her voice and pointed beyond them. "I must be on the right track. Coffee?"

The man gave a thumbs up. "Just around that corner."

"Such as it is." The woman lifted her mug, wrinkling her perfect nose. "We're in search of a coffee shop. You don't know a good one here, do you?"

"Sorry, I just got in last night. Good luck."

They gave her perfunctory nods, already deep in conversation again.

She rounded the corner, inhaling, hoping for a whiff of strong coffee, but not detecting anything. The kitchen was tucked into a separate wing of the house with French doors leading from a formal dining room.

The doors were open a few inches and no one was in the kitchen, but an empty, stained carafe sat on a warming plate at one end of the cluttered counter and a Keurig machine at the other. Beside the Keurig was a half-empty carousel of off-brand coffee pods. No wonder the couple was still in search of coffee. But this would have to do until she could get into town for the real stuff. A light pulsed from the machine, indicating it needed water. She filled the reservoir at the sink, selected a pod, and popped it in the slot.

Waiting for the machine to finish brewing, she perused the kitchen. No signs or labels or any other indication that this space was intended for guests. Except maybe the basket of granola bars? Maybe she'd misunderstood. Looking over her shoulder, she willed the Keurig to hurry up. She did not want to have to admit to Grumpy that she *still* hadn't read the instructions in his precious little notebook.

Checking behind her, she opened the refrigerator door and gave a little sigh of relief when she saw the basket on one shelf with a neatly labeled sign: *Guests, help yourself to anything in this basket.*

The refrigerator was almost empty except for a carton of eggs and a few half-empty condiment jars. She selected a bottle of caramel flavored coffee creamer from the labeled basket and carried it to the counter where her mug was filling. Voices from the yard floated in through the open window.

"What does she want from me, Jason? How much longer is this going to drag out? I'm ready for it to just be *over.*"

She recognized her host's voice. Zach. He sounded stressed.

Another masculine voice answered in a low murmur she couldn't quite catch. Something about insurance and attorneys.

"Well, I could have saved her a ton of time." Zach again. "Like I told you, I'm not interested in litigation. Just tell me what I need to do to put this behind me. And get her off my back!"

Liesl took a long-handled spoon from a bouquet of utensils in a small pitcher and stirred her coffee quietly, straining to listen, even as she felt guilty for eavesdropping. It sounded like maybe things weren't so rosy in paradise. No wonder she hadn't seen his wife around.

More unintelligible murmuring, then the sound of tires on gravel.

She jumped when the back door opened and her host stepped inside. "Oh!" Her spoon clattered on the counter, splashing drops of coffee. "Um...good morning." She grabbed a napkin from a stack near the coffeemaker and daubed at the mess.

He frowned. "Sorry. I didn't mean to scare you. Find everything you need?"

"Yes. I'm good."

With a curt nod, he turned his back on her and went through to the dining room. She waited until all was quiet in the house before heading back upstairs.

Zach heard his guest—Liesl—on the stairs and quietly closed the door to his study. According to her profile on the app, the woman was a writer—no doubt the snoopy type—and he didn't need anyone overhearing the conversation he was about to have.

He dialed Marta Snelling's office and waited, his jaw clenched. He'd been trying to get this attorney off his back for two years. She was adamant that he should sue the county for neglect. The roads had been slick with rain that night and branches hadn't been cleared after the storm. Snelling felt certain Zach could get a judgment and a nice payday at the expense of the county's treasury.

He wasn't interested. Not in suing the fine county he lived in and not in dragging out this whole drama any longer than it already had been. Once the insurance money was finally paid, he would be fine. But he was starting to suspect that the attorney was somehow, for some reason, impeding the insurance payment that was owed him.

Maybe that was paranoid thinking, but Marta had been beyond aggressive in her campaign to convince him to sue. Jason, his insurance agent, seemed to be on Team Marta too. Zach didn't like it one bit. Like he'd told them—again and again—he just wanted this whole thing to be over. But Jason was adamant that they had to wait until all investigations were complete before they could settle the claim.

The phone went to voicemail and he hung up without leaving a message, frustration rising. It wouldn't do any good to leave a voicemail. It would just be ignored like his others had. Unless he was calling to agree to sue, of course.

He pulled up the inn's reservation app on his computer and checked the week's schedule. The other two rooms were both reserved through Friday, so he was off the hook for laundry and cleaning until then. And of course, he would freshen the attic suite that day too. Unless his guest—Liesl—requested he wait. He wished he could always book guests for weeks on end. But then how would he fill his hours? What Jenny had enjoyed about vacuuming and laundry and making beds, he had no idea. But then Jenny had always been an enigma. A wonderful, delightful enigma.

A knock on the door made him jump. He rose and went to open it.

Liesl stood there, a hair dryer in hand, her hair looking curlier than it had when she arrived. "I'm sorry to bother you, but this doesn't seem to be working."

He stared at the plug she held up. "Oh, that? You have to plug it in."

She gave him a sidewise glance, apparently not getting his joke. Or not appreciating it.

"Sorry. I'm kidding. It doesn't come on at all?"

She shook her head. "You don't happen to have another one do you? I didn't pack one since the app said you provide hair dryers."

It sounded like an accusation.

"We do." He reached for the appliance. "Let me take a look. Maybe I can fix this one."

She handed it to him, then reached up and squeezed the hair clip, letting a few damp shoulder-length tendrils escape. "If it's going to be a while, I'll need to run downtown and locate one. Do you know anywhere that sells them?"

A memory came: Jenny hurrying through breakfast, telling him, "If I don't dry my hair right this minute, I'll have to start all over." He'd always thought that was ridiculous, but apparently it was a thing. "If you can hang on three minutes, I'll see if I have another one somewhere."

"Thanks." She offered a smile that was probably meant to hold apology, but merely looked pained.

"Be right back." He scooted around her and headed downstairs to his room, inspecting the defective dryer as he went. Who was he fooling? He was not mechanical.

In his room, he opened the closet where the last of Jenny's things were stored. Her mom had helped him box up Jenny's clothes a few days after the funeral. That same week, he'd moved into the one finished room in the basement, knowing he'd need the extra income the suite could provide, but also knowing he couldn't stay in the suite he and his wife had shared, the attic nest where they'd laughed—and sometimes fought. Where they'd made love and snuggled together afterward.

But he hadn't had the heart to get rid of every trace of Jenny yet. Last winter, in a fit of delayed grief, tired of the reminders everywhere, he'd finally packed up all her toiletries and hair paraphernalia, stuffing everything into an oversized moving box. It had sat in a corner of the closet for six months now, and he hadn't had the courage to sort through things.

He tossed the defective hair dryer in the trashcan under the sink and dragged the box to the middle of the bedroom floor. He sat on the bed and untucked the box flaps, steeling himself for the assault that seeing Jenny's belongings usually brought.

He caught a familiar coconut scent, but for the first time in a long while, he felt nothing. He was on a mission to secure a hair dryer for a guest. Nothing more. He pushed aside half-empty shampoo bottles, cosmetic bags, and a pile of scarves and hair ties to reveal a hair dryer identical to the one Liesl had brought him. He plugged it in and tested it. Good, it worked.

Hair dryer tucked under one arm, he quickly secured the box again, returned it to the corner of the closet, and went back up to the entryway outside his office.

Liesl gave the appliance in his hand a questioning look. "You fixed it? That was fast."

"No. Just found another one like it. This one works. I tested it."

"Oh good." She took it from him as though it were a lifeline in a stormy sea. "Thank you."

He watched as she raced up the stairs, taking the steps two at a time. A strange sensation toyed with his emotions. She disappeared around the corner into the upstairs hall, but he kept his eyes on the stairway long after she'd gone.

There was something so ordinary, so achingly familiar about the way she moved, the graceful way she flew up the stairs, as if she owned the place.

He finally shook himself out of an unsettling daydream and went back to his office. He checked the app again, but finding nothing that needed his immediate attention, he clicked on Liesl Bachman's reservation and scrolled back through the messages they'd exchanged when she reserved the suite three weeks ago.

> Liesl: I'll be there on a research trip for a book I'm working on, and I'll need a desk and chair and a good wifi connection. Is that possible?

> Jenny & Zach: Yes. The attic suite has all of the above.

> Liesl: Wonderful.

> Jenny & Zach: Let us know if there's anything else we can do to make your stay more enjoyable.

That last line was a copy-and-paste from stock messages Jenny had prepared. He would never take the time for all those pleasantries.

Before he could talk himself out of it, he went into his account and pulled up his profile. Feeling like an axe murderer, he deleted Jenny's name from the profile. She stared back at him from the round profile photo—the two of them in an embrace, Jenny looking up at him with so much love in those dark brown eyes of hers.

Pressing the little camera icon, he tried zooming in on his own face in the current image but they were standing too close together, and Jenny's bright yellow dress at the bottom of the circle made it look like he was wearing a ruffled, floral shirt. He deleted the photo and uploaded one he'd used on an old LinkedIn account. He hit Save before he could change his mind.

But the profile description was still all about how he and Jenny had remodeled her grandparents' cottage, carefully refurbishing everything except for the happy memories from her childhood summers spent in Willowtree.

He logged back in to LinkedIn and copied his profile from there—all except the line that said: *Zachary and his wife, Jenny, an innkeeper, make their home in the Blue Ridge Mountains of North Carolina.*

He deleted that line from the LinkedIn bio as well. Never mind the bio still said he was employed as an account manager for Stephan Landers Corp. He'd update the rest of it later.

Back on the inn's app, he pasted in the new bio, hit Save, and quickly logged out.

A pang of guilt hit the minute the screen went dark. How long before Jenny's mom noticed that he'd erased her daughter from the profile? He half expected Glory's name to show up in his text messages.

But if that happened, he'd deal with her. It was time. It had been time for a long while now.

Chapter Four

On Friday the usual raucous chorus of birdsong woke Liesl earlier than she wanted to be up, but after trying for almost an hour to fall back asleep, she finally got up and showered. By the time she'd dressed, the birds were being drowned out by the roar of a lawnmower. She gave a little huff, then chided herself. She couldn't be annoyed by the lawnmower and the unkempt lawn at the same time.

She tugged the curtains across the window as if they could deaden the racket and pulled out the desk chair.

She'd worked most of the day yesterday catching up on e-mail, editing a magazine article, and assuring her editor that she was on track to finish this book by the original deadline. This morning she would write the intro for her *Best-Kept Secrets: Blue Ridge Mountains/North Carolina* edition. That seemed backwards. Most writers wrote the intro or foreword after the book was finished, but she always worked better when there was a promise to readers she could then fulfill as she did her research. Yes, she might have to change a paragraph here or there and fill in some blanks as she researched, but this method had served her well with the other books in the series.

She'd taken a cursory drive through the streets of Willowtree just before dark last night, but so far, she'd yet to find any secrets, best-kept or otherwise. Although there did seem to be something going on with her host given that the hostess pictured on the app was mysteriously absent from the inn. Not that Liesl had any intention of putting hospitality industry hosts in her book. If statistics proved out, the inn would likely fold before her book was published. Although it did appear that this place had been around a while.

On a whim, she opened the app on her phone, looking for the date the inn had opened. A photo of Zach appeared. Wait a minute...

She refreshed the page. She could have sworn there'd been a woman in the photo with him at the time she booked. No, even more recently than that. When she'd looked up the address after getting into town, she was certain it listed a couple as the hosts. For safety's sake, she usually gravitated away from inns run by only a man.

She remembered the overheard conversation from yesterday morning. Apparently, she'd arrived in the midst of some sort of drama. She hoped it wouldn't affect her ability to work here. She had a book to write—albeit a short one—in a little over a month's time.

Sighing, she settled in at the desk, opened her laptop, and filled in the template for a new book. This would be the seventeenth volume of her *Best Kept Secrets* travel guides. There'd been a time not that long ago when she could have seen herself writing a hundred of these. The success of her first book—about St. Simons and Jekyll Islands off the coast of Georgia—had been heady and caused her to dream of a glamorous life traveling the world. The shine had worn off about two years in, and while her subsequent titles had sold well enough to secure her place with the publisher, and magazine work filled in the gaps, she wouldn't be retiring independently wealthy anytime soon.

Worse, the lure of travel had dimmed considerably when she realized that traveling the country, never mind the world, meant putting down shallow roots if she put down roots at all. And it was painful to be uprooted. It meant ninety percent of her family's celebrations—such as they were—happened via FaceTime or Zoom. It meant not having a church family or a group of friends she could call when she just wanted to hang out with someone she had a history with.

The lawnmower grew louder, apparently mowing underneath her window now. She got up and rummaged in her backpack for earbuds, glad for a distraction from her troubling thoughts. But those thoughts didn't miss a beat.

Bottom line: she was lonely. For a while—at her brother's urging—she'd found a church to attend for the month or six weeks she was in one town working on a book. But as she'd told Brad, always being the visitor got old quick. What she hadn't told him was how awkward and painful it was to sit in church alone. She'd started making excuses and just watching online services from her church back in Iowa. But recently, she'd pretty much given up on that too. It just wasn't the same as being a part of a close-knit group the way she'd been during college and that first year after graduation when she'd lived at home.

Now, she found herself avoiding the topic of church when it came up with her parents or with Brad and Heather. If they'd pressed her, she would have told them—truthfully—that she hadn't given up on God. Sometimes she felt closest to Him in the beautiful places she visited and wrote about. Okay, maybe not the breweries or souvenir shops or casinos. But the hiking trails leading to waterfalls and mountain overlooks and stunning sunsets on placid lakes made her feel closer to God than any church sanctuary.

It was the people she missed. Talking with not just her peers, but also with friends who were a few seasons ahead of her in life—about how to live in a way that honored the One who'd created her. How to live so that when she got to the end of her life, she'd have no regrets.

Because right now, she had a few. And she'd barely been on this earth for three decades. The math was not looking good.

She glanced at the blinking cursor on her screen, then at the clock. Still nothing but a blank page, and it was almost ten o'clock. She tucked the earbuds in tighter. She needed to get this intro finished so she could get out and explore the village of Willowtree and find those "best kept secrets" she'd earned a reputation for ferreting out.

Maybe a second cup of coffee would help. Such as the coffee was here. She headed downstairs, treading lightly, hoping the proprietor was nowhere to be found.

Zach cut the ignition on the lawn mower and headed for the kitchen, hoping not to run into any of his guests before he'd had a chance to shower. He quietly opened the back door only to see Liesl standing at the coffeemaker, just as she had yesterday morning. He ran a hand over his stubbled jaw, then through his hair, knowing how wild it always looked after working in the yard. "You're getting a late start there, aren't you?"

"Excuse me?" She didn't exactly glare, but her expression wouldn't win any Miss Congeniality awards either.

"Sorry. It's just that you were down a lot earlier yesterday."

"Well, if it's a big concern for you, you'll be happy to know this is my second cup. I was down at six for my first."

Before he could think better of it, he clapped a hand to his chest as if in shock. "Sorry. *My* bad."

To his surprise, she laughed. "Do you always monitor your guests' coffee habits?"

"Nah, I was just...making conversation." Now he felt genuinely apologetic. "And please excuse my sweaty clothes. I was hoping to sneak through."

"Hey, it's *your* house. No apology needed."

"Speaking of which, I hope the lawn mower wasn't too loud."

For a minute, he thought she was going to protest, but she seemed to think better of it and merely pointed to the side of her head. "I've got earbuds. But...how often do you mow?"

"Once a week. Why?"

"Nothing. I was just hoping it wasn't an every-morning thing."

Did she really think people mowed their lawns daily? "No, just once a week...maybe more like every ten days once the weather cools down in the fall."

"Shouldn't be a problem."

"All right then." He nodded, wondering what she expected him to do if it *was* a problem for her. "Well... I'm going to go clean up. Have a good day. Do you have anything planned?" And to think he'd accused *her*—in his head anyway—of being the snoopy type. What was wrong with him?

Her expression seemed to ask the same question, but she answered politely, "Nothing special."

"You'll do Asheville. And the Biltmore, I assume. That seems to be on everyone's not-to-be-missed list."

"No, actually... My thing is writing about some of the more off-the-beaten-path stuff—places most people might overlook."

"Oh. Well, that makes sense."

"You don't have any suggestions, do you?"

He thought for a minute, then shrugged. "I guess I'm so used to giving people the expected answers, I've never really thought about the more unusual places people might enjoy. Let me think on that and I'll get back to you."

"Sure. Thanks." She held up her cup of coffee. "Now, I need to get some words on the page before I do anything else."

"Of course. Sorry to keep you."

"Oh, no problem." She turned and glided up the stairs, holding her coffee cup level. Watching her a moment too long— again—he let himself remember what it had been like to have a woman in the house. Not just a woman, but a companion. A confidante. A beloved friend. A lover...

He stopped himself. That season of his life was over. There was nothing to be gained by harboring those memories.

Chapter Five

L iesl parked the Accord on a side street, gathered her backpack and water bottle, and locked the car. She still hadn't finished the intro to her book as planned—

She stopped mid-thought. Who was she kidding? She'd barely *started* it. But maybe her exploration of this tourist town would inspire her. Walking a block over to Main Street, she snapped a few photos of the rows of shops on either side of the street. The street shot had become her trademark in the books and if a magazine ever picked up her articles, the street shot was the one they usually requested to use from the book.

She scrolled through the half a dozen photos, viewing them with a critical eye. There were too many cars parked on the street this time of day, although with few exceptions, they were late model, high-dollar vehicles and would make the place look more upscale than it probably was. But she would come back at sunrise to get an empty-street shot that showed off the buildings better than this one. Still those puffy clouds in a blue sky made for a striking photograph.

She ambled up the street, noting shops she might like to research and visit later. Her routine on the first day of an assignment was to simply stroll the streets and get the lay of the land.

See where tourists tended to congregate, then eavesdrop on conversations to see what spots were creating buzz. Later she would scout out the local Chamber of Commerce office or a visitor center, assuming Willowtree had one.

She'd had that second cup of coffee at the inn in lieu of breakfast and now her stomach grumbled. She glanced at her phone. Almost eleven. Most of the cafés and diners would be serving lunch by now, and it would be less crowded than if she waited until noon.

She spotted a cute place across the street and walked to the end of the block before crossing to the other side. The outdoor seating and string lights under the awnings would make a great nighttime photo. She spoke a note into her phone to remind her to come back here after dark some evening, then she ducked inside the cafe. There was already a line at the counter and several tables filled behind her, but the queue moved quickly and after deciding it was too warm to sit outside, she took her avocado toast with a side of coleslaw to a two-top by the window.

A table full of older men drank coffee to her left—early morning golfers judging by their attire—and their raucous laughter and corny jokes made her hide a grin behind her hand. Nothing here that could be fodder for her book. She slipped her laptop out of her backpack and rummaged in one pocket for her earbuds. But before she could put the earbuds in, the conversation at the golfers' table turned serious, and something about the tone made her focus on their words.

She opened her mostly empty manuscript file and pretended to work, feeling guilty for the ruse. But not guilty enough to stop eavesdropping.

"You can't blame the poor guy," a man in green shorts and white socks pulled high on even whiter calves was saying. "Not sure what I would have done in his shoes."

"I sure as blazes wouldn't have tried to keep the place open. Can you see me making beds and serving breakfast?"

"I can see you cleaning toilets," a bald man jabbed. More

laughter, then Baldy added, "But I don't think he serves breakfast, does he?"

"*She* did. When she was there."

For a minute Liesl wondered if they were talking about her host and his mysterious ex. But then she remembered how many inns and Airbnbs there were in this little tourist town and she realized it could have been any one of dozens of couples.

"Yeah, Jessica definitely served breakfast. I'm surprised you didn't know that, Randy." White Socks crumpled his napkin and pushed his chair away from the table.

"Jenny. Her name was Jenny," Baldy—or *Randy*—corrected. "Short for Jennifer, maybe? I don't know…"

"Whatever… I knew it started with a J. Anyway," White Socks continued, "Marcella and some of her friends stayed there for a weekend hen party thing a couple years ago. She said Jenny fixed them a big breakfast. Good cook too. Marcie was trying to get me out there on a little getaway of our own."

"Did you go?"

White Socks scoffed. "Why would I stay in some strange place when my own bed is two blocks away?"

A lanky man who'd been quiet till now piped up. "I think the point might have been that *Marcella* needed a getaway."

"Yeah, well, Marcie can get away any time she wants to. As long as she makes me a big pan of her famous cinnamon rolls before she goes."

"You'd better be good to her, Bob." Randy elbowed his friend in the white socks. "You'd starve without that woman."

Elbows on the table, the tall man tented his hands and leaned forward. "Whatever happened with the settlement in that deal?"

"Still not settled last I heard." Bob looked grim.

"What? It's been over a year hasn't it?"

"More like two. Sad thing to happen to such a nice couple. Marcie said Zach and Jenny seemed like the happiest couple."

Zach and Jenny? Liesl's breath caught. It *was* her host they were talking about. Something must have gone south somewhere along the way, and it must have been a messy divorce if things still weren't settled after two years. But apparently he got the house.

"You just never know, do you?" The tall man shook his head.

The mood at the golfers' table had shifted from jovial to somber and Liesl felt her own mood shift with it. That was exactly why marriage terrified her. You just never knew. It seemed like half of her married friends were either divorced or just going through the motions. Not that she knew firsthand. But if social media was any indication, the statistics were depressing.

Even her own parents had been through struggles—separated and on the verge of divorce when Liesl was in high school. Thankfully, they'd toughed it out and seemed genuinely happy together now, but like Brad always said, there were no guarantees. "Except with me and Heather, of course."

Liesl smiled at the memory. Those two were the real deal, and Brad's wife was one of Liesl's favorite people in the world. But then, it sounded like everyone at the table to her left had thought the same thing about Zach and Jenny.

The golfers had moved on to a different topic now, but Liesl couldn't quit thinking about the seemingly happy couple that had once owned a bed and breakfast together.

What had gone wrong? Zach seemed like a decent guy. Maybe a little serious. But that was likely the *effect* of the divorce, not the cause.

She turned back to her laptop and started typing. She had to get some words on the page even if they were sloppy ones. Easier to fix pathetic writing than face a blank page. And right now, all she had was a whole bunch of those.

"Looks good. Thanks Sadie."

"No problem. Do I need to come again tomorrow?" The girl stole a glance toward the front window, clearly distracted.

"No. Everybody's here through the weekend, so if you can

just come Monday morning, as usual, that should be enough. And if you could wash the bedding in the attic suite then, that'd be good. The guest isn't checking out yet, but it'd be nice to tidy up the room. She's here for over a month, so we'll want to clean and change the bedding at least once a week, okay?"

Sadie nodded and Zach followed his young housekeeper to the front door. A dark blue car waited on the drive, but not the minivan Sadie's mom drove. Zach caught a glimpse of the driver. It looked like a guy. One too old for Sadie Mitchell, judging by his physique. Granted she was mature for her age, but she'd just graduated high school a week ago and was living at home so she could save up for college.

"Anything else before I leave?" Sadie waved at the driver of the waiting car. He waved back, but Zach couldn't see his face. She reached for the doorknob.

"No... Well, except for your paycheck."

She giggled. "I almost forgot."

"Hang on a minute and I'll grab it." He slipped into his office and retrieved the check he'd written yesterday from his desk drawer. He didn't pay her nearly enough, but he paid what he could afford, and she seemed content. Appreciative even.

No one had ever done such a good job cleaning the inn, including Jenny herself, and he did not want to lose Sadie. Especially not to some guy.

Thanking Sadie again, he followed her to the front porch. Liesl's Honda pulled up just then. She offered a nod from behind the wheel but waited until Sadie got in the waiting car. It drove away and Liesl took the parking spot it had occupied.

Zach resisted the urge to escape into the house so he wouldn't have to talk to her. But that might seem rude, since she'd acknowledged him on the porch. Unlike Jenny, he'd never made a lot of effort to engage their guests. A polite hello and he was out of there. But Liesl... There was something different about her. Something that invited conversation. Jenny would have already made a lunch date with the writer from Iowa and by the time Liesl checked out next month, she and Jenny would have been fast friends, promising to keep in touch. Jenny would have done it too. He smiled at the thought.

"Hi there." Liesl climbed the steps.

"Hello. How'd your research go today?"

"It went okay, I guess." A strange expression flitted through her blue eyes, but just as quickly, her pretty smile was back. "I'm just getting started with the research part, but at least I got my intro fleshed out."

"Not that I know anything about writing, but I trust that's good?"

"It's very good. Sometimes the hardest part is getting started. Once I have an idea where I'm going with a chapter, it gets a little easier and then... Never mind."

He nodded absently, only half listening. "Oh, before I forget... That was Sadie Mitchell, my housekeeper, who just left." He gestured in the direction of the driveway. "I asked her to change the bedding and make up your room on Monday morning. Will that be a problem? She usually comes around ten."

"That should be fine. Hopefully I'll be exploring some good places to write about by then."

"About that... I've been thinking about your 'best-kept-secret' assignment." He chalked quote marks in the air.

"You've been creeping on me?" She tilted her head and eyed him, but he couldn't tell if she was teasing or angry.

"Creeping?"

"Cyber stalking. How do you know about my series?" Her growing smile suggested she was toying with him.

"Um...maybe because it's in your bio? On the reservation app, I mean." That much was true, but he *had* been creeping on her. At least that was how she'd likely see it if she knew.

Color rose to her cheeks. "Oh, yeah. That."

Now he felt bad for embarrassing her. "Anyway, I thought of a place you might be interested in. It's one *I* think is definitely a best-kept secret. I actually have an appointment near there tomorrow." He hesitated, hearing Jenny's oft repeated plea for him to interact more with their guests. "I guess...I could take you there if you want."

She shifted from one foot to the other. "Um... I'd probably want to check it out first before I spend a lot of time there."

"So, is that a no?"

"Oh. No. I appreciate the offer, but I'll just take my car. It's not too far from here, is it? Except for a few honorable mentions, I try to only write about places in the same county as my feature city—Willowtree, in this case. Or at least within a twenty-mile circle."

"Not a problem. You won't cross the county line."

"Okay. So what is this mystery location? Do you have an address?" She waited, phone poised.

"It's bigger than one address. Maybe you could follow me there? I'll buy you breakfast and show you around a little—and then you can be on your own from there." He swallowed. Where had *that* come from? Seriously. The woman had said no as politely as possible. What was he *doing*?

But she grinned. "I guess I can't turn down a free breakfast. So what time is your appointment? When would we need to leave?"

"Is seven thirty too early?"

"In case you haven't noticed, I'm an early riser."

"We could go earlier if you like."

"Oh, no. That's fine. I sleep in a little on weekends."

"Great, then seven thirty. It's a date." *No!* He hadn't meant it that way. Not *that* kind of date anyway. But if he tried to clarify now, it would just make things stickier. "I'll... I'll see you in the morning. Um...you'll want to wear comfortable shoes."

"I don't own any other kind." She turned and ran up the stairs while he stood at the bottom wondering what he'd just done.

Chapter Six

The next morning Liesl changed outfits three times before settling on navy drawstring pants and a sleeveless linen top. Eyeing her reflection in the mirror in the suite's spacious bathroom, she frowned. She'd waited too long to blow-dry her hair and it had dried wonky. Her mascara was already smudged, and she was afraid her outfit was too casual for the day. But Zach had said "comfy shoes." And it wasn't as if this was a date.

At least she hoped that wasn't what he meant when he'd said "It's a date." Still, she barely knew Zach Freylan and from what she did know there were a dozen reasons to steer clear. Not least of those being his apparently messy divorce. And from what she could gather, that might not even be final yet.

But it was too late now. Zach would be waiting for her. She unplugged her phone from the charger, grabbed her backpack, and locked her room behind her before heading downstairs.

Sure enough, he was waiting by the front door. "Ready?"

"I am. Do I need to take anything with me?"

"You have your camera?"

She patted her backpack. "I've got my phone and my laptop. If I need my good camera, I'll go back another day."

"Okay then." He opened the door and motioned to where his pickup sat idling in front of the house. "We're headed up the highway to Sorrel Hollow—in case we get separated. There's parking near the college there. It's only about ten minutes."

"Got it. I'll stick close." She gave a little wave and hurried to her car. But when she turned the key in the ignition, nothing happened. Not even a click to indicate it was trying to start. She tried again with the same results. Great.

Leaving her things on the passenger seat, she ran back to Zach's pickup. "My car won't start."

"Have you had problems with it before?"

"Hardly ever. It sometimes takes a few tries to start when it's cold out, but that's sure not the problem today." She glanced eastward where the sun was already warming the morning air.

"I'll warn you, I'm not very mechanical, but I can take a look."

"You don't need to do that. I can just call...someone." She'd let her Triple A membership expire when they raised her rates last fall. She'd never had to use it before.

"Let me check it over first—if that's okay with you."

"Sure. Thanks." She handed him her keys and followed him to the Honda.

He slid behind the wheel and turned the key. Nothing. He reached under the dash for the hood release then went to the front of the vehicle and popped the hood. He fiddled with some cables, then went to his truck and brought back jumper cables.

When that didn't work, he dropped the hood back in place. "Sorry, but that's all I know to try. I can give you the name of some places in town where you could get it fixed. In fact, let me call a friend who might be able to come look at it here so you don't have to pay for towing."

"That would be good. Thanks." She sighed. This stupid assignment was going to cost her more than it earned.

"Do you want to wait here with your car? Or I can call Jim's shop for you, and we can go on to breakfast. He can call you if he has any questions."

"If you're sure you don't mind." She hated feeling beholden.

"Of course not. Like I said, I have an appointment in Sorrel Hollow anyway. You can explore while I'm in my meeting and I'll bring you home whenever you're ready."

While Zach called his friend, she retrieved her things from her car and followed Zach to the pickup. He opened the passenger door for her before trotting around to the driver's side.

As he slid behind the wheel, she caught a pleasant soapy scent. He was clean-shaven today, his wavy hair tamed with gel.

"So where is this mysterious place? Sorrel Hollow?" she asked once they were on the road.

"Don't laugh, but it's a college campus."

She gave him a quizzical look. "College?"

"My alma mater. Sorrel Hollow College. Have you heard of it?"

"I don't think so. But that doesn't exactly sound like a tourist attraction."

"You've never heard of a little place called Harvard University? You know...in Boston? Mecca for tourists. Besides, I thought you were looking for unexpected attractions."

"I am." She put up a hand. "I'll reserve judgment until I've seen the place. Would people have to have an ID to get on campus?"

"Nothing like that. The campus is pretty quiet, especially in the summer."

"Okay, I promise to keep an open mind." Sure, Harvard was a tourist attraction, but a little college nobody had ever heard of?

Looking smug, he wound expertly through country roads where mountain laurel was in its full misty pink glory and butterflies flitted above the bushes. A few minutes later he slowed the truck as they approached a stone archway with *Sorrel Hollow* spelled out in script letters at the top of the structure. Beyond the entrance was a small village that could have been a twin of Willowtree. The same wooded, hilly terrain, with stone walls and outcroppings on either side. A little creek ambled lazily alongside the road, peeking through the trees at intervals.

"The college is just up here." Zach pointed through the windshield.

A huge, smooth-as-glass lake snugly ringed by stone walls and bridges appeared on their right. Ancient-looking stone buildings hugged its banks, and Liesl spotted an inviting stack of aqua and green paddleboats on one side of the lake. "Wow. This lake is on the campus?"

"Yes, Laurel Cove Lake. It's kind of the crown jewel."

"I'll say! It's beautiful."

"It's kind of like a smaller version of Sourwood Lake."

"Oh? Where's that?"

"You haven't discovered our lake yet? In town?"

She shook her head. "In Willowtree?" How could she have missed a lake bigger than this one?

"Well, there's another best-kept secret for you then. I'll drive you by it on our way back."

"That would be great. If you have time."

He nodded. "Let's eat first, if you don't mind, but then would you like to walk around the rest of the campus? It's really best seen on foot."

"Sure."

He parked his truck in a shady spot overlooking the creek. Liesl followed him across the stone bridge to a building that appeared to hold several shops. He opened the door to one called The Bagel Station.

"I probably should have warned you that the breakfast choices are bagels, bagels, or bagels."

She laughed. "Good thing I like bagels, huh?"

"We could go to the bakery downtown for a bigger selection if you'd rather."

"No, this is fine. A bagel sounds good, actually."

The young man behind the counter started to ask if he could take their order, but seeing Zach, he stopped mid-sentence.

Zach reached across the counter to shake the guy's hand. "Oh, hey there. Davis, isn't it?"

He ignored the offered hand. "Yeah. Davis."

"I didn't know you worked here."

"Just started a couple weeks ago." Davis mumbled, head down. "Are you ready to order?"

Zach seemed a little taken aback by the young man's dismissal, but he turned to Liesl and asked, "Do you know what you want?"

"Yes, I'll have the egg and bagel sandwich and coffee with cream, please."

"Make that two," Zach told the server.

"I can bring it to you."

The way he avoided eye contact made Liesl wonder if the young man might be autistic or have some kind of mental disability. But watching him a little longer, she decided he was just socially awkward.

"Sure. We'll be on the deck."

They settled at a table with a view of the lake and a few minutes later, an older woman in a barista's apron brought their coffee and bagels.

Zach glanced past the server to the counter, then lowered his voice to a whisper, looking concerned. "How's Davis getting along?"

"Oh? You know him?"

"Not well. But I met him at the scholarship banquet in September."

"Oh, yeah. Davis told me about the scholarship." The server tucked her pencil behind her ear. "He's doing really well here. He caught on real quick."

"Glad to hear it."

"You two enjoy. Let me know if you need anything else."

"So this is where you went to school?" Liesl asked after the server disappeared inside.

"It is. It's been a while, but being on campus...it always feels like I'm a student again."

"What's your degree in?"

"You don't want to know."

"Well, *now* I do."

He laughed. "Take a guess."

She rolled her eyes. "I do not like guessing games. But I'll go with hotel management. For obvious reasons."

"Not even close."

"Okay, then accounting."

His eyes went wide. "How'd you know?"

She laughed. "Am I right? I just figured that's as far from the hospitality industry as you could get."

"Account manager, actually. For a corporation. But you do realize that there's accounting involved in the innkeeping business. Any business."

"Sure, but it probably doesn't require a degree. So how'd you end up running an inn? Or is that just a hobby?"

A faraway look came to his eyes and she wished she hadn't asked that question. No doubt the answer had something to do with his ex.

"It's a long story."

She waited, but for a long minute he said nothing.

"My wife's grandparents ran the The Inn at Rosebud Lane," he finally said, his voice noticeably softer. "When her grandpa died and her grandma couldn't handle it on her own, they asked Jenny if she would help. Then her grandma went into a nursing home, and Jenny just kept going with the inn. She loved it. When her grandma died, Jenny inherited the house and the business." Strangely, there was no trace of animosity or bitterness in his voice.

"And...you ended up with the house?" There had to be a story there. Why would he have even *wanted* his ex's family home? Unless of course, it was for the income. But what about his ex? That must have felt like a slap—

He frowned. "Ended up with the house? What do you mean?"

"I just meant... I mean, I assumed..." She let her voice trail off, feeling like she'd stuck both of her size-nine feet in her mouth. She waited for him to explain where this mystery wife was now. But instead, he took a large bite of his bagel sandwich and looked out over the lake, chewing.

"That's a strange way to put it," he said finally. "But yes, I guess you could say I got the house when my wife passed away."

"Oh—" Liesl stifled a gasp. "No... Oh, I'm so sorry. I didn't know."

"Of course not. Why would you?"

"I'm so very sorry. I thought— For some reason, I thought you were divorced." Her voice dwindled to a whisper. "Or separated."

He looked askance at her. "Why would you think that?"

"It was...something I overheard, I guess."

"Where?" His tone turned harsh. "From who?"

"I— I really don't know who it was. Just a conversation I overheard in the coffee shop. In Willowtree."

"What exactly did they say?" Without waiting for her reply, he rose and went to the railing, gazing out over the lake.

She stayed in her seat, afraid to go to him, thankful there was no one else on the deck. "I honestly don't even remember for sure, Zach. Something about a settlement. So I just assumed—" She stopped herself, mortified that she could have been so wrong. "I'm so sorry. And I'm...I'm sorry about your wife. I didn't know."

No response. He stood with his back to her, stiff and distant.

What was she supposed to do now?

Chapter Seven

Zach blew out a breath and turned to face Liesl. He should have been prepared for this moment. Or he should have kept his mouth shut. Now he owed her an explanation. "I don't know what you heard, but you misunderstood."

"It was none of my business." She lowered her gaze. "I shouldn't have said anything. I'm sorry."

He returned to his seat and forced a calmness to his voice that he didn't feel. "You didn't do anything wrong. I'm still just a little —" He picked up the paper napkin that lay crumpled on his plate. "I'm not sure how to talk about it."

"You don't have to if you don't want. It's none of my business," she said again.

"It's not that I don't want to. I just don't need people feeling sorry for me. And I sure don't need them gossiping about me." He'd made it a habit not to tell his guests about Jenny. When he'd done so in the beginning, the undisguised sympathy was too awkward and difficult to respond to. And now, Liesl would be no exception, especially since her probing questions went beyond small-talk or even innocent curiosity, and leaned toward snoopiness. He'd told himself he would keep his distance—though he probably wouldn't be sitting here with her if he'd been serious about that. Either way, it wouldn't be easy to avoid her given that she'd booked the suite for a month. And given that she was a talker.

Jenny had been a talker too, but not in an annoying way. He missed the sound of her voice every single day.

"When...when did it happen?" Liesl asked softly.

He gave a humorless laugh. "That's the thing. It's been two years now. I should be way past this." He ran a hand through his hair, embarrassed. But what had he expected when he invited her to breakfast? He was an idiot.

"Why would you say that?" The genuine compassion in Liesl's voice didn't help his emotions. "I've heard people say the second year is actually the hardest."

He shrugged. "Maybe it was. Depends on the day, I guess. Sometimes I think I'm doing great...that things are getting better. And then—"

"I can imagine." She chewed her bottom lip. "Actually, I *can't* imagine. I mean, I've never been married. But I can guess how hard it must be."

For the first time, he wondered if she had a boyfriend. And if he was honest, it bothered him a little that she'd agreed to come with him when, for all she knew, he was still legally married. Not that he'd intended this to be a date. But still. He wouldn't have liked it if Jenny had let some guy take her on a tour of the town.

"Do you mind me asking what happened? What took her so young, I mean?"

"Car accident."

Liesl shook her head, her blue eyes holding genuine empathy. "How awful. Were you with her? In the accident?"

"No. She was on her way home from visiting her mom. Jenny's car went off the road and rolled. Into a ravine. They're not really sure what happened even now."

"Oh, that would be the hardest."

"She lived for thirty-six days after the accident. She died on her twenty-eighth birthday."

"Oh, Zach..." Liesl covered her mouth with her hands. "That seems almost...cruel."

"No. It was actually a gift—two hard days on the calendar combined into one," he explained at her quizzical look.

"I'm glad you can look at it that way." She swallowed the lump in her throat. "I'm so very sorry."

He knew it was sympathy, even empathy, but both always felt like pity to him. "She never regained consciousness, so I don't think she suffered. There's some comfort in that."

"But *you* did. You suffered."

He nodded. She spoke it like a fact and he found surprising comfort in her words. Because they were true.

"That must have been so hard. Did they ever think she would survive?"

"No. They never gave me any hope. And honestly, if she had survived, it would have been horrific. For her, I mean. Her injuries were...catastrophic. She had a traumatic brain injury."

"That must have been awful for you. Must *be* awful. Still."

He gave a shrug that he knew belied what he'd just told her. "It happened. Life goes on."

"You...you don't really mean that?" She made it a question, seeming disconcerted by his nonchalant attitude.

"But it's true. Life does go on. What else is there? What other option, I mean."

She didn't respond.

"I'm doing the best I can. With God's help." He tossed the now shredded napkin onto the table. "That's all I can do."

"Of course. I didn't mean—"

"Hey. Can we change the subject?" He cleared his throat. "I appreciate your sympathy. I really do. But I didn't intend to put such a damper on this day. And"—he checked his watch—"I need to head over for my appointment. I don't want to be late."

"Oh. I'm sorry. I almost forgot."

"It's fine. I have time. And my meeting shouldn't take more than half an hour. Maybe forty-five minutes. You can get another coffee and wait here if you like—maybe you have some work to do?" He glanced at the backpack she'd brought. "Or you can walk around campus if you'd rather. I'll text you when I'm finished."

"Okay. I have e-mails to answer, so I'll just wait here until you're finished. Besides, I wouldn't really know where to go on campus."

"I was hoping you'd say that. I'd like to be the one to give you the tour." He pushed back his chair again. "Can I get you a coffee before I go?"

"Don't be ridiculous. I can get it."

"Okay. Sure. I'll make it quick." He gathered his trash and tossed it in a nearby receptacle, then headed toward the campus center, praying his meeting didn't last as long as it had last time.

WATCHING ZACH WALK AWAY, Liesl wondered for the first time what his appointment was here at the college. The fact that he hadn't offered that information, coupled with the news about his wife made her wonder if it was with a counselor or something. But he said his wife had been gone for two years. She tried to remember the conversation she'd overheard that first morning she'd gone down for coffee and wondered what that had been about if not the ex-wife her imagination had invented for him.

She flushed at the thought and wished desperately that she could take back that part of their conversation. The sun grew warm, and she fished in her purse for a hair clip. Her hair was finally long enough to tuck into a bun and it felt good to get it off her neck. Leaving her used plate on the table to hold her spot, she went inside to order another coffee.

There were several people seated in the coffee shop now, and Davis, the young man Zach had spoken to, was behind the counter again. He greeted her professionally as if he didn't recognize her from before. He seemed perfectly normal now, speaking clearly, and writing her name in neat letters—and spelled correctly —on a disposable cup.

While she waited for him to make her Americano, the front door opened and two police officers wearing black uniforms walked in, laughing and chatting amiably.

"I'll grab us a table," the older officer told his partner. "You know how I like my coffee."

Liesl turned to see if her Americano was ready yet, but the empty cup with her name on it sat under the espresso dispenser, and Davis had disappeared. She walked to the other end of the counter where a door opened to the kitchen. Just then, the woman who'd served her and Zach came out and greeted the policemen, but behind the woman, in the kitchen, Liesl saw Davis with his back to her, standing by a large industrial sink, clutching the steel rim as if he were going to be sick.

Apparently unaware anyone was watching, he held one hand up in front of him and even from fifteen feet away, she could see that his fingers were shaking like leaves in a storm. He was either very ill or he was on something...or maybe coming down from a high.

He turned and took a step toward her, but seemed oblivious to her watching him. His gaze trailed to the booth where both policemen were now seated. Looking panicked, Davis ducked back into the kitchen and disappeared from sight. There was definitely something going on with him. Something not good. She'd have to ask Zach when she saw him.

WALKING BACK FROM HIS MEETING, Zach purposely took the long way around so he could approach Liesl from the opposite direction, partly because he wanted to avoid her perusal, but if he were honest, it was also because he wanted to watch her.

She was definitely easy on the eyes, but that wasn't his reason for wanting to watch her. Well, not his only reason. She intrigued him. Her work, for one. Not that he wanted to be a writer, but to not be tied down to a job he hated was more than just a dream. It felt like his ticket out of the suffering he'd known for the past two years.

She apparently made enough money to support herself. He had a list of questions for her, but he didn't want to risk doing what she'd done to him: assume things that weren't true. For all he knew, she was living on an inheritance. Or maybe writers just made a lot more than he'd assumed. There was that word again.

Whatever the case, something about this woman had made him feel, for the first time since Jenny's death, that there might be a way out of this trap he was in. He checked the thought immediately. He'd made promises to Glory, Jenny's mom. To Jenny too, in a way. Her dream had been to live out their lives here. Raise a family here. And even though Glory couldn't take on the responsibility of managing the inn her parents had run since Glory was a child, The Inn at Rosebud Lane was all Jenny's mom had left of the generation before her and the one that came after too.

In his grief, Zach had promised Glory that he would keep the inn going. That she would always have a place to come home to. In truth, maybe he was trying as hard as Glory was to hang on to the only thing they had left of Jenny.

That first year, Glory had driven up from Charlotte and stayed at the inn four or five times. But she'd visited only once this past year, and then she'd only stayed two days. Zach wasn't sure whether it was because Glory was healing and needed the comfort of her childhood home less and less. Or if it just hurt too much to be surrounded by such vivid memories. He sure understood that.

But even without that promise to Glory hanging over his head, he had obligations. A few months before her accident, he and Jenny had paid off one of the loans they'd taken out to refurbish the inn. They'd been so relieved and hopeful. But they—*he*— still owed on the loan for the new roof and finishing out the basement where he lived now. Once that was paid off, the inn would provide a comfortable living. And once the insurance mess was settled, he'd be fine. Except for the fact that running a bed and breakfast was the last thing he would have chosen to do with his life.

He rounded the curve coming up from the lake and spotted Liesl, still at their table, drinking coffee and looking at her phone. She was scheduled to be at the inn for another month, and he was eager to pick her brain about her freelance work. Her travel. He envied her freedom? Not that he had any skills as a writer. But he was pretty good with a camera. Maybe he could turn that into a career somehow. Or was he grasping at straws?

Her back was to him, her hair pulled up now in what Jenny always called a messy bun. The curve of her long neck, the arch of her back evoked a familiar, but unwelcome emotion. Yet he couldn't seem to look away.

This fair-haired guest from Iowa was turning out to be more trouble than she was worth. He shook his head and forced himself to think of something else. It wasn't her fault after all. She was just trying to do her job. He was the one who'd suggested taking her to Sorrel Hollow. He was the one who—

He gave a low growl. There he went again.

Chapter Eight

L iesl sensed him before she saw him. But the sound of Zach's voice made her smile. She rose and turned to face him, lifting the long strap of her crossbody bag over her head and adjusting it on her shoulder.

"Hope you didn't get too bored."

"Not at all." She lifted her phone. "I got all my email answered and even posted a couple of photos."

"Good. You ready for the tour?"

"Sure. Lead the way."

As they passed in front of The Bagel Station, the two police officers were exiting. Zach nodded a greeting. Liesl opened her mouth to ask him about Davis, but Zach spoke first. "We'll walk around the lake and then I'll give you a little tour of the campus, but first, I need something to drink. Do you want a Coke?"

"No thanks. The giant Americano I drank should hold me."

"Okay. I'll be right back."

Keeping one eye on the door, making sure the cops didn't come back, he inhaled and let out a slow breath. The line at the counter *wasn't bad. He could duck out early and still make his appointment on time. He sent a quick text, then looked up at the sound of the door opening.*

He inhaled sharply.

Zach Freylan. Why was he here again? Heart racing, he turned as casually as he could manage and headed down the hallway toward the restrooms.

Thank God he'd parked in the lower lot, out of view. He watched from the small hallway, waited until Zach was distracted placing his order, then slipped out the back. He should have let Mindy know where he was going, but she'd figure it out.

He ran through campus to where his car was parked, climbed in, and locked the doors. He should have driven away immediately, but his hands were shaking too hard after the close encounter. He rolled down the window and stretched across the seat to adjust the passenger side-view mirror. He straightened and studied his reflection in the visor mirror. His face appeared pale, despite the sunburn he'd gotten at the beach last weekend.

He ran the window back up, trying—and failing—to ignore the subtle difference in the paint colors where the side mirror connected to the car. But it was only obvious when the sun hit it just right. No one else would notice. Would they?

He waited another minute, forcing his hands to stop trembling before finally turning the key in the ignition. Despite the familiar flood of guilt, something made a decidedly unfamiliar *hope nudge at his consciousness, lifting the weight from his shoulders ever so slightly. Had it merely been his imagination that Zach Freylan looked a little better? Maybe it was just the fresh haircut and button-down instead of the jeans and T-shirt that seemed to have become his uniform since the accident. But that was a good sign. Wasn't it?*

Liesl followed while Zach led at a brisk pace, sipping his Coke and pointing toward the stone buildings across the lake. "That's the campus center over there—where my meeting was—and that big building on the hill is the inn...lodging for visitors and the conference center."

"Do you mind if I stop and take a few photos?"

"Of course not. But let me get out of the way." He took a step back while she framed a panoramic image with her phone's camera.

She clicked, then checked her screen. "That is just gorgeous."

"The inn?" He followed her gaze to the small mountain rising up behind a palatial stone building pocked with arched windows. "Or the Appalachian Mountains?"

"The whole scene. I love the reflections in the lake." The lush trees and greenery reflected in the smooth surface of Laurel Cove Lake looked like a scene out of a European travel magazine. "Is that what those mountains are? The Appalachians? Not the Blue Ridge Mountains?"

"The Blue Ridge is just what they call the front range of the Appalachian Mountains—a subrange, I think it's called. And the Great Smoky Mountains are part of the Blue Ridge."

She made a face. "How does anybody keep track of all that?"

"I'm sure there's a more scientific explanation but that's all I've got. With all the traveling you do, I'm surprised you don't know all about that."

"Believe it or not, this is the first mountain town I've written about." She didn't tell him she'd grown up right here in North Carolina. "I wrote my first travel guide on a whim, after a trip to the Georgia coast, but then I moved to Iowa and I couldn't afford to go far. So I started in on the little towns—Des Moines, St. Louis, Omaha, Kansas City, Wichita..." She shook a finger at him. "I did do Chicago. That was a biggie. And it paid enough to get me to the Pacific coast."

"Was that your goal? The ocean?"

While they wound single file along a path that followed the

lake, she thought for a moment, not wanting to tell him that her goal had been to get *out* of North Carolina. "No. The goal was just to see the world, I guess. Or at least the country."

He opened his mouth to say something, then seemed to think better of it.

"What?" She was genuinely curious.

"I was just wondering if it's been everything you hoped it would be?"

She arched a brow. "Why do you ask?"

"No reason. It's just...something I've considered."

"Being a travel writer?"

"Most definitely not." He shook his head. "I am anything but a writer. But I wouldn't mind the traveling part. Maybe what I should have asked is if you know of any other ways to make a living traveling?"

"You'd sell the inn?"

He shrugged and shook his head. "Probably not. I like living here. But running the inn is rather confining. But it's all Jenny's mom has left of her family home, so I wouldn't feel right selling it. At least not yet. I guess I could hire someone to manage it, except I can't really afford that. But in case you haven't already noticed, hospitality is not one of my gifts."

She made a goofy face. "Well, I didn't want to say anything, but..."

He laughed. "You didn't have to. Your horrified expression pretty much said it all."

"What? When did I have a horrified expression?"

"I'm just giving you a hard time."

"So I noticed." She was glad he didn't press her on that note because she *had* wondered why he'd chosen to run an inn. Not that he'd been rude, but neither had he been friendly toward her or his other guests. He just didn't seem the type to choose innkeeping as an occupation.

They climbed the stairs up to a sheltered street and walked beside a rustic rock retaining wall that formed a platform for a group of massive old stone edifices built high on a hill. Ancient bare-rooted trees stood sentinal around the most imposing building.

Liesl snapped several photos on her phone and wrote clever captions in her head, hoping she'd remember when she got back to the inn. "You were right about this place. It's like being in Europe. Not that I've ever been, but I've watched enough British TV to feel like I have."

"Pretty cool, isn't it?"

"It's gorgeous. I love it!" She knew she was gushing, but he seemed so pleased with her reaction that she didn't care. She pointed to the building labeled Winston Hall. "So is this a dorm?"

"It's a lodge. The main dorms are over there." He waved a hand to the west. "I was in Barker Hall. Jenny was in Anthony." He spun slightly south.

"Jenny? Your wife? This is where you met?"

"In the dining hall first day of her freshman year. I'm a year— I *was* a year older than her," he corrected himself, and a faraway look came to his eyes.

"College sweethearts, huh?" She swallowed hard, wanting to acknowledge his words, his obvious love for his wife. But she couldn't label the emotion that welled inside her as anything but jealousy.

"Yes. And then while we were still engaged, her grandparents asked Jenny to run the B&B. They ran the inn for almost forty years and before that, it was their family home. But both of them were having health issues, and Jenny jumped at the chance. After our wedding, we moved into the attic suite, and came back from our honeymoon to our first paying guests."

"Wow. Talk about baptism by fire." But she was still thinking about what he'd said about him and Jenny living in the attic suite. Where she was staying now. The knowledge was oddly disconcerting.

"Oh, but it was the perfect gig for Jenny. Everyone loved her the minute they met her. She was all sweetness and light." He gave her the side eye. "As you may have noticed, I am *not*."

She laughed, thankful for the levity. "You might have a few rough edges."

"More than a few as I'm sure you'll discover—since you're staying a while, I mean."

And there it was. She was staying another month and a few days and then she'd be off on the next assignment. The story of her life. But Zach seemed unlike anyone she'd ever met. And she flattered herself to assume that perhaps she was unlike any other guest he'd hosted since Jenny's death.

And he was still in love with his wife. That much was crystal clear.

HE AND LIESL walked for miles around campus and the little town of Sorrel Hollow with Zach pointing out the places he thought visitors might like and some of the shops that had been Jenny's favorites. Being on campus brought back memories—but good ones—and he regaled Liesl with some of them.

After they'd walked for over an hour, he drove her out to the downhill end of the Point Lookout trailhead and they hiked a short way through the Pisgah National Forest, talking the whole way. She'd had so many interesting experiences in her travels, and she shared the stories with wit and brevity, not hogging the conversation, but showing interest in his contributions to their discussion. He found himself wishing they were on a date. Maybe she thought they *were*. But not likely. She wasn't acting flirtatious or coy. Just friendly and engaging. A lot like Jenny, he had to admit. But different too. In interesting and sweet ways. He was determined not to compare them.

Liesl was obviously delighted with the hiking path and spent several minutes photographing the train tunnel once it came into view below the trail.

But the trail was almost eight miles roundtrip, and from where they'd started, the back half of the hike was a slow but significant incline. "We probably ought to turn around now. It's a little over a mile back and it's all uphill."

She wrinkled her nose, looking disappointed.

"Was that face about having to go back already or having to walk uphill?"

She laughed. "A little bit of both. But I don't have the energy to do the whole thing today. Not after all the walking we've already done."

"The *right* way to do this trail is on bikes. And starting at the uphill end."

"I'd love that!" Her blue eyes brightened. "Is there a place to rent bikes around here?"

"There is, but why rent when I have one you can use?"

"Really? That would be awesome."

"If you don't mind an e-bike. I know some people think they're for wimps, but don't worry, you still have to work for those uphill miles."

"I'd be grateful for the boost. I might just come back next week—if the bike's available then. But where do I get on the uphill trailhead?"

"I can show you. Would you want company?"

She looked at him a few seconds too long before she answered. "Sure. I'd love company."

"It's a deal then. Just let me know what time and I can work around it." That was one good thing about running an inn—he could rearrange his schedule fairly easily most days.

They hiked in silence up to where his truck was parked. He wondered if she regretted agreeing to his company and tried to tell himself that he'd originally only offered to go with her to help out one of his guests. But he wasn't very convincing.

They drove back through town and when they passed Laurel Cove Lake, Liesl pointed to The Bagel Station. "Did you know the guy who waited on us there this morning? Davis, I think you called him? At the counter?"

"Yeah. That's Davis Simmons. I don't know him well, but I know who he is. Why?"

"I think there might be something...*strange* going on with him." She described how she'd seen him hide out in the kitchen from two police officers who came in. "He was really sweating it. His hands were shaking. Not that it's any of my business, but I wondered if maybe he was on something."

"I sure hope not. This was his first year at Sorrel Hollow—the college—and he's a straight A student. There on scholarship."

She tilted her head at him. "I thought you didn't know him well."

"I guess you could say I know him on paper. He won the scholarship we started in Jenny's honor." He had—maybe foolishly, if the auto insurance fell through—formed the scholarship in Jenny's name with the small life insurance policy Jenny's mom had held for her.

He didn't tell Liesl that Davis had ducked out when he'd come in for the Coke after his meeting, seeming eager to avoid him. But it had struck him as strange, especially after what Liesl told him. "I'm on the selection committee, so I saw his info and read his essay. He graduated high school in three years. Turned seventeen just before his first semester of college. He's young. And maybe a little immature socially. I hope I didn't misjudge."

"I'm sure you didn't," she said too quickly. "I shouldn't have said anything."

She turned and stared out the windshield, and he guessed she was thinking of this morning when she'd uttered those same words about her assumption that he and Jenny were divorced. He sought to relieve her of the notion. "I'm glad you gave me a heads up. He's applied for it this year too— Actually, that's what my meeting was about. So I'll be a little more cautious and make sure everything is on the up and up before we renew it for next year."

She didn't respond for a minute, then turned to him, a look

of chagrin on her pretty face. "Listen, I want to apologize again for what I said...about your marriage."

"No big deal." It kind of was, but she couldn't have known, and he'd get over it.

"I'm so sorry about Jenny. It's obvious—from the way you talk about her—that you had a really good marriage. And that you loved her deeply. I feel awful that I ever threw the D-word out there. And...just so I'm clear, I probably just misunderstood what people were saying."

He should leave it alone, but curiosity wouldn't let him. "So what exactly did they say? Is there a rumor going around that we were getting a divorce?"

"No! No, of course not." She dropped her head. "I guess I need to make a confession."

Chapter Nine

"The rumor actually started that first morning at the inn, not in the coffee shop." Liesl closed her eyes and sighed softly.

Zach didn't know what he thought her big confession was going to be, but not what she was saying now. He stared at her in the passenger seat beside him, a mixture of sheepishness and relief fighting within him.

"I didn't really intend to eavesdrop. But I couldn't help but overhear." Her words gathered steam. "I know I should have just left, but my coffee was brewing and I didn't want you to come in the kitchen and think I'd left it unattended. So I just—"

"Hey." He held up a hand. "I shouldn't have been having that kind of conversation where the whole world could hear." It was true. And he wondered how many other guests had overheard that exchange or others like it.

"I guess... I hope that explains why I thought what I did."

"Well, just so you know, the 'she' in that conversation wasn't Jenny. It's too long and boring to go into, but so you don't jump to any more conclusions, it was about an ongoing insurance mess. And I was referring to an attorney."

She shook her head. "You don't owe me any explanation. It was none of my business."

"I know I don't, but at the same time, I feel like I need to defend my integrity."

"You don't, Zach. I understand that it was a misunderstanding."

He smiled at her antithetical statement.

She smiled back, apparently realizing what she'd said.

"Okay. We're good?"

She nodded. "We're good. Thank you."

"One other thing though..."

She tilted her head, waiting.

"You said you overheard a conversation at the coffee shop? You heard something else there?" He made it a question, easing his truck onto the road as he waited for her reply.

"Yes." She sighed and covered her face briefly with her hands. "You must think I'm the biggest busybody that ever lived."

He laughed. Sometimes she talked like an old lady. "No, I just think your hearing must be a whole lot better than mine."

"Well, I hereby pledge that even if I overhear something super juicy, I will keep it to myself and try to forget I ever heard it."

"No, don't do that. I'm sure it's that quality that makes you a good writer. And besides, it's boring enough around here without eliminating all the gossip."

Grinning, she looked pointedly out the window. "There's no way all this beauty could ever be boring."

"That wasn't fair. I just don't get to enjoy it very often." He checked himself. "No, that's not exactly true either. I don't *let* myself enjoy it very often."

"Why not?"

"I tell myself it's because the inn requires so much of me. I'm doing Jenny's job and mine and it's still not all getting done."

"You couldn't hire someone?"

"Oh, we have a girl who comes in to clean. Sadie. She worked for us when Jenny was still here. I'd let her go if I thought I could take on one more thing, but I just can't."

"I'm sorry. I guess running an inn gets romanticized."

"That's for sure. Jenny and I always laughed when we saw it portrayed in one of those Hallmark Christmas specials she loved. It's not *at all* like that. And we—*I* have a best case scenario with the inn fully booked year round."

"I guess I'll erase that off my bucket list then."

"What? You wanted to run an inn?" It surprised him a little, but then he was jaded.

"Oh, not really. I'd probably get bored with it. But staying in rentals as much as I do makes me feel like it would be kind of fun."

"I bet you'd be good at it."

"No. I'm not good with numbers. I'd have to hire someone to do the bookwork right off the bat and—"

"See? That's why it pays to be an accountant."

Her laughter was musical. "I'm sorry I said anything. I'll be eating those words for the next month, won't I?"

He chuckled, but her words were a harsh reminder that she would be checking out a few weeks from now. And already he knew he would miss her. He hadn't even known her a whole week, but she'd sparked something inside him that he'd thought was lost.

"By the way..." Her voice broke into his reverie. "Just so you know, what I overheard at the coffee shop wasn't anything bad. Especially now that I know they were talking about your beloved wife, not an ex."

His curiosity escalated. "So what *did* they say?"

"I'll tell you what I can remember. But just this once, and then, like I said, no more gossip."

"Got it." He slowed the car as they entered the Willowtree city limits.

"It wasn't anything bad really. Someone asked about whether you served breakfast and they said *she* did. Meaning Jenny, I assume. It was some older guys. Golfers, I think. But I don't want to jump to any conclusions."

He grinned. "Good point."

"Anyway, they said Jenny served a big breakfast and that she was a great cook, then the subject changed and somebody said something about waiting on a settlement and how it was a sad thing to happen to such a nice young couple. Putting that with what I overheard in your kitchen made me think they were talking about a divorce settlement."

"I see."

"But don't worry. I learned my lesson. No more jumping to conclusions."

"And no more gossip."

"Hey, you asked."

"I'm kidding. And thank you."

"Oh, one last thing, just so you know, they spoke very kindly of you and sounded really sorry for what happened—which, again, is why I thought they were talking about a divorce. Now I know better."

"Thanks for sharing all that." He glanced at the clock on the dashboard. "It's almost lunchtime. Would you want to stop and get something to eat?"

She hesitated. "You're sweet to ask but I really need to get some work done. If I don't get these pictures labeled, I'll forget where we were."

"Of course. I probably ought to get back too." She seemed to have forgotten that he'd offered to show her Sourwood Lake. But he wouldn't push things. Her rejection stung, even though it didn't sound like she was just making an excuse.

"But maybe another time. And I *would* love to go on that bike ride."

That eased the sting a little. "Sure. Just let me know when you have time. Oh, and I'll text you the mechanic's number so you can put him in your contacts."

"That'd be great. Thank you."

He parked in front of the house near her car and turned off the engine. "Do you want to try to start it one more time? In case it was just flooded or something?"

"Sure, I can try." Car keys in hand, she hopped out and went to her car. Same results as earlier. Nothing. She shrugged and shook her head before walking back to his truck.

He grimaced, matching her expression. "I'm sure Jim will get back to you as soon as he can."

"Why does stuff like this always happen on the weekend?"

"Yeah, I'm sorry about that. He may be out of town. But if you call or leave a message now, maybe you'll be at the top of the list for Monday. I can try him again if you'd like? It might save you a tow."

"No need. I can call."

It felt like another rejection, but he played it cool. "Okay. See you around." He waited until she was inside then went around to the backyard to do some much-needed weeding.

Chapter Ten

A quiet knock on her door made Liesl look up from her laptop. Closing the lid, she went to answer the door.

A dark-haired girl she guessed to be a teenager stood there with a shy smile, a bucket of cleaning supplies in hand. "So sorry to bother you. Would this be a good time to change your bedding and tidy up? I could come back later..."

"Oh, no. That's fine. I can go down on the porch until you're done. Just give me a minute to gather a few things."

"Of course."

The girl waited in the hallway until Liesl appeared with her laptop and bottled water.

"It shouldn't take me more than twenty minutes or so. I'm Sadie, by the way."

"Thanks, Sadie. And no rush. I'll be on the back porch."

Just yesterday, only after she thoroughly read the instructions that Zach had nagged her about on her arrival—she'd discovered there was a covered porch that overlooked his backyard. The porch was open to guests of the inn, and at least half of the reviews of the inn mentioned it as a highlight, so she was eager to check it out.

She wondered where her host had been. Of course, she'd

mostly kept to her room the rest of the weekend while she waited for them to come and fix her car.

Zach had texted her the mechanic's number without comment, but she hadn't seen him since their trip to Sorrel Hollow on Saturday. The mechanic, Jim, stopped by Saturday afternoon and confirmed that her battery was, indeed, dead, but apparently, that wasn't the only issue. He informed her he wouldn't be able to put in a new one until Monday.

Now it was Monday, almost noon, and the mechanic still hadn't showed up, which worried her a little since she'd given him her car keys. But Zach had said he was a friend, so she would trust that everything was on the up and up.

At least she'd gotten some work done, editing and polishing the book's introduction and writing a first draft of the section on Sorrel Hollow. She'd mostly focused on the campus but planned to go back into Sorrel Hollow for a day or two this week and pick out a few more places in town to highlight. After she and Zach biked the Point Lookout Trail, she would make that a feature as well—assuming the rest of the trail was as great as the part they'd hiked. And assuming it wasn't teeming with tourists.

After that, she needed to concentrate on Willowtree and its shops and restaurants. And find that lake Zach had talked about. Sourwood. She was beginning to feel as if she needed to apologize to the place of her birth and her childhood. She'd misjudged North Carolina through no fault of this beautiful state. She was eager to pick her older—and wiser—brother's brain. She'd always assumed Brad had the same low opinion of North Carolina— after all, he'd moved away practically the day he graduated high school. But now she wondered if she was wrong about that too.

She checked the time when she got down to the kitchen and decided it wasn't too late for a second cup of coffee, so she poured that and took it out to the porch. An older couple was just getting up from a glider swing as she scouted out a place to sit.

"You're welcome to the glider, honey," the woman said. "We've had all the sittin' around we can take for one day."

"Thanks, but I kind of need a table to work at."

"I thought they called that thing a *lap*top," the man said, eyeing her computer.

She laughed. "You're right, but it doesn't work that way for me. At least not when I have serious work to do. I need to spread things out around me." She gravitated to a small table in one corner, hoping they'd take a hint.

The man opened his mouth to say something, but the woman—his wife, Liesl was pretty sure—nudged him toward the door, tossing a knowing wink her way. "You have a good day, honey. Don't work too hard."

Grateful, Liesl blew out a sigh and settled into the comfy chair, taking in the charming porch. A vine-covered latticework trellis provided privacy but with a few empty spots that allowed her to peer through to the sprawling lawn. A choir of birds sang from the tall trees that enclosed and shaded the yard. One would have never known this was behind the house until they came through that door off the kitchen—the one Zach had come through the day he'd caught her eavesdropping.

She flushed at the thought and opened her laptop. The flowerpots were in need of some deadheading and the lawn showed signs of neglect but the overall effect was charming. It was clear the yard had once been the showpiece of the house. She wondered why the garden hadn't been pictured in the listing photos. Maybe it had and she just hadn't paid attention. After all, she hadn't read the instructions.

She smiled, remembering her first exchange with Zach. How different the man had turned out to be from her first impression of him.

The temperature was supposed to reach the eighties today, but here in the shade with a gentle breeze wafting from the ceiling fan, it was as close to perfect as it got. She scrolled through the photos she'd taken at Sorrel Hollow and selected a few to include in the book, writing captions to match, then editing and cropping the images.

She was almost finished when the back door opened and Sadie stuck her head out. "I'm finished, ma'am, whenever you want to get back in your room."

"Thank you. I appreciate it."

"Oh, and isn't that your white Honda out front?"

"Yes."

"There's a guy out there working on it. He's got the hood up. I thought you'd want to know."

A horn tooted from around front.

"Oh, good. Thanks. They must need to talk to me." She closed her laptop and scooted her chair back.

But Sadie laughed. "They might. I don't know. But that horn is my ride. I'd know that honk anywhere."

"Ah. I didn't think it sounded like mine." She rose and tucked her laptop under one arm. "I should probably go talk to them anyway. Hopefully I won't have to pledge my firstborn to pay the bill."

"Oh, you have kids?" Sadie brightened.

"Oh, no, no. Just an expression. I'm not even married yet." She quickly plumped the throw pillow on her chair and followed Sadie back through the house and out to the front porch.

The girl scooped up her bag and they exchanged farewells before Sadie jogged to the waiting vehicle. When she opened the passenger side door of the blue car, the driver reached over to move something off the seat and Liesl realized it was the guy—Davis—from the coffee shop in Sorrel Hollow. Strange that Zach hadn't mentioned the guy was dating Sadie. Maybe he didn't know. Or maybe they were just friends. But something about Sadie's demeanor when she'd greeted him said otherwise.

Not that she was *about* to say anything to Zach. She'd learned her lesson there. For all she knew, Davis was Sadie's older brother. But surely Zach would have mentioned that, too. They'd talked about both of them on Saturday.

Whatever the relationship was, Sadie seemed like a really sweet girl. Liesl hoped she hadn't gotten caught up with a bad influence.

Maybe she'd have a chance to talk with the girl over the next few weeks and try to plant some seeds.

FROM HIS OFFICE, Zach heard voices at the front of the house and went to pull the curtain aside. Jim's pickup was parked beside Liesl's car, and she was standing beside the open hood of her Honda talking to him.

The guy who'd picked up Sadie was also parked in front. At least it looked like the same vehicle. Dark blue, an older model he didn't recognize. It appeared Sadie was already in the car, and from the looks of her expressive hands, they were having a lively discussion. Or maybe a heated one? He couldn't see either of their faces.

He watched for a minute, wondering if he should go see what was going on, but he thought better of it. It really wasn't any of his business. Especially not after his "busybody" discussion with Liesl. He smiled to himself, thinking of the way she'd said it.

He made a note to get the e-bikes out and cleaned up first thing in the morning so they'd be ready for the bike ride he'd promised Liesl. He found himself praying it didn't rain this week, even though the lawn could use the moisture.

He pushed away a thought that had dogged him ever since he'd taken Liesl to Sorrel Hollow on Saturday. But it pushed itself right back to the forefront: Liesl's time at the inn was already one quarter over. She would be leaving in three weeks. The short time he'd spent with her had given him the first glimpse of hope he'd felt since losing Jenny. But the truth was, whether he treated her as a friend, or pursued her as something more, he was only setting himself up for disappointment.

But maybe that was okay. Maybe—and nothing disrespectful meant toward Liesl—but maybe she could be like a practice round for him getting back into the dating game. He gave a low growl. The thought made him sick. He'd been happy in marriage, happy to be settled with someone he adored, someone who made his life, if not exciting, certainly interesting. And comforting. That's how he felt about Liesl. She was interesting and comforting. And fun.

But it could never just be friendship with a woman. There was always the specter of romance lurking. And even if she wasn't remotely thinking about a romance with him—and he was certain she *wasn't*—eventually, that possibility would come up. And then what?

Drop it, Freylan. In three weeks she'll be history.

Chapter Eleven

With her car fixed, Liesl spent Tuesday and most of Wednesday thoroughly exploring the downtown areas of both Willowtree and Sorrel Hollow, and now she was up early and settled in to edit photos on the inn's back porch—a spot that had become her favorite "office."

She hadn't seen Zach once since Saturday, although last night she'd heard his now familiar voice in the hallway at the bottom of the stairs to her suite. She was starting to think he was avoiding her. But maybe he always tried to stay out of sight to afford his guests their privacy. She would have appreciated that from her hosts most places she'd stayed. But she had to admit, she looked forward to seeing him again.

And she hoped he hadn't forgotten about the bike ride. If she hadn't run into him before this weekend, maybe she'd use the promised bike ride as an excuse to seek him out.

Her phone buzzed on the table beside her and she smiled at the photo of Brad and Heather that filled the screen. "Hey, bro! What's up?"

"Does something have to be up for me to call my baby sister?"

"No, but it usually is."

"Well, okay then. I'll start with my short list."

"Ah ha, told ya!"

Her brother's rich laughter made her smile and she suddenly missed him deeply, even though she'd spent several days with him and Heather a few weeks before she'd left for North Carolina.

"Okay, three items on my list. Number one: did you know you left that purple water bottle here?"

"I didn't know that because I don't own a purple water bottle."

"Really? Okay, must have been somebody else. Number two: Not nagging, but just strongly urging you to give mom a call. She thinks she did something to offend you, and she's scared to call you because she can't take the rejection if you hang up on her and yada yada yada."

Liesl tensed then deflected. "You do know that nobody says that anymore, right?"

"Yada yada? What are you talking about? I *just* said it."

She laughed.

"Just call her, Lees. Please. Otherwise Heather and I are the ones that have to listen to the whining."

"Fine. I'll call her." She loved her mom, but there was no winning with that woman. "I'll call her, but I have no idea what we'll talk about."

"Maybe I can help with that."

"What do you mean?"

"Number 3: Heather's pregnant."

"Wait. What?" Liesl heard the words but they took a second to register. "Are you serious?"

"Would I kid you about something like that?"

"Brad! Oh, man, that it just the best news ever! When's she due? I need details! Did you know this when I was there? Do you know what you're having?"

"A baby. Pretty sure it's a human baby."

"Cut it out. You know what I mean."

He laughed. "We don't know. It's too soon. Heather just had her first baby appointment last week. And don't put it on Facebook or anything. We're just telling family for now. She's due mid-December-ish. The twentieth, I think. Hopefully not on Christmas day because that would stink."

She feigned a gasp. "To share a birthday with baby Jesus? Watch it, bro. You trying to get struck by lightning?"

"You know what I mean."

"I do. Oh, man, I am so happy for you guys!" She truly was. But despite her happiness, a selfish question pushed its way in. *Will I ever get to share this same happy news?* She forced the thought away. "Is Heather excited?"

"Ha! She can't talk about anything else." Her brother sounded a little bummed by the fact.

"Well, of course not. This is every woman's dream."

"Really? Is it yours?"

"Well, sure. Not right away or anything. But sure. Someday." Had he sensed her hesitation earlier? Thrown off by his question, she opted for levity. "I thought I'd work on the husband part first."

"Yeah, that's a good plan. A very good plan. Be sure and tell Mom that."

She would have given him a shove if he'd been sitting beside her. "So Mom knows about the baby?"

"Yeah, and she's pretty chuffed about it too."

"Chuffed? Um, I think that's another one nobody says anymore. Like since the 1950s?"

"Just call Mom, and don't worry your pretty little head about my language. I've made it this far in the world...I think I'll be okay."

She gave a little snort. "Okay, fine. And I'll call her tonight. That'll actually be something fun to talk about."

"See there. Don't say I never did anything for you."

"Are you kidding? You're making me an aunt! That's huge."

He laughed. "I thought you might like that."

She turned serious, surprised by the lump in her throat. "I'm really thrilled for you guys. Tell Heather I can't wait to see her belly."

"You can't even tell yet. But shhh...don't tell her that. She has a little pizza belly and she's already shopping for maternity clothes online."

"Ha! She won't be so happy about that with the next one."

"Whoa! Whoa, who said anything about a next one?"

"Brad! You wouldn't deprive your baby of a sibling, would you? A little mini me?"

"Oh, man. That seals the deal. We're having an only child."

She laughed, but her spirits soared. Brad and Heather had been trying for a while and Heather had confided at least a year ago that they were starting to fear it might not happen. Now they'd have a baby before the New Year. And *she* was going to be an aunt.

"Well, that's all I've got. Well, except one kind of big prayer request."

"Oh?" She braced herself, hearing the tension in Brad's voice.

"I'm a little nervous about my job."

"Uh-oh. What's going on?"

"There've been some rumors about layoffs. I don't think my department will be hit, but then I didn't think they'd let two of the vice presidents go either."

"Ouch. That doesn't sound good. But you've been there forever." Brad worked for a large construction company in Dallas and he'd been very successful.

"Yeah...not as long as the VPs they laid off though."

"I'm sorry. That's scary. I'll definitely be praying."

"Thanks. This would not be a good time to lose my job."

"Is there ever a good time to lose a job?"

"Good point. Thanks for praying though. But enough about me. Everything good on your end? You like South Carolina?"

She grinned into the phone. "I don't know, I've never been there."

"Wait. *Where* are you?"

"*North* Carolina."

"Oh, yeah. Back home, huh?"

She gave a little growl. "I don't claim this as home."

"I know, I know. Just another spot on the map. I can't keep track of you. Have you found a church there yet?"

"Not yet, Brad. I'm only here for three more weeks."

"Too bad. I'll be in Asheville in September for a seminar."

"Bummer. That's really close to where I'm staying, but I'll be long gone by then."

"I figured."

She was grateful for the change of subject.

But he circled right back. "Well, like I was saying, sis—about church—don't let yourself get out of the habit because it's—"

"Don't worry, bro, I'm still reading my Bible and praying." But not much of either if she was being honest.

"That's good. That's good, but it's—"

"I know, I know, it's not the same."

"Okay, fine. I can take a hint. I'll let Mom take over from here."

She heard the smile in his voice and groaned.

"Well, I need to go pick up Heather. Her car's in the shop."

"Oh, man, I'm sorry." She told him briefly about her own car woes, and they hung up amidst more congratulations and "I love yous"—and the roar of a lawn mower.

Zach appeared around the corner of the house, pushing a dusty lawn mower. When he spotted her, he waved, then left the mower idling and came over to the porch railing.

"Sorry about the noise. It'll only take half an hour or so."

"No problem. I was about to go in anyway."

"Everything going okay? You need anything?"

"Everything's good. They got my car fixed."

"That's good. Dead battery?"

"That and a couple of other issues. But it didn't end up being too terrible. Not as much as I feared anyway."

"Good."

"Oh, and I saw that lake you told me about. Sourwood. It's beautiful."

"Yeah. It's nice." He took a step back and eyed the mower over his shoulder.

"I'd better get back to work." A bit taken aback by his formal, almost detached tone, she rose and started gathering her belongings. But before she could change her mind, she blurted out, "I was wondering... I thought I'd go to church Sunday morning. Is there one you'd recommend?"

And now that the question was out there, she made up her mind. She would go to church on Sunday. She wanted to set a good example for her little niece or nephew. And besides making her brother happy, she'd get major brownie points when she told her parents.

ZACH TURNED off the mower and took a step toward Liesl, happier to answer her question than it warranted. "Do you have a church in mind?"

"I'm open to suggestions." Her cheeks flushed. "To be honest, I haven't been in a while. Even back home."

"Yeah, me neither. Not for a couple of years now."

"Really? Since...Jenny?"

He nodded.

"But you used to go?"

"Oh, every Sunday." Did he really want to get into this conversation with her? But something compelled him. "When Jenny was in the coma, I was afraid to leave the hospital for more than a few minutes. And then after she died... It was just hard to go and...sit by myself." He didn't tell her that the few times he had gone, people either smothered him with pity or behaved as if a car crash was a communicable disease. There didn't seem to be a happy medium. Worse, he'd been ashamed to realize that before Jenny's death, he himself had been solidly in the "avoid 'em like the plague" camp with people who'd experienced a tragedy. So he didn't blame them. He got it. But that didn't make it any easier to walk through the doors.

Still, he hadn't lost his faith. Far from it. He was grateful for a good counselor who'd helped him through that first year. And he had a couple of good friends he could talk to about God and matters of faith. Even so, he missed the fellowship of being part of a church. But when he thought about walking into that sanctuary where he and Jenny had worshipped together, it paralyzed him. And the longer he didn't go, the easier it was to find an excuse to stay home.

"Well, I know how that is. Not losing someone, of course," she added quickly. "But walking in alone. Sitting alone. Being afraid you're accidentally sitting in someone else's seat..."

It shouldn't have, but it surprised him to realize that she might experience the same loneliness. "Would you like to go with me? I can't this Sunday, but maybe next?"

"Where do you go?"

"Well, if you don't mind, I was thinking of going somewhere new. I've heard good things about a church called Cornerstone here in Willowtree."

"Sounds good to me. Do you know what time services are?"

"Not for sure. I'll let you know though."

"Thanks. I'd like that. Having someone to sit with too."

"If you like... Maybe we could make a day of it. Get breakfast first and then ride bikes at Point Lookout? If you want to."

"I do. That would be great."

"I think there's rain in the forecast for next weekend, but that could easily change. We can play the bike ride by ear, okay?"

"Sure. I'll look forward to it. And thanks."

She gave a little wave and disappeared into the house. Zach started the mower again, shaking his head. What had just happened? Hadn't he decided just two days ago that he would *not* pursue this guest? The one who would be checking out in *less* than three weeks now, never to be seen again?

He should be feeling frustrated and angry at his lack of self-control. So why did he feel happy and hopeful instead?

Chapter Twelve

June

"You're sure I'm not dressed too casually?" Fastening her seatbelt, Liesl looked down at her black leggings and sleeveless tunic, her outfit chosen more for the biking they'd do later than for the church service. She'd brought along a light jacket since they'd be in air conditioning at breakfast and in the sanctuary.

For the past week and a half, they'd only seen each other briefly, coming and going in the inn. Thanks to a rainy week, she'd managed to get some writing done, but she was grateful for sunshine today and a chance to get out and do something besides stay holed up in her room.

"If *you're* too casual"—Zach looked down at his khaki shorts, black polo, and leather sandals—"then I'll definitely get kicked out. But you're fine. You look nice."

"Thanks." She hadn't been fishing for a compliment but it made her smile, even though he said it the way her brother might have.

"Seriously, most of the churches around here cater to tourists and expect shorts and T-shirts."

"I hope you're right."

He tossed her a conspiratorial grin. "We'll sit in the back so we can escape if it looks like we're seriously underdressed."

She laughed, liking this playful side of him. "Sounds like a plan."

They were quiet on the short ride to the church but the way he kept wiping his palms on the knees of his pants made her think he was nervous. She was too, but probably not for the same reasons.

She decided to meet it head-on. "Are you afraid you might run into someone you know?"

"Maybe a little." He turned into a large gravel parking lot, parked the car, and turned to study her. "Can I be honest?"

"Of course."

A wry smile quirked his lips. "I'm mostly worried about how to introduce you. You know, if I do see someone."

"You could say I'm your cousin visiting from Iowa." She winked.

"I'm not sure telling a lie in church is a good idea."

"Good point. How about saying I'm your *friend* from Iowa. That would be true."

"Yes. It would. But when they ask how we met? Then what?"

She made a face. "I see your point. Then it kind of feels like a lie again." She glanced at her phone. "What time did you say the service starts?"

He chuckled. "I see where you're going with that. Let's drive around the block a couple of times and go in after it's already started."

"And sit in the back. And leave before it's over."

He touched her hand briefly before putting the car back in gear. "Listen, I'm happy to be seen with you. I hope that didn't sound...otherwise. It's just that if I show up with a beautiful woman on my arm, anyone who knows me is going to think... well, you know. And then rumors will be all over town and then I'll have to explain—"

"I'm not offended, Zach." She grinned up at him. "In fact, I rather liked that part about some beautiful woman. How about if I don't go in on your arm?"

He laughed. "I don't think that's going to change anything."

He meandered down a winding street, a charming one she hadn't yet discovered on her explorations of the town. She made a mental note to come back here tomorrow and see if there was anything worth highlighting for her book.

Half a mile down, he pointed to a steepled church. "That's where I usually go."

"It's pretty." The sign in front said Willowtree Christian Church. "Were you married there?"

"No. Jenny was from Charlotte. We got married there. In the church she grew up in."

"What about you? I'm guessing by your accent—or lack of one—that you didn't grow up around here."

"I get that a lot. My homogenized accent, I mean. I grew up all over the place. I was in seven different schools before I left for college. My dad was always looking for something better. Finally, the year before I started high school, he found something better." He closed his eyes. "Something better than my mom and me...and that was that. I haven't seen him since."

"Oh, Zach. I'm so sorry."

"Yeah. It was rough. For Mom more than me. Those years are kind of a blur, to be honest."

"I can imagine." She shook her head, already understanding him better. "Has your mom remarried?"

His smile came slowly. "No. She never did. Mom passed away three years ago. But she was a strong believer. I know where she is now and that gives me a lot of peace."

"I'm sorry. I'm happy for her, but sad for you. She must have been very young."

"She was sixty-two. Her death certificate says acute hypertension—or something like that. I honestly think she died of a broken heart. But she was strong for me until the end."

"So you lost your mom and your wife only a year apart?"

He nodded. "Just a little more than a year."

"I can't even imagine."

"It was hard. But I actually find comfort in knowing Mom and Jenny are together now."

She paused for a moment, watching him, trying to put herself in his shoes. "Yes, I can understand that."

"They really loved each other." That same faraway look came to his eyes, then he glanced at the clock on the dashboard and sucked in a breath. "We're going to be later than fashionably late if we don't turn around right now."

They drove back to the church in silence, then jogged up the stairs into the building, arriving in the foyer out of breath and laughing quietly at themselves.

A friendly middle-aged couple greeted them near the open doors to the sanctuary where the congregation stood singing a worship song that Liesl didn't recognize. The woman handed them each a folded program, and the man indicated some empty seats near the front.

Zach thanked the greeters but once they were inside the sanctuary, he shot Liesl a conspiratorial grin and with a light hand at the small of her back, steered her to an empty pew on the back row of the far side of the auditorium.

She responded with a discreet thumbs up, and they slipped into the row, remaining standing along with the congregation. The words to the song were on screens up front, and Zach immediately joined in singing. He had a rich baritone voice and for some reason, it surprised her that he sang so confidently.

She had a decent voice and could carry a tune, but she didn't know the song, so she sang quietly beside him, dropping her voice even lower where the tune was uncertain and just enjoying the sound of his voice harmonizing with the congregation. She was almost disappointed when the song ended and a man she assumed was the pastor took the stage.

When the Scripture was read, Zach silently offered to share his

Bible. She was embarrassed she'd forgotten to bring her own, but she declined and followed along in a Bible provided in the back of the pew. As the sermon progressed, she noticed Zach slowly panning the small crowd, no doubt checking to see if he knew anyone here.

The message was solid, if not riveting. And while she was glad she'd come, guilt pinched her to realize that she was more thankful she'd be able to tell Brad and her parents that she'd been to church than she was to be back in church after so many weeks. Even so, she was glad to be here, especially since she had someone to sit with.

She forced her attention back to the sermon. In case Zach wanted to discuss it later, she didn't want to have to admit that she'd daydreamed through most of it.

As the last song came to a close, she threw Zach a questioning look, wondering if he wanted to slip out early. He leaned close and whispered, "It's okay. I didn't see anyone I know."

They stayed till the end, but since they were in the back row, they were able to leave with a minimum of polite greetings. Zach walked with her to the passenger side of his truck, the two bicycles in the truck bed reminding her that their day together was just getting started. The thought made her inexplicably happy.

He opened her door for her and she thanked him. She couldn't remember a date ever opening a car door for her—not that she'd had that many dates in her life. The courtesy might be old-fashioned, but she liked it.

Once behind the wheel, he turned to her with a teasing smile. "That wasn't so bad, was it?"

"Not at all. I thought the sermon was good."

He nodded. "It was. Thanks for going with me. It kind of broke the ice. Maybe it won't be quite so hard to go alone now."

"I'll be here for a couple more Sundays...if you want company." It didn't feel natural being so forward, but she wanted him to know.

"Did you like that church enough to go back again?"

"I did. It seemed like there were quite a few young people there, especially for an early service. But don't you want to go back to your own church?"

He released a slow breath. "I don't know. The truth is, our church was really more Jenny's church. I mean, I liked it fine, and we were starting to get involved. But I think I might like a fresh start somewhere else."

"I can understand that."

"Okay, well... Let's play it by ear. But I'll talk to you before next Sunday."

"Sure." She tried not to take it personally that he'd put her off.

IT WAS ALMOST ten by the time they got out of the church parking lot and drove to the café Liesl had chosen. But they got seated right away, and Zach was grateful to learn that the breakfast menu was still being offered.

An hour later, bellies full, driving away from the café, Zach realized that he could barely remember what he'd eaten. He only knew that he hadn't felt so carefree in a very long time. He and Liesl had compared notes about their less-than-ideal school years, dissected the sermon, and talked about favorite books and movies. They had similar tastes, but just different enough to keep things interesting.

He hadn't dated much before he met Jenny, but enough to remember that one of the things he'd liked most about her was that he could be completely himself with her. Liesl made him feel the same. Likely because there was no pressure on either of them. She was only in town for a while. And this wasn't a date. Not really.

His phone buzzed in his pocket and he excused himself and slipped the phone from his pocket. A message from the inn's reservation app. "Sorry, I'd better take this."

"Of course."

He pulled over and checked the app. A guest was arriving earlier than expected and asking whether they could check in at three instead of four. He reluctantly agreed. He still needed to make up the room since a couple had checked out late this morning, and Sadie wouldn't be in until tomorrow. Three-plus hours would still give him and Liesl plenty of time to ride the trail, and though the clear skies belied it, there was rain in the forecast. Still, he hated to put a deadline on this day.

Looking up from his phone, he caught her watching him, and in that fleeting glance, he felt sure she was feeling the same emotions he was.

Maybe this guest's message was divine intervention. Because if he let himself pay attention, that nagging little voice was still whispering in his ear, reminding him that nothing could come of this thing that was sparking between them.

Before he could change his mind, he typed a reply to his guest. "Sure, no problem. We'll have your room ready by three p.m."

Chapter Thirteen

Out of breath but elated with the exercise and glorious views, Liesl dismounted the e-bike and put the kickstand down. She walked to the edge of the trail where it towered over the same railroad tunnel where they'd walked this path before.

She framed the image with her phone's camera and took several shots, then checked the resulting photos, zooming in on the tunnels. The light was even better in these pictures than it had been before, and today there was a bank of fluffy clouds reflecting the light and casting stunning shadows.

She heard Zach's footsteps behind her. "It's all downhill from here."

She turned to roll her eyes at him. "Haha. I wish."

"No. I'm serious. We've been climbing since we left the parking lot. It's just that the pedal-assist makes it easier. But we're almost to the end of the trail, and then we get to turn around and go back down." His smile said he relished revealing that fact.

"Well, that is the best news ever. Even with an e-bike, that was hard work! But it was fun," she added quickly, not wanting him to feel bad for suggesting the trail. "I don't know when the last time I rode a bike was. And that little boost up the hills is great. I might have to get me one of these."

"You should. You could easily add a rack to the back of your car."

"I'll have to think about it. Sadly, being a travel writer isn't the most lucrative job in the world."

"But if you love what you do, I guess it's worth it?" He made it a question.

"I guess. I do enjoy my work. I just don't know if I want to be on the road the rest of my life."

"What would you do if you weren't a writer?"

He seemed genuinely interested, so she risked an honest reply. "I'd probably still write. I'd love to try my hand at a novel some-day." That would likely be when she was in her empty nest years. If she ever got to have a *full* nest in the first place. But she wasn't ready to be *that* honest with him.

"Wow, a novel. That seems...daunting."

"I'm sure it would be. But I'd love to give it a try." She rolled her eyes. "I suppose every writer thinks they have a novel in them. And of course, mine will be an instant bestseller and will be made into a blockbuster movie."

He laughed then put a hand over his mouth as if he thought maybe she was serious.

Which made her laugh. "Don't worry. I'm kidding. What about you? What would you do if you didn't run the inn?"

"Well, as you know, in my former life—when Jenny was running the inn—I worked as an accountant. Her accident happened in the middle of tax season and after I missed so much work caring for her, my firm let me go."

She frowned. "That was kind of a dirty trick."

He shrugged. "I would have had to quit that job anyway in order to keep the inn running. It's what Jenny would have wanted. And it would have felt like a betrayal to sell the inn."

"Are you glad you kept it though? Now that some time has passed?"

"I am." He hesitated, as if deciding how much he wanted to say. "It's not what I would have chosen, and I'm aware it's not my area of gifting but it's what I was handed. And I think Jenny would be happy that I've kept it going."

Liesl didn't know how to reply so she kept silent. But she wanted to tell him that she thought his wife would have wanted him to do whatever made him happiest, whatever helped him heal from his grief. Feeling awkward in the silence, she went back to stand by her bike, waiting for him to mount his.

"You rested up?" He looked pointedly at her bicycle.

"Whenever you are."

"We could go back from here, but we'd miss a really pretty overlook at the top of the hill. It's not far though. We can turn around up there and coast all the way back down."

"I'll follow you." It felt rude that she'd essentially shut down the conversation. And yet, it suddenly seemed too personal and too fraught with risks.

They rode to the top and she got some stunning photos of the layers of shadowed mountains fading from dark green to shades of blue to misty purple. These rolling peaks were quintessential North Carolina even if they'd become a bit cliché among the photographs in travel magazines. But she actually preferred these mountains to the Rockies. They were no less majestic, and looking at them now, mist hovering just below each peak, she thought of the psalm she'd read this morning. ...*May the Lord rejoice in his works, who looks on the earth and it trembles, who touches the mountains and they smoke!* The mist looked a little like smoke, and she wondered if this sight was something like the image that had inspired the psalmist.

They'd met a few hikers and other bicyclists coming down the trail as they ascended, but now they mostly had the trail to themselves, and Zach slowed, waiting for her to catch up with him, then keeping pace and riding beside her.

"You doing okay?" he asked, after they'd ridden side by side for several minutes. "You're awfully quiet."

"I'm doing great. This is awesome, actually. I forgot how much fun it was to ride a bike. Especially downhill." She smirked.

"Yeah, that's the reward, for sure. The first time Jenny and I rode, we started out up here at the top, not realizing it would be all uphill coming back. And that was before we got the e-bikes."

Liesl laughed. "I bet that was depressing."

"We were young and dumb. And in a lot better shape than I am now."

That was hard to imagine. Zach's shorts and T-shirt showed off his physique, and she'd been admiring him, watching tan, muscular legs pedal, broad shoulders taut over the handlebars.

She took a deep breath and made a decision. If they were only short-term friends getting to know each other, there was no reason to avoid the subject of Jenny. And if anything deeper were to spark between them, then it was a subject they must broach. "So did you and Jenny ride here a lot? This was her bike, I assume?"

"It was. We didn't ride as much as we would have liked." He pedaled and kept looking forward. "I really regret that now. But between my job and the church and, of course, the inn, life was pretty chaotic most of the time."

"Are her parents still in Charlotte—Jenny's? Do you see them often?"

He seemed grateful when he had to slow and ride single file to let a group of hikers pass. But he maneuvered back beside her once the trail was clear again. "No. Her dad passed about ten years ago, and I've only seen Glory—Jenny's mom—a handful of times since Jenny died. I think it's hard for Glory to be around me. I'm a reminder of what she lost, you know? And... I don't know." He shrugged. "Maybe she blames me a little for what happened."

Liesl wasn't sure how to respond. This man had lost so much. And all fairly recently. She needed to remember that. And offer grace. But curiosity won out. "Blame you? But I thought you said she was alone in the car."

"She was. I don't mean Glory blames me for *causing* the accident, but I think maybe she thinks I should have gone with Jenny that night. That it wouldn't have happened if I'd been driving. Or that it should have been me who was killed instead of her."

"That's awful, Zach. She actually said that?"

"No. No, of course not. Not in so many words."

"Then don't take that on for a minute. I can't imagine anyone actually blaming you."

He shrugged and changed the subject. "So what about you? Are your parents still in Iowa?"

"Oh, I didn't grow up in Iowa. I moved there four years ago. My parents live in Colorado now. But I grew up mostly in Cumberland County, near Fayetteville. Fayetteville, North Carolina, not Arkansas. Couldn't get out of there fast enough."

"Really? Why?" He cocked his head, looking genuinely curious. "I've never been in that part of the state... I think I've seen the exits for Fayetteville on the way to the beach once maybe."

"You didn't miss anything." She suddenly felt like a traitor. "I'm sure it's a very nice town. I just have some not-so-great memories of living there. My parents had a lot of struggles—both financially and in their marriage—when we lived there. Those are years I'd just as soon forget."

"But your parents are still together?"

"They are. They actually seem to be doing really well now." Her countenance brightened. "They both have good jobs now and things are better financially, plus they don't have my brother and me wreaking havoc on their lives."

"Oh, you have a brother?"

She released a little huff. "Yeah. One of those love-hate relationships when we were growing up, but Brad is one of my dearest friends now. They live in Dallas. Well, a suburb. He's married," she explained, "and he and Heather have a baby on the way. I just found out last week."

"That's cool. You'll be an aunt. I always wondered what it would be like to have a brother or sister."

"I'm sure there are advantages to being an only too." But she'd never thought about the fact that only children would never have nieces or nephews—unless it was by marriage.

"I suppose there were advantages. But I could have used a brother or sister these past couple of years."

"Oh, I'm sure." She felt bad for making light of his only-child status. And appreciated Brad all the more.

A volley of raindrops fell from the leaves overhead. She was grateful for the distraction, but a few minutes later the skies opened and the trees no longer offered protection.

"We're only about a half mile from the end of the trail," Zach yelled over the cacophony of the rain, pedaling faster. "We're parked just around that curve up ahead. Follow me!"

Pedaling hard to keep up, she squealed as her clothes quickly became soaked. A bolt of lightning cracked across the sky and she squealed again and pedaled faster.

"You okay?" he hollered, looking back over his shoulder at her.

"I'm fine. Just drenched!"

Finally they reached the parking lot and laughing, they parked their bikes behind his truck and hopped off.

"You go ahead and get in." He motioned toward the passenger side door.

"It's okay. I doubt I could get any wetter."

"Good point."

Zach lowered the tailgate and she helped him lift the heavy bikes into the bed of the truck. He hopped up on the tailgate and laid them over on their sides, then jumped down and unlocked her door.

"Do you have a towel or a blanket or...anything I could sit on?" She was scared to look in the mirror, knowing she must look like a drowned cat.

"Sorry, I don't. But it won't hurt these seats to get a little wet."

She climbed in and he looked up at her with concern. "Are you cold?"

"No, I'm fine. Just glad we're not too far from home and dry clothes."

"That's for sure." Chuckling, he closed her door and jogged around to climb behind the wheel.

He pulled out of the parking lot and turned out onto the road the way they'd come, but they'd only gone a couple of miles when he tapped the brakes. In front of them, a raging river of muddy brown water gushed across the roadway.

Chapter Fourteen

Two cars waiting on the other side of the road seemed to indicate the water had just now breached the pavement, but it was rushing with such velocity that Zach didn't dare try to cross here. Especially not with Liesl in the truck beside him.

Resting his right arm across the top of the seat, he checked the road behind him and slowly backed to the side of the road. The embankment was steep and the road narrow. "My truck has decent clearance, but I don't think I'm going to risk crossing here. That water's moving pretty fast."

"Have we gotten that much rain that it would flood?" Her eyes were wide and she sat on her hands as if trying to keep them steady.

"That came down hard and fast. And when it's raining upstream, the river can rise really fast. But it's not unusual on this road. Once it stops raining, it'll subside as quickly as it came up."

"So now what do we do?"

"We can turn around and take a different road." *Or they could wait.* But she was shivering and miserable, and there was only one reason *not* to take the other route.

Jaw clenched, he checked his mirrors and made a tight three-point turn in the road and headed the other way. He'd managed to avoid this scenario for more than two years, but it was inevitable now. When they reached the crossroads, he turned right, forcing his foot to stay on the accelerator when everything in him wanted to hit the brakes hard.

He sensed her watching him and loosened his iron grip on the steering wheel, hoping she hadn't noticed his white knuckles.

"Are you worried we won't be able to get across here either?"

"No, we're fine. It would take a lot more rain than this to flood this road. It's just that…" He blew out a heavy breath. "This is a route I try to avoid."

"Oh? Not a good road."

"Not for me." He closed his eyes briefly. "Up ahead is where Jenny's accident happened."

"Oh, Zach. I'm so sorry. There's not another way we could go?"

"It's okay. It's high time I faced it. I'm glad I'm not alone."

"You haven't been here since the accident?"

He sucked in a shallow breath. "Just once. When they pulled her car out. The day after it happened. She was in the hospital in a coma then, but for some reason I felt like I needed to be there when they pulled out the car. Like maybe that would give me some answers."

"Did it?"

"No. It was just so strange that she drove safely all the way back from Charlotte—and then died just a few minutes from home."

"I'm so sorry, Zach. Do you…want me to drive?"

He shook his head and gave her what he hoped was a grateful smile. "I'm okay. It'll be good to get it over with, actually. It's stupid that I haven't done it before now."

"It isn't stupid at all, Zach. I don't blame you. I'd feel the same."

"Well, thank you. I appreciate you not calling me a wuss." He tried to laugh, but it came out more like a groan.

"Don't even think like that. Nobody would blame you for wanting to avoid this road." She turned slightly in her seat, as if to bolster him. "Will you show me where it was? When we go by?"

"I will." He felt stronger already, just having her beside him. It was a disconcerting thought. Especially coupled with the reminder of her check-out date, June 23. He'd looked it up in the reservation app this morning before they left for church—just to remind himself what this could *not* be.

He slowed the truck, and for a minute, wondered if he'd even recognize the spot after all these months. But then suddenly, they were upon it, the unmistakable scarred oak still standing off to the right of the road where Jenny's car had careened into the tree.

"Right there." He indicated a tree trunk, a deep gash in its gray bark revealing the lighter flesh of the wood. "You see that tree."

She shivered harder and put her hands over her mouth. "That's where her car hit?"

He nodded again, not trusting his voice. He slowed further and slid as far to the right in the road as he could as they climbed the steep rise of the hill. "It was raining that night. Probably a lot like this...except it was dark. She was coming the other way, and when she started down this hill, apparently the road was slick from rain and she lost control of the car."

"No one saw it happen."

"No. When she wasn't home twenty minutes after I was expecting her—and her mom said she'd left almost three hours before that—I knew something was wrong."

"Oh, Zach."

"I called the sheriff, and after searching along her route, they discovered what had happened. Her car sideswiped the tree and was airborne another few hundred feet into the woods down there. The ambulance had already taken her to the ER by the time I got—"

He hit the brakes hard when he realized the car at the top of the hill wasn't moving. Thankfully he'd only been doing about twenty miles an hour, but even so, Liesl gave a little gasp and braced her palms on the dashboard.

Zach started to pull around the car but stopped again when he saw someone scramble up the steep ditch and climb behind the wheel.

"What on earth is he doing?" Liesl sat forward, peering through the windshield. "Hey, isn't that the guy from the coffee shop? In Sorrel Hollow?"

"Davis?" Zach turned to look beside them. It looked like the blue car that had been waiting for Sadie that day at the inn. "Hmmm. That car looks familiar. I wonder if he's got engine trouble."

He put the truck in Park and climbed out, but before he'd taken two steps, the blue car sped away, disappearing over the next hill in a spray of sand and muddy rainwater.

He brushed himself off and climbed back into the truck. "That was strange."

"Was it him?"

How would she know what vehicle Davis Simmons drove? "Did you see the driver? What made you think it was Davis?"

Liesl was quiet for a few seconds, then blurted, "I didn't notice the plate number at the inn the other day, but that car had the same Chislan Automotive plate holder."

"The car at the inn?"

She nodded.

"Hmm... That dealership is a couple counties over."

"I'm pretty sure that's the car that picked up the girl who cleans for you—Sadie—the other day. Judging by how they acted with each other, I'd guess they're a couple."

He remembered then. Seeing Sadie run out to a blue car like the one that had just sped off. And not being able to get a good look at the driver, but having the impression that it was a man he thought too old for Sadie to be hanging out with. He told Liesl what he'd seen. "I couldn't tell who it was, but that makes sense now. But if he's messed up in something he shouldn't be..."

What was he supposed to do though? Though he thought of her as much younger, Sadie was probably eighteen or close to it. She could do what she wanted. Besides, she wasn't his responsibility. Neither was Davis, although if the guy had done something that violated his scholarship eligibility, it shouldn't go unreported. The possibility that someone thought so little of Jenny's scholarship made him fume. He inhaled deeply. No use jumping to conclusions. He, of all people, knew that things weren't always as they seemed.

Heart hammering, he raced up the highway, eyes darting between the road and the view behind him in the passenger-side mirror. That mirror had caused all this trouble in the first place. Right after the accident, he'd hidden his car behind their house, not wanting to face his father's wrath for tearing up the car. It was so stupid that something like this could happen the first time he'd driven by himself with his brand new driver's license.

He'd found the right replacement mirror. It was just the wrong color. But even though he'd gotten it at a salvage yard, it had cost him half a week's wages. He couldn't afford to have it painted, especially since that might make people ask questions. The black paint wasn't that different than the navy blue of his car, especially if he let it get dirty. And for almost a year he'd let himself forget about it. Thought he was home free.

But then the dominoes had started to fall. Three weeks ago he'd driven by the spot where it happened, alarmed to see a black car parked on the shoulder of the narrow road. Just across from where Zach Freylan was stopped now. The car that day wasn't a cop car, unless it was an unmarked vehicle. But it had strange tags that looked "official" somehow. Government tags? And two men were rummaging around in the woods below.

He knew what they were looking for. And he had to find it before they did. Maybe they already had. But he didn't think so.

Otherwise, they would have already knocked on his door. Taken him away.

He'd searched the accident site hard right after it happened, but not finding the mirror, he figured if he didn't find it neither would they. But then he overheard that conversation and a new urgency struck him.

He was only sixteen when it happened. They would have put him in juvie. That was bad enough. But last week he turned eighteen. If they caught him now, he was probably looking at prison. He'd read all about what happened to kids like him in prison. He'd kill himself first.

He had to find the evidence. But he couldn't let anyone discover him down there combing through the dense underbrush. Even so, he had a story ready if anyone discovered him. He even had a collar for his imaginary little dog who'd run away into the dark woods when he stopped to let the dog relieve herself. A cheap, frayed collar he'd gotten from the Goodwill. That would be more convincing than a brand new Walmart collar. So now, he "owned" a dog. Her name was Daisy and she was a mutt. He'd decided she would be a mutt in case he ever had to actually go get an actual dog from the pound to corroborate his story.

Sometimes he thought he was losing his mind. He hated how this whole mess had forced him to live in an imaginary world half the time. And the other half? He didn't know if it was imaginary or not. Didn't know if those cops at The Bagel Station had come to check him out or if they were just having an innocent snack break. Didn't know if Zach Freylan suspected something and that's why he'd suddenly showed up at the shop. Or if that was a coincidence too.

But today, when he picked up Sadie at the inn, she'd noticed the mirror. She was messing with her stupid hair and bent down to check her reflection in the side-mirror.

"Hey, did you know this mirror is a different color than the rest of your car? Look, the paint isn't the same."

He froze up and tried to change the subject. But she just kept going on and on about it. Wouldn't shut up. He finally told her he couldn't take her home. Said he forgot something and had to leave right away.

He could tell it hurt her feelings. He hated that. Sadie was pretty much his only friend in the world now. And she, at least, wasn't imaginary. But something told him it was urgent that he get back to the woods and search one more time.

And then Freylan had showed up there too. Pulled up right behind him on the side of the road. Looked him in the eye.

The net was closing in.

THE SUN DIPPED behind the tallest mountain peak as they rode back to the inn in silence. Liesl watched Zach surreptitiously. He seemed deep in thought. And sad. She struggled with whether to give him some space and silence or try to draw him out.

After a few uncomfortable moments, she touched his arm briefly. "Are you okay?"

He nodded. "I'm fine. Kind of glad to get that over with actually." He turned to meet her gaze. "Thanks."

"For what?"

"Just for being here. Without talking."

"I wasn't sure which you'd prefer." She still wasn't.

He smiled. "You managed to come up with the perfect ratio of quiet to noise."

"Well, that's a first." She forced herself to be quiet again. To wait on him.

Finally, he spoke again. "Jenny would have liked you."

She swallowed hard, surprised by the compliment. "Thank you, Zach. That's such a sweet thing to say."

"It's just the truth. Granted, there weren't many people Jenny *didn't* like, but she especially valued genuineness."

"I'm glad you think I'm genuine."

"Why? You're not?"

A glimmer of a smile let her know he was teasing.

"I try. I'm sure I'm not always successful, but I do try." She gave him a sidewise glance. "When I'm not being *noisy*, that is."

But he ignored her ribbing. "I think you're nailing it."

"Well, you make it easy." She looked away and pretended to inspect her manicure, uncomfortable with how personal the conversation had become.

"I'm really grateful you were with me. I don't think it will be so hard to take that road after this."

"I'm glad."

"But Liesl, I— There's something I feel like I need to say."

"Okay..." She waited, nervous yet extremely curious.

"It's just that I don't want you to think I make a habit of dating my guests. To be honest, I haven't had a date since Jenny died. Maybe I shouldn't tell you this, but until the week you checked in, the inn still listed Jenny and me as the proprietors."

She thought back to one of their earliest exchanges on the inn's reservation app. "I *thought* there was a woman in that bio. No wonder I thought you were married. But wait... You changed it that week?"

He nodded. "Even though I had no idea what you would become to me, something about that day made me feel like it was time to let go of the past. And Liesl, I'm aware—very aware, that you are leaving in a few weeks. I'm not under any delusions that this"—he motioned between them—"could go anywhere. But for what it's worth... I wish things were different."

"I do too." The words were out before she realized how true they were. "So...I guess we just enjoy a few days of friendship, say our goodbyes, and write it off as—" She shrugged, at a loss for the right word.

"As a good month," he finished. "But just so you know, if you were sticking around, you're the kind of woman I'd want to ask out."

"I'm honored." She smirked. "I think."

He laughed. "I bet that's not a conversation you've ever had before."

She eyed him. "What do you mean?"

"I'm not asking you out but"—he did a goofy imitation of himself—"if I *was* asking anyone out, it'd be you."

She giggled. "No, can't say as I've ever had that conversation."

"But I'm serious, Liesl." He reached across the seat and brushed his hand over hers. "You're going to sweep some lucky guy off his feet."

She couldn't answer. Because right now, she only wanted Zachary Freylan to be that guy. And she couldn't stop wondering about his revelation that the week she'd checked in, Zach had taken Jenny off the bio.

Chapter Fifteen

They arrived back at the inn to find Sadie sitting on the front porch steps, elbows on her knees, chin propped on clasped hands. Zach couldn't make out her expression in the shadows of the overhanging branches, but her demeanor made him think something was wrong.

"Is she working today?" Liesl watched the young girl closely through the windshield, her own expression holding concern.

He frowned. "Not on Sunday. Not sure what's going on. Let me talk to her and make sure everything's okay and then I'll help you carry your stuff."

"You don't need to, Zach. I know you have a room to get ready."

He checked his phone. "It's okay. There's still time. And we can leave the bikes in the back and maybe ride again later this week. If you want to." He jumped out of the truck without waiting for an answer, not wanting Liesl to feel pressured. Or himself to be disappointed if she declined.

"Hey, Sadie..." He got out of the truck and approached the porch slowly, hoping he wasn't walking into a minefield.

Sadie glanced up, as if she hadn't heard them pull into the driveway. "Oh, hi."

"Everything okay?"

She shrugged. "Yeah. Um— I hope it's okay if I worked today. Something came up and I need to take tomorrow off?" She said it like a question.

"That's all right, I guess. For this time. Let's not make a habit of it though, okay? I kind of like Sundays to be a day of rest. For you, too."

"Okay. Sorry." She dropped her head. "I tried to text you but I never heard back."

He checked his phone and saw the text she'd sent while he and Liesl were in church. "Yes, I see you sent it. Sorry. Just haven't checked my messages in a while."

"I went ahead and got the east room ready too since they already checked out. I saw you have someone checking in tonight."

"Oh, wow. You're good! Thanks, Sadie. I'm glad to have that done." So he was free to spend more time with Liesl. He wouldn't tell Sadie that, of course.

"I figured you'd be okay with that." She gave a little smile, but it didn't quite reach her eyes. In fact, she looked near tears.

"For sure. Thanks again." He glanced up the driveway. "You sure everything's okay? Do you need a ride home?"

She shook her head. "My mom's picking me up."

"Oh. Okay. If you're sure." He wondered now if she and Davis were in an argument. Maybe that explained the young man driving away in such a hurry. And Sadie's demeanor. But he wasn't about to insert himself into that mess. It was none of his business.

He went back to his truck where Liesl was shaking out the passenger side floor mat, looking contrite. "I got some mud on your mat. I think most of it shook off, but I should probably take a vacuum to it."

He waved her words away. "Don't worry about it. I need to wash the truck and vacuum the whole thing out anyway."

She tipped her head toward the inn. "Do you need help getting that room ready?"

"Sadie already took care of it." He smiled. "You wouldn't want to go drive through for ice cream, would you?"

She shook her head. "I shouldn't." But then she brightened and quirked an eyebrow. "I did pedal all those miles though, didn't I?"

"You sure did. I'd say you've earned it. Do you want to change into dry clothes first?"

"I'm okay." She held out her arms. "I'm almost dry."

"Let's go then."

She beamed and put the floor mat back in place. "You driving?"

"Hop in."

THEY WALKED BACK to the truck licking ice cream cones that melted almost as fast as they could eat them. Liesl glanced over in time to see Zach dive in for a bite and end up with a big dollop of mint chocolate chip on his nose.

She swiped at his nose with her paper napkin. "Were you saving that for later?"

He rubbed at his face, looking embarrassed. "Did I get it all?"

Laughing, she stopped on the sidewalk and gave his nose another pass with her napkin, happy for an excuse to inspect his handsome face. "You're good. I take it you're happy with your choice?"

"Mmm... I think the last time I ordered anything *besides* mint chocolate chip was 1998."

"Seriously? I'm all about trying every flavor there is." She held up her cone. "Hence, marshmallow creme on the bottom and mocha fudge on the top."

"To each his own."

"I guess. But you'll never know what you're missing."

He hurried to open the door of the truck for her and she climbed in and fastened her seatbelt taking care to protect her cone.

Zach started the engine and got the AC running, but after a minute, seeing Liesl shiver, he turned it off. "Sorry. I guess we don't really need the air, do we?"

"That's the best thing about ice cream. Internal AC. That, and maybe my clothes weren't quite as dry as I thought." Grinning, she broke off another bite of her cone and savored the creamy sweetness. "Why don't you go through the car wash and I'll vacuum the truck out for you. I feel bad about the mud I tracked in."

He nodded toward the back of the truck. "I don't want to do that with the bikes in here, but if it's going to bother you so much, we can go use their vacuum."

"I'd feel better if we did."

"But first"—Zach held up his half-eaten cone—"I'm going to enjoy my mint chocolate chip."

They ate in silence for a few minutes until Liesl felt his eyes on her. She took another bite and met his quizzical gaze. "What?"

"Nothing. Just enjoying the moment."

She smiled, feeling unaccountably sad. "It's been a fun day, hasn't it."

He nodded. "I wish there could be more of them."

"Zach—"

"I know, I know. I'm trying to just enjoy the moment. But I don't get it."

She tilted her head, not understanding.

"For the first time since Jenny died, I feel like I'm living my life in Forward gear instead of in Reverse."

"Oh, Zach—" She let a sigh escape. "I wish things could be different."

"Yeah, me too. Because it's not actually Forward, is it? I'm really just revving my engine in Neutral."

"Neutral can be nice too." She knew it was lame—and she didn't even really believe it—but she didn't know what else to say. Were they both just torturing themselves when this attraction couldn't ultimately lead to anything but *goodbye*? And the more time she spent with Zach, the harder that goodbye was going to be.

He seemed to read her mind. "I'd be okay with this"—he motioned between them—"if you were just going to go your way at the end of this month and that was that. But I'm starting to feel like it won't be like that for me."

"Like what?" She dared to hope he meant what she thought he was implying.

"Just going our separate ways. No harm, no foul. But Liesl, as hard as I'm trying to guard my heart, it's not working."

"No, not for me either," she admitted.

"So what do we do about that?"

She shrugged. She truly didn't have an answer. But she was so afraid he was going to suggest that it was a waste of time for them to see each other, to spend time together. And maybe he was right. But the thought of letting this budding friendship go made her feel profoundly sad.

"It seems to me like we have two choices." He put an arm on the back of the seat and shifted behind the wheel to face her.

"I'm listening."

"Either we say goodbye now—tonight—before one of us gets hurt..."

"Or?" She didn't think much of Option 1.

"Or we go all in and see where we are in two weeks."

"Eighteen days, to be exact. But I do like that option better. All in."

The smile he offered in response cheered her. "Can we set some ground rules though?"

"Like?"

"No kissing."

"No kissing? Where's the fun in that?"

"I know. But let's not get physical. As much as I want to. It... muddies the waters."

She knew he was right, as much as she didn't like it. "Agreed. What else?"

"No trying to figure out the future. For eighteen days we just have fun. Enjoy each other's company. Get to know each other. Figure out if there's more than friendship between us."

She affected a pout. "Well, how can we figure that out if there's no kissing allowed?"

He grinned. "Tell you what: If things are still going well in eighteen days, I'll kiss you when you check out. If you hate it, then we'll know."

"That's *really* not fair." She put the last of her cone in her mouth.

"Why not?"

"Because now," she said over the ice cream, "You're making me want these eighteen days to go by really fast."

He laughed.

"But seriously"—she frowned—"if you want to kiss me after eighteen days but we're not allowed to figure out the future before I check out, *then* what am I supposed to do? Just drive off not knowing if I'll ever see you again?"

"How about this: Save some time for me your last night here? If we both agree there's something *to* figure out, we'll stay up all night until we have an answer."

"And there will be kissing?"

"When you check out."

"You drive a hard bargain, buddy."

He winked. "I know." The smile that followed grabbed onto her heart and wouldn't let go.

And she was pretty sure they'd be staying up all night on June 22.

Chapter Sixteen

What had they been thinking? Liesl closed the door to her suite behind her and started down the stairs for coffee, not sure if she hoped Zach was in the kitchen or not. Something had changed between them last night and as wonderful as it was, she wasn't sure this morning how to be with him.

"Good morning, sunshine." He popped out of the office smiling that same sweet grin from yesterday. The one she'd dreamed about all night long. He touched her arm briefly in a way that was innocent, yet intimate at the same time.

And suddenly she didn't even have to think about how to "be" with him. They just were. And it felt like the most natural thing in the world to see him and...*love* him.

The revelation startled her. Was this what Mom meant when she said, "When you know, you know"? *Did* she love Zach? No. Of course not. They'd barely known each other for two and a half weeks. And she didn't believe in love at first sight—or even second sight. But she did know that she'd never felt as deeply for any other guy the way she did for Zachary Freylan. And she didn't know what she was going to do about that.

God, show me what you want for my life. The prayer came as a quiet whisper in her heart. And it startled her as much as her growing feelings for Zach had. But maybe the two were connected. Despite all he'd been through, Zach's faith was quiet, but strong. Her own had been silent and weak. But talking to Zach—and her brother—seeing how they lived out their faith made her want to get back on track with God.

It wasn't that she'd ever stopped believing in Him or even trusting in Him. It was just that she hadn't given God the place of priority He'd once had in her life. She had a feeling her brother had sensed that when they'd last talked. It made her sad to think she'd disappointed Brad. And according to him, her parents too. But now that she was going to have a little niece or nephew looking up to her, she wanted to be someone Brad and Heather would want to play a big role in their baby's life. Even if they did live much too far away.

"What's that frown about?" Zach brushed a finger lightly under her chin.

"Was I frowning?" She took in a quavering breath and forced a smile. He was *not* making his "no kissing" rule easy to follow. "I was thinking about my niece- or nephew-to-be."

"Oh?" Zach's forehead furrowed. "Is everything okay?"

"Oh, yes. At least the last time I talked to Brad. I was just thinking..." She hesitated. "I'll tell you why the frown later, okay."

"Okay..." He looked disappointed.

"Everything's fine. Honest." She gave him a smile meant to reassure. "More than fine."

"So where are you headed today? Or is this a writing day?"

"Both. I need to get serious about getting some good photos. I've got a ton on my phone, but I want to take my good camera today and revisit some of the places I'll be writing about. But first, coffee."

He laughed. "Of course. I just put a fresh pot on."

"Wow, am I that late that you've already gone through one pot?"

"The couple in the West room filled big travel mugs before they checked out."

"Ah. Well, lucky me. What about you?"

"I've got a cup in my office."

"No, I meant what are your plans for the day?"

"Paying bills. Writing checks. My favorite thing to do, actually."

"Ah, the accountant in you gets to come out and play?"

"The nerd, you mean?" He scrunched up his nose, looking adorable. "Oh, by the way, Sadie will be in today after all. I'll have her give your room a good cleaning if that won't disturb you. She should be here by nine."

"I'm going to finish my coffee and grab my things, then I won't be back to write until after lunch, so if she can do it later this morning that'd be great. It's really not too bad though if she wants to skip it until next time."

"Up to you, but you're paying for cleaning services."

"Well, then let her have at it. I'd better run. Have a good day." She gave a little wave and started toward the kitchen.

"Hey, Liesl..."

She turned back and something in his expression stopped her. Reluctance? Was he having second thoughts about their conversation yesterday?

He opened his mouth to say something but just then, his phone rang. "Sorry..." He held up a hand for her to wait, then shook his head. "Sorry. I need to take this and it might be a while. We'll talk later, okay?"

"Sure."

He punched Answer, then with the same brief wave she'd given him a moment earlier, he turned his attention to his phone and started back to his office. "Hi Glory. How are you?"

He closed the door to his office quietly, but not before Liesl caught snatches of his conversation. "Who said that? ...Are you sure? ...No, Glory. Calm down. I'll take care of it. They had no right to—"

He must have moved to the other side of the room because his words turned to an unintelligible drone.

Glory? That was Jenny's mom. Zach had said he rarely talked to her. But the person on the other end of the phone was upset about something.

Feeling guilty that she was essentially eavesdropping—again—Liesl turned and hurried to the kitchen.

"GLORY, please don't worry about this. I'll call the office here and get them off your back. They never should have contacted you in the first place." Zach stared at the blotter calendar on his desk. He wanted to strangle Robert Langford—or Langford's boss, Marta. She was ultimately the one to blame. Somehow, they had tracked Glory down in Charlotte and were trying to get her to do what he'd been unwilling to do: file charges against the county for Jenny's accident.

"I appreciate that, Zach," Glory said, her voice still quavering. "But what did he mean that Marta Snelling thought I could encourage the sheriff's office to speed up the investigation into Jenny's accident? What are they investigating? I thought that was all finished."

"It is." It came out more harshly than he'd intended. He lowered his voice. "It is, Glory, and I'll be sure they don't call you again."

"But the guy that called me said something about a lawsuit pending...that if there was a lawsuit pending against the county for the damages it might speed things along. What damages do they mean. It's not like they can fix this."

Zach sighed into the phone. "No, of course not. The same guy contacted me. He said something about finding parts from another vehicle—a mirror, I think he said—near the scene. This guy seemed to think there might have been another vehicle involved and that—"

"You mean someone ran her off the road?"

"No... No, he didn't say that. It wasn't malicious."

"It was if they didn't own up to it. If someone caused her accident."

"I'll talk to him again, Glory. To be honest, until you called, I didn't think there was anything to it. It's been almost three weeks since I heard from anybody in Snelling's office. I think they're just ambulance chasers looking for a quick buck."

"I'm sorry I even talked to them then."

"I'm sorry they dragged you into it. I'll call Langford as soon as I hang up and try to find out what's going on. And I'll tell them to leave you out of it. Assuming that's what you want."

"Of course. I mean, if someone did cause Jenny's accident, they should do what's right. But it does seem odd they're just now discovering evidence. So-called evidence."

"That's what I thought. But I'll talk to them and make sure."

"Thank you, Zach. I'm sorry to bother you."

"You're never a bother, Glory. You know that. And the door is always open to you here, you know that."

"I know it is. I need to come visit. It's been too long. I miss the inn. And seeing you, of course," she added quickly.

Zach laughed. "I see where I am on your list."

"You know I didn't mean it that way."

"I know, Glory. I'm just giving you a hard time."

"You always were a big tease." He was thankful for the smile her voice held.

"I guess some things don't change." But so much *had* changed. For both of them. He pushed away the melancholy thought. Best to hang up on a happier note. "Listen, I need to run, but you let me know whenever you want to come and stay and I'll make sure the suite is ready for you."

"I just might do that. Thanks, Zach."

He didn't tell her that her suite was currently occupied by a beautiful woman he was fast falling for. He'd cross that bridge when he came to it. "I'll get back to you as soon as I can get through to Langford. Knowing them, it might be later this week."

"No rush. I trust you, Zachary. I already feel better just talking to you."

"I'm glad. You take care, Glory. I'll be in touch." He hung up, feeling the familiar nostalgic gloom that conversations with Jenny's mom usually brought.

And now he had the added weight of a conversation with Marta Snelling looming. Why did anyone think a big fat check would relieve one ounce of the pain Jenny's death had inflicted? No amount of money could bring her back. And dragging things out like this only caused more grief. For him and for Glory.

His heart went out to her. He'd been a little relieved when she didn't take him up immediately on his invitation. He hoped he could put her off until after Liesl checked out.

But what if Liesl didn't check out. What if their feelings grew and they figured out a way to make things work. He didn't relish telling Glory about her, knowing it would likely be hurtful and—

He was getting ahead of himself. Right now he needed to call off the dogs in Marta Snelling's office. And everything depended on what he found out from the investigation. If there even was one.

Chapter Seventeen

L iesl finished her coffee at her desk while she scrolled through e-mails, then got ready to go. She had her purse over one shoulder and car keys in hand when an idea for a chapter she'd been working on struck her. She tossed the purse and keys on the unmade bed and opened her laptop to capture the thoughts before they escaped.

An hour later, she'd finished the difficult chapter and had a brilliant opening for the next one. At least it seemed brilliant right now. Sometimes these bursts of genius backfired on her. She might come back and read what she'd thought was so inspired and not even be able to figure out what she'd been trying to say. But at least it was words on a page. That was infinitely easier to face than a blinking cursor on a blank screen.

She jumped ahead in her outline and made notes on some other photos she wanted to capture when she went downtown. She hoped to talk to the woman at the visitor center again too. She'd been very helpful. She glanced up from her screen when a soft knock sounded on her door, followed immediately by a key turning and the door creaking open.

Sadie peeked around the door, and when she saw Liesl, gave a horrified gasp. "I'm so sorry! I thought—" She closed the door and spoke through it. "Zach said you were gone for the morning and I was going to clean. I'm so sorry."

Liesl jumped up and opened the door, beckoning the girl in. "It's fine, Sadie. Something came up and I changed my mind. I'm just about finished here and you're welcome to get started."

"I can come back later if you'd rather." As she had the day before, Sadie looked near tears.

"No, it's perfectly fine. Please don't feel bad."

The girl burst into tears and stood with her head hanging, gripping a basket of cleaning supplies.

"Sadie... Please don't cry. I'm so sorry if I startled you. It's truly fine. I know you only came in because Zach told you I would be gone—"

"No, no... It's not you. I'm sorry. I'm just having a rough day. I didn't mean to lose it in front of you."

"You want to talk about it?" Liesl didn't really want to hear some teenage sob story, but it would be pretty heartless to ignore her tears.

"It's just stupid boyfriend issues." Sadie set the cleaning supplies on the floor and swiped at her freckled cheeks with the hem of her T-shirt.

Feeling awkward, Liesl touched Sadie's arm. "I'm sorry. I remember what that was like." That much was true. Maybe even *currently* true, given everything that was going on with Zach.

"Did you ever have a guy who just clammed up and wouldn't talk to you?"

She gave a wry laugh. "Mine were more on the order of wouldn't shut up. Do you mean like...he ghosted you or something?"

"Oh, no. Not that. I mean, he talks, but he's just making small talk. Something's wrong though. I can tell. And he refuses to tell me what it is."

"Maybe he just needs a little space. I mean, you probably

don't always tell *him* everything, right?" She was in so deep she couldn't even touch the bottom.

"That's just it. I do!" Sadie plopped on the bed and put her face in her hands, then immediately jumped up. "I'm so sorry! I don't know what I was thinking sitting on your bed. That was so unprofessional. Please don't say anything to Zach. I—" Her gaze darted to the door. "I should leave you alone. I'm so sorry."

"Sadie, I was the one who invited you in. And started the conversation. It's okay. You're not in trouble. But here—" She pulled up the extra chair by the door and motioned for Sadie to sit there so she wouldn't be in trouble if Zach happened to come up.

"Thank you," Sadie whispered.

"Do you have any idea at all what might be bothering him? It's Davis, right?"

Sadie's head jerked up. "How do you know that?"

"Zach knows him, and when we saw him in the snack shop, Zach told me his name."

"I didn't know Zach knew him. He told you we were dating? Zach, I mean..."

Liesl smiled. "Actually *I* told Zach. I saw your boyfriend pick you up the other day."

"Oh." She worried the end of her ponytail that hung over one shoulder. "Zach wasn't mad?"

"Why would he be mad?"

She shrugged. "I don't know. It just seems like he might."

"As long as Davis isn't here while you're working, I don't know why there'd be a problem."

Sadie frowned. "How does Zach know him? Davis never said anything."

"I guess because of the scholarship." The words were out of her mouth before she realized it might be confidential information.

"What do you mean?"

She hesitated, feeling like she'd overstepped her bounds. "You did know that Davis got a scholarship, right?"

"I think he mentioned something about it. But what does that have to do with Zach?"

"Maybe you should be asking Davis these questions. I'm not really sure I should say any more, Sadie."

Her brow furrowed. "Is he in trouble? About the scholarship?"

"Not that I know of. Why do you think he'd be in trouble?" She had a feeling Sadie suspected Davis was mixed up in something, but she dared not press the girl. For all she knew, she'd completely misinterpreted what she'd witnessed in the deli.

"I don't know. I just know something's wrong. He's been acting so weird lately, and like I told him, I can't help him if he won't tell me what's wrong."

"Sadie... It's none of my business, but if Davis is in some kind of trouble, I hope you won't get tangled up in it."

"What kind of trouble?"

"I have no idea." It wasn't quite the whole truth, but now wasn't the time to toss out best guesses. "But you seem to think maybe he *is* in trouble. You'd certainly know better than I do."

"Something's bothering him. That's for sure. I just don't know what."

"Have you talked to your parents about this?"

The girl's frustrated huff answered the question. "They're not crazy about Davis. They don't even really know him though."

"Just...be careful, please. If he won't talk to you, that's not good. And if you think he's messed up in something—I don't know...drugs maybe or—"

Sadie's eyes widened. "No! Oh, it's nothing like that." She gave a humorless laugh. "He would never do anything like that. He's too worried about keeping up his grades and getting his precious degree."

"Well, that's good, I guess. And I'm glad. I didn't mean to accuse him of anything. I don't know him at all. But you seem so concerned. You should probably trust your instincts." Liesl kept seeing flashes of Davis in the snack shop, "hiding" from the police and obviously shaken. But how could she tell this girl that? She might have completely misunderstood. And even if she hadn't, it wasn't her business. She'd already done enough prying into other people's business.

She rose and reached for her purse and keys on the bed. "I hope everything turns out okay, Sadie. I really hope you'll talk to your parents about this. I wish I'd talked to mine more when I was your age." She gave a sheepish smile. "They were a lot wiser than I gave them credit for back then."

The girl took her broad hint and stood and returned the chair to its place. "I'm sorry for taking up your time." She looked like a little dog who'd been scolded.

Liesl felt bad for dismissing her. And yet, she had no business trying to counsel this young woman she barely knew. Especially when Sadie was on the clock. She didn't want to get the girl in trouble with Zach.

And *she* had work to do as well. But she wasn't going to get it done in her room. Maybe she'd stay at the inn though and just sneak out to the back porch to work. She could go into Willowtree later. "I'd better get going. Thanks for taking care of my room."

"You're welcome. Thanks for listening." She reached for the basket of cleaning supplies.

"Sadie... Wait. I—I don't know how you feel about this, but I just want you to know I'll be praying for you."

The girl gave a knowing nod. "Thank you. I could use it."

A few minutes later as she settled in on the porch, the thing Liesl couldn't quit thinking about was the fact that she had offered to pray for someone. And genuinely meant it—and followed through. Maybe there was hope for her after all.

THE FOLLOWING morning found Zach sitting in the waiting room of Snelling & Snelling downtown. Tourists already clogged the narrow streets of Willowtree, but he'd decided he would rather talk to Marta Snelling in person than play phone tag with her office. He was ready to be done with this once and for all, especially now that they'd involved Jenny's mother.

The attorney came out of her office and extended a hand. "Thanks for coming in, Zach."

"Of course." After weeks of refusing to talk with her or her minions, he was tempted to remind her that *he* was the one who'd initiated this meeting, but he bit back the words. There was no reason to start off on the wrong foot.

"Why don't you come on back to my office." She turned and led the way down a maze of hallways. Marta Snelling's father, Carl, had handled the paperwork when they'd inherited the inn from Jenny's grandparents. The man had always had a stellar reputation in town. Marta had taken over the firm after Carl's death, and Zach wondered what he would have thought about the ambulance-chasing direction his daughter was taking.

As they entered the office, Marta offered coffee. He declined and once seated at her tidy desk, she pulled a folder from a desk drawer—a little too conveniently located, he thought, given the massive wall of hanging files to her right. Had the woman been so sure he would acquiesce that she had his information waiting at her fingertips?

"Have you reconsidered litigation?"

"No, I have not."

Her face fell but she waited for him to explain.

"First of all, I do not appreciate you trying to involve Jenny's mother in this."

"Well, it would certainly be her right to seek remuneration for her daughter's wrongful death."

"Did she tell you she wants to do that?" It was a test and he felt a little disingenuous asking the question.

"Actually, she said to talk to you." Snelling actually chuckled.

"But she also informed us about the will, which, as I'm sure you know, leaves the decision whether to prosecute in your court."

"And I've given you my decision."

"Zach, let me remind you that you would pay nothing up front to hire us. We wouldn't collect any legal fee whatsoever unless we win your case and there is a settlement."

"As I told Mr. Langford, I have no desire to sue the county I live in. Or any other county for that matter." He hesitated, not wanting to give her an inroad, but needing to know the truth. "Langford said something—and Glory mentioned it too—about thinking another car might have been involved. Is that investigation ongoing?"

Marta leaned back in her chair and cleared her throat. "The findings were inconclusive. I really think your best bet is holding the county responsible for what was obviously gross negligence on their part. And we can get that rolling as soon as—"

"What do you mean they were inconclusive?"

She opened the folder she'd retrieved from her desk and scanned a document. "Basically, they couldn't prove conclusively that the vehicle part they found was from the same accident. And"—she sounded resigned—"they were unable to trace that part back to a specific car."

"So you're saying that investigation is over?"

"I'd say so. Yes." Was that hesitation he heard in her voice?

"So we can close this case and move on?"

"Zach, I'll say it again, I would strongly encourage you to pursue litigation. Think how many people might be affected if the county is made accountable for their negligence. Lives could even be saved. You wouldn't have to testify or anything. You likely wouldn't even have to appear in court. The bottom line is"—she all but glared at him—"your basic insurance is paltry compared to what you would get from a settlement."

"You're grasping at straws. It's not the county's fault the roads were slick or that a tree just happened to grow where it did."

The attorney opened her mouth to say something but stopped when Zach rose.

Her pathetic speech only convinced him all the more that he was ready to be done with this. "I haven't changed my mind and I am going to ask you on behalf of Jenny's family, please do not contact us again."

Chapter Eighteen

The sun was beginning its descent behind the mountain peaks when Liesl got back to the inn. After writing for several hours on the porch, she'd had a productive day in town, talking with the woman at the visitor center, taking photos, and collecting new ideas for the book. She was going to have trouble staying within the page count her editor had mandated. But always better to have too much good stuff than to be trying to find enough filler to meet the count.

Sadie's car wasn't in the driveway, and Liesl felt a twinge of guilt at the relief washing over her to not have to talk to the girl again. But she whispered another prayer for Sadie, and she did mean the words wholeheartedly. It wasn't that she didn't want to help if she could, but it had taken everything out of her emotionally to console Sadie this morning.

She'd debated whether or not to say anything to Zach about their conversation. Sadie hadn't asked her not to, but if she'd been in Sadie's shoes, she would have assumed that what she said was in confidence. Still, if there was something sinister going on, she would feel awful if she didn't say something.

As if her thoughts had summoned him, Zach stepped out of the office as she opened the front door.

"Hey there." He touched her arm in that sweet, almost shy way he'd adopted with her since Sunday. "How was your day?"

"Good. I accomplished a ton."

"I was beginning to wonder if you were ever coming back."

"Oh, I ended up writing this morning, so I didn't leave here until about one."

"Ah, no wonder." He went back and pulled his office door closed. "Have you eaten?"

"I had a kind of early lunch." She hoped he was hinting at a dinner invitation, but she didn't want to assume.

"Silly girl. It's almost seven o'clock."

"No wonder my stomach is growling."

"I was just about to go make a Chef's Salad. You want to share it with me?"

"I'd love to. Just let me take my things upstairs and I'll be right down." She held up her right arm with a shopping bag looped over it. "I got some cherry tomatoes at the farmers market downtown. I'll bring them down to contribute."

"Great." His smile said he was as happy as she was about the unplanned time together. But a spark came to his eye. "Just be sure none of those tomatoes get on my side of the salad."

"What? You don't like tomatoes?"

He frowned. "Can't stand them. Sorry."

"What is wrong with you?"

"Lots more than not liking tomatoes. And if it helps my reputation at all, I love marinara sauce, ketchup... I'll even choke down salsa if it isn't too chunky."

"You don't know what you're missing."

"Oh yes I do. I tasted a tomato once. It about killed me."

"How long ago was that? Taste buds change, you know."

"Not that much, they don't. I was ten, I think, when I had my first ill-fated encounter with a tomato."

"Ten? You're not allergic are you?" She playfully held the shopping bag away from him.

"Well, if I have to lie and say yes to avoid ever tasting another tomato, then"—he crossed his fingers on both hands—"I am *highly* allergic to tomatoes."

She laughed. "You liar!"

"I admit it."

"Fine. I'll leave the tomatoes in my room and eat them for a midnight snack."

"Bring them. I don't care. Just as long as they don't touch *my* lettuce." Tossing a smirk across one shoulder, he headed to the kitchen.

Feeling lighthearted, she ran up to her room, changed clothes quickly, and met him in the kitchen a few minutes later.

Chopping vegetables, hard-boiled eggs, and smoked ham side by side at the island counter, they talked non-stop until two beautiful bowls of salad stood before them. When they'd both liberally doused their salads in dressing—ranch for him and honey mustard for her—and croutons, Zach pushed the kitchen curtains aside and peeked out the window, then turned to her. "There are some guests on the porch, would you be comfortable eating outside my apartment?"

"Outside?"

"Follow me. I'll show you." He snatched forks, a handful of paper napkins, and motioned for her to bring her salad and follow him.

He opened the door at the end of the kitchen, flipped on a light, and led her downstairs.

"We're headed outside, I promise. We're just using the secret passageway so we don't have to talk to anyone."

Intrigued, she balanced her heavy salad bowl and followed him down a narrow stairway. At the bottom, she caught a glimpse of a cozy living room to the right and a set of double doors to the left. Zach opened one of the doors and beckoned her outside.

"Zach! This is lovely!" The flagstone patio just outside the door was shaded by a pergola thick with trumpet vine. Hummingbirds flitted in and out of the deep orange blossoms. On one side of the patio a small table and three chairs were surrounded by flowering pots, and on the other side a rattan love seat with navy and white striped cushions was tucked in front of a rose trellis. There were only a few roses blooming, but their heady fragrance wafted to her on the breeze. "I can't believe this has been here all this time and I had no idea!"

"It's my best-kept secret." He pulled out a chair at the table. "Here, sit."

"Thank you." She set her salad on the table and settled into the comfy chair. "Speaking of best-kept secrets, I wish I could put this in my book."

He shot her the evil eye. "Don't you dare!"

"Don't worry. I wouldn't want to share this."

"Exactly. Let me get us something to drink." He went inside and returned a few minutes later with lemonade over ice.

She took a sip and savored the tart-sweet liquid. "Mmm. Delicious."

"Just store-bought. But it is good." He sat across from her and offered a quick prayer over the food.

She surveyed the space, admiring the flowerpots. "Did you plant these pots, Zach? This is just a little slice of heaven."

"I did. But don't give me too much credit. We planted the same flowers in the same pots every year. Jenny always said, 'Don't mess with success.'"

"They're lovely. And I bet the basement doesn't even feel like one with these double doors and all this right outside." Her gaze swept over the space.

Zach nodded. "We finished the basement as soon as we could afford to. We had planned to live down here when we started the project, but once we'd finished this little patio, we knew we could rent out the basement for more than the attic—the suite you're in—and frankly, we needed the extra money." He gestured back to the doorway. "Since there's a full apartment down here—living room, bedroom, kitchenette, and bath—we could rent it for double the other rooms."

"Nice."

He nodded. "But after Jenny's accident, I just couldn't stay in our...upstairs. And it's been good to have a more private place to get away to. Especially this patio. I'm not as crazy about people as Jenny was." He shot her a sheepish look.

"Well, it's absolutely gorgeous. I feel honored that I made the cut to share it with you."

"You're the first woman who's made the cut." He took a bite of salad and looked away. "Well, except for Glory—Jenny's mom. We usually have coffee down here when she stays."

"Then I'm doubly honored."

Zach put down his fork and met her eyes. "I'm sorry if that came out too forward. I didn't mean for it to sound like I'm flattering you—or pursuing you. I know we had an...agreement."

She smiled at him over a forkful of lettuce. "Right. No kissing."

He offered a smug smile that she couldn't quite read.

"What was that look?"

He took another large bite and mumbled over it. "You don't want to know."

"Hey, don't tell me what I do or don't want to know. I *do*."

He swallowed, took a swig of lemonade, then met her eyes again. "I may regret that stupid rule."

At a loss for how to answer, she just smiled and turned her attention to her salad.

"Do you need a refill?" Looking at Liesl's half-empty glass of lemonade, Zach let her tacit changing of the subject stand.

He didn't know whether to be glad he'd pressed the "kissing" issue—or rather the "*no* kissing" issue—or whether he should downplay it. But he valued honesty above almost every other quality and he was not going to let this relationship—such as it was—be one in which he had to play games and pretend that things were different than reality.

And he *did* want to kiss her. It was a revelation that, in some ways, caused him great relief. Because for the first time since Jenny's death, he felt hope that the rest of his life didn't have to be spent alone. That God might even have another woman, another *wife* in his future. He didn't want to think about the reality that it might not be Liesl, but she was the first woman who'd made him feel alive again. And that gave him deep hope.

She held up a hand. "I'm fine. This is heavenly." She stabbed another bite of salad. "I did want to talk to you about something though."

"Oh?"

"My conversation with Sadie this morning."

He tensed. "Please don't tell me she's going to quit on me."

"Oh no... Nothing like that. More like boy problems."

"Davis?"

She nodded and took a sip from her glass. "She thinks he's hiding something from her. She said she can tell something's wrong but he won't talk to her about it. Denies anything is wrong in fact."

"And you think that's connected to what you saw when we were on campus?"

"I don't know. But it would make sense they are." She put her fork down and wiped the corners of her mouth with her napkin. "I never should have gotten involved, but Sadie was crying and I couldn't just pretend I didn't notice. But I hope I didn't tell her more than I should have."

"What did you tell her?" A frisson of alarm shot through him.

"You're going to think I'm the biggest busybody in the world." She hesitated. "Sadie asked how you knew Davis, and I said I thought it was because of his scholarship. Sadie didn't seem to know the scholarship was connected to you. To Jenny. I didn't say anything about you or Jenny, but I hope I didn't blab about something that's confidential. The scholarship, I mean."

"No, Liesl. Of course not. I mean it's probably best if Davis is the one who tells her about it. If he chooses to. But they publish the scholarship winners in the paper every year. Ours... Jenny's is listed as the Jennifer Freylan Memorial Scholarship, so it's public knowledge for anybody who wants to find it."

She blew out a relieved breath. "I'm so glad. And that's really neat about the scholarship being in her name."

"And that was very sweet of you to listen to Sadie's woes." Zach raked a hand through his hair. "I'm sorry if she bothered you while you were trying to work. I'll speak to her about it."

"No, please don't do that, Zach. I encouraged her. Please don't say anything. I didn't mean to get her in trouble. And honestly, Sadie didn't do anything wrong. If I'd just ignored her I think she would have just gone about her work and left. But I could tell she was upset and I couldn't ignore her. And that's a good thing." A pensive look crossed her face.

"There's that look again."

Her brow furrowed. "What look?"

"Remember this morning when I asked you why you were frowning?"

A knowing smile came.

Now he was curious. "I'm sorry my phone call cut you off."

"Oh, no. It wasn't anything urgent. But... I would like to share something with you."

"Of course." He scooted his empty salad plate out of the way and leaned in, waiting, not taking for granted the delight of having a beautiful, kind woman in his life again. For however brief their time together might be.

Chapter Nineteen

Liesl stacked her mostly empty plate on top of his and shifted in her chair. She'd prayed for an opening to share with Zach, and it touched her that he'd remembered her "frown" and asked about it again.

"First of all, I wasn't frowning. Apparently my thinking face looks like a scowl."

"*Scowl* might be too strong. But you did look...thoughtful, I guess?"

She closed her eyes, gathering the right words. Finally she said, "I'm a writer. You'd think I could put two words together in real life, but I'm struggling to say this in a way that will make sense to you."

His worried frown made her laugh.

She nudged his arm playfully. "Now who's scowling?"

He shook his head. "Not scowling. Just very curious."

"This might sound silly to you, Zach, but something has happened to me—*is* happening to me—since I got here."

"Here? To North Carolina?"

"Yes, but more specifically this place. The Inn at Rosebud Lane." She loved the way the name rolled off her tongue. It didn't hurt that she was sitting in this beautiful garden surrounded by the fragrant roses of the inn's name.

Zach's confused expression made her question whether she should have started this conversation. But she wanted him to know. Even if he misunderstood. "When I got here, my life was in cruise mode. Another assignment, another reservation, just checking off boxes. I think I'd kind of settled in to a routine that was...good enough. I mean, I do like my job. I enjoy traveling and seeing new things, meeting new people. But something has been missing, and for some reason, I feel like I've found it while I've been here."

"And what is it that you've found?" He leaned closer.

For a minute she was afraid he'd misunderstood. That maybe he thought she was about to make a declaration of love. But studying his face, she saw that he was genuinely interested.

"I think I've found God again."

He cocked his head. "Again?"

"God and I were pretty tight when I was younger. Especially when my parents were going through their struggles. But somehow—so gradually I almost didn't notice—I just lost my way. I mean, it's not like I was an atheist or anything. I never stopped believing in God, but I guess I quit looking to Him to guide my life. Until a few days ago, I'd pretty much quit praying in any meaningful way."

He waited. And his patience drew her out.

"My frown this morning was because I realized that while I have a long way to go, I've been making progress. Slow progress, but still..." She shrugged. "And when I prayed for Sadie, for the first time in ages—maybe in my entire life—I thought of someone else before myself. And it felt really good. Really right, you know?"

"I do." He nodded. "Not necessarily from experience. I'm quite good at being a self-centered jerk myself. But I try—"

"No, I've watched you. You're anything but self-centered, Zach.

And I think watching you, hearing your story, is part of what has made me want to get back on track with God again. For some reason, God got crowded out by other things. Things that have no real meaning, yet somehow they had the power to distract me and get me way off track. This gig was no different than dozens of others, and I don't get why everything I've encountered since I got here has seemed to draw me closer to the God who was once the most important thing in my life. Anyway, that's the long story of why I was frowning."

"Well, it's a good story. And I'm glad you're back on track now."

She smiled up at him. "Me too. And whether you realize it or not, you're a big part of that, Zach. And I'm grateful. Thank you for living out your faith in a way that shines a light for everyone who sees you."

He dipped his head and rubbed a hand over his face. "You're giving me way too much credit. But I am really thankful you've found your way back."

"Am finding," she corrected. "I'm sure not where I want to be yet. But I feel like I'm taking steps forward now. And not taking two steps back for every one step in the right direction." She rolled her eyes. "Famous last words, no doubt."

"Well, in the interest of keeping that forward momentum, would you want to go to church with me Sunday?"

"I would. That was another thing that—" She groped for the right words. "I felt like God used...not just the sermon but our conversation about it afterwards to make me start thinking about what's been missing in my life."

"I'm glad." He touched her hand briefly. "I'm really happy for you, Liesl."

"Being on that bike trail was another...*domino* in the whole lineup of things God's been pointing out to me since I got here. I mean, how can anyone look at those incredible mountains and not believe there's a Creator behind all that beauty?"

Zach nodded. "I agree. It's really cool to hear all this. How he's working in your life."

"I hope—" She winced. "I hope all that doesn't sound callous in light of everything you've been through these past few years. I'm sure you had to wonder where God was in all this."

He thought for a moment before answering. "Like you, I never stopped believing God existed. Even that He still loved me. And I know Jenny has gone to be with Him. And that I'll see her again. All those things *do* comfort me. I guess I just went through a time when I didn't understand *why* it all happened. Honestly, I still don't. But I'm finally okay with not understanding. I figure I'll know someday—or else I won't *need* to know. It kind of boils down to the fact that we live in a fallen world."

She clicked her tongue. "That darned Adam and Eve blew it for us all."

"Yes, but I don't doubt for one minute that if *they* hadn't sinned, I would have been right there in line behind them waiting to get my hands on that apple."

"Yep. And I would have probably been the one handing it to you."

He laughed. "And still"—he spread his arms to encompass the little Eden where they sat—"He gave us all this to enjoy."

"All this and so much more." Her voice broke. "Finding out Brad and Heather are pregnant kind of sealed the deal for me."

"The deal?"

"God's goodness. All the miracles I've taken for granted." She didn't tell him that she hoped to some day experience a miracle like Brad and Heather's. Because she would have been too tempted to confess that she also hoped for a miracle like having Zach Freylan for a husband. Or at least someone like him.

THE REST of the week was a run-of-the-mill work week, and yet something had changed. It had a lot to do with Zach and a lot more to do with the fact that she'd gotten in the habit of starting her days with intentional prayer. Not the quick bless-me-Lord she'd carelessly tossed up in the past whenever she happened to remember, but a sincere prayer for God's blessing on those she loved, and an offering of gratitude to the One who'd made her.

Somehow that one change had transformed everything. Acknowledging God in her life again had opened her eyes to the beauty around her in a brand new way. Her job had always required that she take in the details of whatever she was writing about. But now it was as though she was seeing everything with new eyes.

God had been extra mindful when He created North Carolina, and Liesl saw his beauty everywhere she turned. From the lush vegetation that seemed to blanket every hill and valley to the majestic green and lavender layers of the Blue Ridge Mountains. But now, she saw the silver threads that tied everything in Creation together. Nothing had been created without reason and purpose, and it all worked together in perfect symmetry. Perfect harmony. The spring flowers brought joy for their beauty alone, but more importantly, they provided nectar for the hummingbirds and bees, who in turn created sweet honey that she enjoyed on her morning toast.

She'd even called and talked to her parents last night. Mom hadn't nagged her once. Of course, they were over the moon about Brad and Heather's baby, and having that to talk about made their conversation less awkward than it sometimes was.

She thought of the miracle Brad and Heather awaited and her heart filled with amazement—and a twinge of envy—at the child they were expecting. So much she'd taken for granted before. And while she couldn't imagine how her friendship with Zach could ever be anything more, simply because so much distance separated them, if nothing else, it had given her hope and a vision for a future she'd only dared to dream of. One where she belonged to someone who would cherish her and with whom she could build a life and family together.

A strange thing had happened while she was staying here at the inn—something that had never happened with any of the other inns where she'd stayed: She was starting to grow sentimental about this place. The Inn at Rosebud Lane felt like... home. And except for the tiny house in Fayetteville where they'd lived for a short time when she was in first grade—before all the trouble started with Mom and Dad—no other place had ever truly felt like home to her.

Of course, the way she felt about this inn had something to do with the man who ran it. She couldn't deny that. But she didn't know what to do about it either.

Chapter Twenty

As they came out of church Sunday morning, Liesl followed Zach's gaze as he looked up toward the sun. It was high in the sky and already in the upper eighties by the feel of it.

He eyed her. "You sure you want to ride? Looks like it's going to be a hot one."

"We'll be in the shade most of the time, won't we?"

"Mostly."

"And we'll make our own breeze on the bikes. I'm game if you are."

"Sure. Let's do it."

"We can reward ourselves with ice cream to cool off afterwards."

"Deal!"

Zach had brought a small cooler packed with sandwiches and fruit and they ate those on the drive to the trailhead in the Pisgah National Forest. When they got to the spot where they'd had to detour for flooding the last time, he slowed and turned onto the road—the place where Jenny had been killed.

"Is there still flooding here?" Maybe that was why he'd tried to give her an out on biking today.

He dipped his head before meeting her eyes. "No, I've just been forcing myself to take this road. There's no reason not to. It's a prettier drive, and it's a shortcut for most of the places I go. I shouldn't have avoided it for so long."

"Nobody would blame you, Zach."

"I know. But it was time. And thank you for being with me the first time. That made it easier, and it gets a little easier each time." He gave a short laugh. "I guess this is only the third time I've been on the road since we were here, but still, it's getting easier."

"I'm glad."

They rode in silence—a very comfortable, pleasant silence—until Zach parked his truck in the parking lot. They worked together getting the bikes out and ready to ride. The sun was warm, but they rode fast enough to fan themselves and Liesl enjoyed pointing out views she remembered from when they'd ridden the trail before.

They rode side by side, only moving to single file for the occasional oncoming riders.

"This is so pretty up here," she told him as they approached the high point overlooking the old railroad tunnel. *Thank you for all this beauty, Lord.* For a minute she wondered if she'd said it aloud. These conversations with God—the truest form of prayer, she supposed—were becoming ordinary to her. Church had felt so different today. Instead of sitting in the back for a quick escape, they'd sat in the middle toward the front. And during the greeting time, so many people had introduced themselves and welcomed them. She would have hated it before, but somehow it had felt genuine and warm today. Was this the difference prayer made? A renewed determination to let God have His way with her life?

She wanted to talk to Zach about it, but she wasn't sure what he would think. And besides, it seemed such an intimate topic, maybe not one he was ready to delve into.

Her phone vibrated in her hip pocket. She'd turned it off before church and hadn't turned it on again but she wasn't expecting a call, so she ignored it. But when it buzzed again, she squeezed the brakes on her handlebars.

"You want to stop for a while?" Zach asked, slowing beside her.

"Sorry... I'm getting a call. This is the second time, so maybe I should see who it is."

"Sure." He guided his bike to the edge of the trail and she parked behind him. Her phone had quit ringing but there was a voicemail waiting. Brad.

She read the brief transcription of his message: *Hey, Lees, call me as soon as you can, please.*

She frowned. Brad rarely left a message, let alone asked her to call back. He usually just wanted to talk. Or nag her to call their parents.

But after clicking Listen and hearing the tremor in her brother's voice, alarm rose in her. "Zach, I need to call my brother."

"Is everything okay?" His expression said he'd sensed her alarm.

"I'm not sure. I'm so sorry. I'll make it quick."

He waved off her apology. "Take your time. I'm not going anywhere."

He wheeled his bike a few yards ahead and leaned it on its kickstand, giving her some privacy.

She was grateful for his thoughtfulness, not knowing what to expect. She pressed Brad's number under Favorites, whispering another prayer, but one she couldn't even put into words.

He answered on the first ring. "Lees. Thank God."

"Brad? What's wrong?"

"We're at the hospital. They think Heather might be having... a miscarriage."

Her breath caught. "Oh, Brad, no! I'm so sorry."

"Well, the baby is still in there so far, but Heather's lost a lot of blood. I think they're trying to prepare us. Please pray—" His voice broke.

Tears sprang to her eyes and she swallowed the lump that lodged in her throat. "Of course."

"Thanks, sis. I don't think I've ever felt so helpless."

"You're there for Heather. That's the best thing you can do right now. And pray, of course."

He gave a mirthless laugh. "I think I've done more of that in the last few hours than I have in my whole life put together." He offered a shortened version of what had landed them in the ER and ultimately the hospital.

"How's Heather handling it?"

"She's been amazing. I mean, I know she's scared— And it'll be different if she loses the baby. But honestly, I think she's taking it better than I am."

"I'm just so sorry. What can I do? Do Mom and Dad know?"

"Yeah. I just got off the phone with them before you called."

"Are they going to come?"

"No. There's really nothing they could do, and I think Mom kind of gets on Heather's nerves."

"Join the club."

It was good to hear Brad laugh.

"Well, please let me know if there's anything I can do. And give Heather my love. And that baby. I'm pulling for him to hang in there."

"Her."

"Huh? I meant the baby."

"I know. It's a girl."

A sob rose in her throat but she choked it back. "A girl? When did you find out?"

"At Heather's last appointment."

"Oh, Brad! That's so exciting! A girl. I love her already." *Oh, please, God. Please don't let them lose her!*

"I can't let myself get excited, sis. I just can't."

She forced her voice to steady. "Well, I'm excited enough for both of us, all of us. And I'm praying this little girl holds tight. She has to."

Liesl ended the call near tears but trying to compose herself before she had to talk to Zach.

He walked his bike back to her, concern in his eyes. "Everything okay?"

She shook her head. "Heather—my brother's wife—is threatening to miscarry."

"Oh, Liesl. I'm so sorry. How far along did you say she is?"

"The baby's due toward the end of December. It's a girl."

"Oh, wow. I'm so sorry," he said again. "So she's what...about four months along?"

She nodded. "It's way too early," she whispered, barely able to find her voice.

"Let's stop a minute and pray for them."

Taken aback, she bowed her head, grateful not to have to hide the tears that came now. But she was even more surprised when she felt Zach's arm come around her and his voice, strong and deep, lifting up her family in prayer.

"Father, please be with Liesl's brother and his wife as they face this scary time. We know that You hold this baby's life in Your hands. If it be Your will, please, God, preserve this child and let it —let *her* live and grow up and bring joy to her family and glory to You." He squeezed her shoulders and briefly pulled her close. "And especially be with Liesl as she worries about how to help her brother from afar. Thank you, God."

Such a simple, humble prayer, but it touched her deeply. She swiped at her cheeks before meeting his gaze. "Thanks so much, Zach."

"Of course." He gripped the handlebars of his bicycle. "Do you want to go back now? I understand if you just want to be alone for a while."

"No, it's okay. Actually, I'd rather *not* be alone."

"Of course. Are you ready to ride again or do you want to sit for a while?"

"I'm okay. We can ride."

"You're sure?"

She nodded, popped up her kickstand, and mounted her bike as if to prove it.

He did likewise and led the way on the trail again.

She pedaled behind him, grateful that he'd been with her when she got the call. She prayed for the baby—her niece—as they rode, in awe at the deep consolation Zach's prayer had brought. She hoped her own silent prayers would give Brad and Heather the same comfort.

SADIE WAS ON TO HIM. And it was his own fault. Why hadn't he just told her the truth from the beginning?

Because. He couldn't trust her. Not that Sadie wasn't trustworthy but because she was. And when she found out the truth of what he'd done, she would turn him in like any decent law-abiding citizen. Sadie always did the right thing. And that was why he loved her.

He leaned over the steering wheel and yanked at his hair, as if pulling it out by the roots might absolve him. But no such luck. It only added pain to his anguish. God, help me!

He heard a noise and looked up to see two bicycles coming up the path. It was them. He wasn't even sure what he had to gain by keeping track of Zachary Freylan. Except that it eased his pain somewhat to see Freylan smiling again. He and the woman—Liesl was her name according to Sadie—were getting pretty close from what he could see. And it gave him a weird sort of comfort to know that Zach hadn't been so utterly devastated by his wife's death that he'd completely quit living.

No. That dubious honor belonged to him alone. He shook his head, trying to clear his thoughts.

The bikes came to a halt beside Freylan's pickup and the two talked while they loaded the bicycles into the truck's bed. He couldn't make out what they were saying, but they wore smiles and were laughing. Flirting maybe? At least Sadie laughed the same way when she was flirting with him, tilting her head, cocking her shoulders just so.

The thought lifted the heaviness in his spirit for a brief moment.

But he sobered when he saw the couple getting in the pickup. He ducked down, heart pounding, afraid they'd spotted him.

He waited until he heard the engine start, then he waited for the silence that said they were gone. When he was sure it was safe, he pulled his baseball cap down low over his forehead and drove the long way to the inn. Sadie had shown him a way to slip through the narrow alleys behind the inn. From her house, it was a shortcut. But if he parked in one of the alleys, he could walk to the inn from there.

He wasn't sure if Sadie was working or not. They hadn't exactly been on speaking terms the last couple of days. His fault again. But if she was there, he would wait for her. Maybe tonight would be the night he would trust her with his secret.

After all, she had secrets of her own. Maybe they could come to a mutual understanding.

When he was sure he was a safe distance away, he parked in an alley a block from the inn. He got out and headed north, keeping to one side of the alleyway, his cap shielding his eyes.

Sadie had refused his offers of a ride to work all week. She insisted her mom was driving her, but he wasn't sure he believed her.

Zach Freylan's pickup was in the driveway, and he and the woman were unloading the bikes from the back of the truck. He hid behind a hedge of overgrown bushes and watched for a few minutes. Edging closer, trying to hear what they were saying, he stepped on a pile of twigs. They snapped loud enough to make Freylan turn and look.

Heart pounding, he retreated and sat on the ground waiting until Zach turned away.

To his surprise, the front door of the inn opened and Sadie came down the porch steps. She approached the woman—Liesl—and whispered something to her. Liesl's smile faded and she said something to

Sadie, looking...sad. Or frustrated? Sadie said something else and the two of them went into the house together.

What had Sadie said to her? His heart clutched. Not that Sadie knew anything except the fact that he was struggling. But she was worried about him. And what if she told someone and they came snooping, trying to figure out exactly what he was struggling about?

It would be just like Sadie to be so concerned about him that she tried to get him help. He loved her for it—even as he realized her concern could be the beginning of the end for him.

Maybe if she knew the stakes, Sadie would keep her mouth shut. He had to make her understand. And maybe if he just went ahead and told her what he'd done, she could help him carry this weight that threatened to crush him to death.

Chapter Twenty-One

arly Monday morning Liesl got a text from Brad.

Brad: Baby is still hanging in there. The bleeding has lessened and they're "cautiously optimistic."

Liesl: That's wonderful news! I'm praying every minute!

Brad: That means a lot, sis. Don't stop.

She was glad she'd planned on staying in and writing all day. She didn't want to go anywhere and risk missing a call from Brad. But after an hour of trying to concentrate, she realized she might have been better off taking photos today because she couldn't seem to put two words together in a way that made sense, never mind come up with a creative turn of phrase.

She finished dressing and put her towels in the hamper since Sadie was supposed to clean her room and change the linens today. She hoped Sadie didn't corner her again wanting to talk the way she had yesterday after riding bikes with Zach.

She genuinely liked the girl and felt sorry for her. But she had no business trying to play counselor with someone she barely knew. And she sure didn't have time to sit and listen while Sadie poured out her woes over what seemed to be an ill-fated romance.

Her instincts told her to warn the girl to just let this Davis guy go. But that wasn't fair. She didn't know enough about either of them to be doling out advice. Sadie kept saying what a sweet guy Davis was. But just because a guy was sweet didn't mean he was "the one."

That goes for you, too, Liesl Bachman.

She laughed at her own reprimand, even as she dared to hope Zach Freylan might *be* "the one" for her.

She went downstairs for coffee and as she settled in at her desk to work on a difficult chapter, her thoughts kept returning to her brother, wondering how the baby was. Her niece. But equally distracting was remembering the way Zach had prayed for her family yesterday. As if God had been sitting in the room with them and Zach trusted Him completely with the request he made for Brad and Heather and the baby. And for her. The memory touched her deeply.

Zach touched her deeply. It felt like something special was beginning. And she didn't want to confuse her growing affection for Zach with a far more profound growing faith in God. But was it possible the two were connected?

She dared to hope.

Yogurt parfaits and bakery croissants weren't Zach's usual bacon and eggs breakfast, but the delightful company made up for the fare's lack of protein.

Liesl had run by a Willowtree bakery and brought breakfast to the patio this morning. "Any excuse to spend time in your secret garden," she'd said last night when she hesitantly made the offer.

Now, he laughed at the memory and scooped a bite of yogurt and berries onto his spoon.

She tilted her head and eyed him. "What's so funny?"

"Just thinking about how you finagled your way down here this morning."

"Finagled? Oh, no. I was completely forthcoming about my motives."

"Were you?" He made his tone serious.

"What do you mean?" Her expression reflected his tenor.

"Was it *only* getting entrance to my garden?"

She shot him a look that said he'd caught her red-handed. "Um...yes. If you consider that the garden comes complete with... *you.*"

"That's what I thought." He tried to curb the smile that wanted to come.

"Is that such a terrible thing?"

"No, it's not. But—" He wanted to be honest with her. "I'm flattered, Liesl. I really am. And I was hoping that would be your answer. I just don't want either of us to get hurt." *But I also want you here across the table from me every morning for the rest of my life.*

"I know." She held her hands out, palms up. "I'm trying to hold...*everything* with an open hand."

"I am too. But I've got to confess I'm not doing a very good job of it."

"Then *I'm* flattered." Her smile was coy.

She was not helping.

"Don't you have work to do?" he asked, his voice gruffer than he'd intended.

He instantly felt bad for the wounded look that crossed her pretty face.

"I'm kidding," he added quickly. "Well, mostly kidding. But you aren't making it easy to keep an open hand, as you say."

"I'm sorry. I'll quit flirting."

"*Were* you flirting?"

She looked toward the sky as if she might find the answer there, then met his eyes. "Probably. I'm sorry."

"No, don't be sorry. It's just—" He sighed and pushed his fruit bowl away. "This isn't working."

"What do you mean?"

"Liesl, I like you. A lot."

"I think we already established that." She was definitely flirting again.

"I know, but what are we doing? There really isn't any place for this to go. I feel like I'm wasting your time."

"I didn't have anything else I was planning to do."

"Well, maybe you didn't..." He let his voice trail off, not sure where that had even come from.

"But you did?" She scooted her chair back. "Zach, if there's someone else you're interested in... Please, I didn't mean to interfere. That was never my intention."

"No. No, I know it wasn't. And there isn't anyone else. That's the problem. There hasn't been anyone I've been remotely interested in. Until I met you."

She gave him a glum look. "So what are we going to do?"

"I have no idea."

"But you don't like the original plan?"

"Waiting until I leave and seeing where we are then?"

He nodded.

"Then what? Do I need to find somewhere else to stay?"

"No, of course not."

"Then we're back at square one?"

To his own surprise, he slid from his chair, knelt beside hers, took her face in his hands, and kissed her. Kissed her good.

She didn't resist. And when he pulled away, she wove her fingers through his hair and drew him in for more.

He rose, pulling her up beside him, and wrapping his arms around her. When they finally drew apart, breathless, she giggled. "Well, *that* was helpful."

He frowned at her. "How do you figure?"

"At least now we know what's at stake."

He laughed. "There *is* that." He touched her cheek and forced himself to resist stealing another kiss. "Oh, Liesl, I'm sorry. I'm just complicating things."

"Why does it have to be complicated? We like each other. We'll see where it goes. End of story."

"And then you'll leave. See there? Right back at square one."

"If it's really serious by the time I need to leave, maybe I won't leave."

"And you'll do what instead?" he challenged.

She shrugged. "I have a little money saved up. That would buy me some time. Till we figure things out."

"You have a great career, Liesl. I don't want to be the reason it ends."

She frowned. "I don't know about the 'great career part.' The pay is just enough that I can keep doing what I do and set a little aside every month."

"But you like what you do. I can tell."

Another shrug. "I do like it. But honestly, the traveling gets old sometimes. It's not like I thought this is what I'd do the rest of my life."

He didn't know how to respond. He wanted to say, "So quit. Find a job here in Willowtree and stay forever." But it was too soon. He couldn't say that. Not yet.

And when her phone rang, he was spared having to say anything.

She picked it up and checked the name on the screen. "It's Brad." Deep worry lines formed between her eyebrows.

He gave a little wave. "Take it, of course. I'll carry our dishes in."

"Thanks." She offered him a grateful smile and put her phone to her ear. "Hey, Brad. Is everything okay?"

Liesl's voice faded as he quietly stacked plates and silverware and carried them into his kitchen, silently praying that her brother's call wasn't bad news.

"THE BABY'S still hanging in there."

Liesl breathed out a sigh of relief. "I'm so glad."

"But I have another problem."

"Oh?"

"They're sending Heather home from the hospital as soon as the doctor has seen her."

"But that's great!" She hesitated. "Isn't it?"

"Oh, it is. Except that they're putting her on complete bed rest. She can get up to use the bathroom and take a three-minute shower and that's pretty much it."

"Oh wow. That won't be easy."

"No. But that's not the worst of it. I was supposed to be flying to Seattle next week—for that seminar I teach at the Expo...you remember?"

"Of course." Brad was a presenter at some construction convention that was held in Washington State every year.

"I might be able to leave a day later, since I don't present until Monday, but I really have to go. Things are still a little tenuous at work, and I can't risk giving them an excuse to can me. We'd lose our insurance and that would be disastrous. Especially after this hospital stay. But I can't leave Heather alone either. I would never forgive myself if anything happened."

"No, of course not. When are you supposed to leave. I'll come and stay with her." The words had tripped off her tongue before she had time to think of the implications. But how could she *not* help her brother at a time like this?

"Would you come, Lees? I know it's a huge ask..."

"Of course I will, Brad."

"I thought about asking Mom but she doesn't get paid if she doesn't work, and—" He cleared his throat. "Well, let's just say that Heather is supposed to stay calm, and Mom isn't exactly the most calming influence."

She laughed softly. "Say no more. I'll leave first thing in the morning and drive straight through."

"Don't you dare. It's...what? A fifteen-hour trip?"

"Well, then I'll make two days of it. Will that be soon enough?"

"I don't fly out until late Friday afternoon, so you have a little time. And remember, you gain an hour coming this way. I'll be back the following Wednesday. But are you sure you can afford to take the time off? I don't want you to risk *your* job either."

"It'll be fine. I can work at your house. Fortunately, I took a ton of photos last weekend so I can do the captioning and finish up those chapters while I sit with Heather."

"Listen, better yet, why don't you fly here? You wouldn't have to come until Thursday that way. I'll pick you up at the airport and you can use one of our cars while you're here. Let me check flights out of Asheville—that's close, right?"

"Yes, but you don't have to do that, Brad. I can drive."

"There's no reason to put the miles on your car. You still driving that beater you had last time—?"

"Hey, watch it. My Honda is not a beater." *Well, except when it wouldn't start a couple of weeks ago.* But Brad didn't need to know that, and the car had been running fine since Zach's friend worked on it. "But let me check on flights before I decide. If I get back to you first thing in the morning is that soon enough?"

"Plenty. As long as you're here anytime before noon Friday, we're golden. You're the best, Lees. And I'm paying for your flights. End of discussion. Just let me know what time you get in and I'll pick you up at the airport. And I'll stock up on groceries and stuff between now and then."

"I can do that when I get there. You just take care of your wife. I'll let you know as soon as I have an ETA."

"You're the best, Lees," he said again. "Seriously. And don't worry, I won't charge you for room and board or anything."

She laughed. "You'd *better* not since I'm going to be cleaning said room and cooking said board."

"Oh, yeah...good point. And I'll make Heather promise not to be too needy so you can still get some writing done."

"Don't you dare tell her that. She *is* needy and for a good reason."

"You know what I mean, but yes, it's for a very good reason. Your niece."

Tears welled in her eyes and she pleaded silently for God to save this precious baby. "See you soon, bro," she whispered.

She hung up the phone and realization washed over her. This change of plans meant she'd be leaving the inn in a day or two. Leaving Zach. And probably never coming back.

Her heart sank. But maybe this was God's way of saying *no* to the dreams she'd barely dared to entertain about Zachary Freylan. Could she be okay with that?

Chapter Twenty-Two

"Everything okay?" Zach stood in the doorway of his basement apartment watching her with concern. "I don't want to intrude, but you were on the phone a long time and every time I looked out the window you looked really worried."

Her hand went to her forehead, trying to smooth the tension there. "Is everything okay? Yes..." She sighed and gripped the back of her chair. "And no."

"Oh?" He took a step closer, then stopped himself, as if he'd breached some imaginary barrier.

"The baby's okay," she told him quickly. "But they've put Heather on complete bedrest, and Brad has a business trip he really can't miss." She supplied an abbreviated version of her visit with Brad. "So, I'm going to go and stay with her while he's gone."

"You're leaving?" His expression registered shock. "When?"

"Probably day after tomorrow."

"I forget where they live. Texas?"

She nodded. "They're in Rockwall, near Dallas."

"Are you driving? That's a long trip."

"Probably. I'm going to check on flights but I doubt I can afford to fly."

He shook his head. "A last-minute flight will be awfully expensive. And then you'd need a rental car."

"No, I can use Heather's car. She's not allowed to drive, of course. And Brad will pick me up at the airport."

He looked skyward for a moment, thinking. "When do you... have to be there?"

"Brad flies out Friday afternoon. But yeah...it's about a fifteen-hour trip so if I drive straight through, I'd need to leave first thing Thursday morning. But maybe I should leave tomorrow and make two days of it. I'm not sure."

"Let me drive you." He blurted it out, as if the idea had just occurred to him. "My truck is more dependable than your—"

"No, Zach." Her mouth had formed the word *no*, but oh, how she wanted to accept his offer. "No, that makes no sense at all. Then *you'd* have a fifteen-hour drive back."

"I know. But if I go with you, with two drivers, we could drive it straight through. That way you wouldn't have to leave until Thursday. And...it would be a chance for us to talk. And find out if we can even stand each other for fifteen hours straight." He affected a cheesy grin.

She laughed but didn't tell him what she was thinking: could she stand to be *without* him for fifteen hours. Instead she said, "You're sweet to offer, but you can't be away from the inn that long... Can you?" She tried—and failed—to keep the longing from her voice.

"I can. And in fact it would be good for me. I honestly haven't had a break since Jenny... Well, in years."

"But on such short notice? Don't you have guests checking in?"

He didn't answer, and instead fished his phone from his pocket and touched the screen. "Let me see if Sadie can fill in for a couple days. If she can, I'll drive you. We can take turns keeping each other awake."

"But who's going to keep *you* awake on the way back?"

"I'll be fine." He sounded like it was a done deal. "I'll drop you off, drive partway back, and stay in a hotel before I drive the rest of the way home the next morning."

"Then let me pay for your hotel." She loved the plan. Even if it did feel like she was taking advantage of his kindness.

As if he'd read her mind, he said, "Just say yes, Liesl."

"But what about my car?"

"We'll figure that out. Maybe you could fly back? It wouldn't cost as much one-way."

She hesitated, then threw caution to the wind. "If Sadie can manage the inn, it's a deal." Maybe she was asking God for a sign —putting out a fleece before Him, the way Gideon did in the Bible—but she needed direction.

"I'll ask Sadie now." Trying unsuccessfully to hide a smile, he turned away from her and finished tapping out a text message. But then he turned back. "Do you think everything is okay with Sadie? I don't mean to pry, but I noticed you two talking after we got back from our bike ride Sunday. It seemed like a kind of heavy conversation."

"It was. Boyfriend problems again. She's just really worried about him—Davis—and from what she's told me, I think she has good reason to be."

"Are you comfortable sharing why?"

She nodded. "Mostly because he won't tell her anything. He apparently has some big issue going on in his life but he won't confide in her. He's 'gone silent.'" She drew quote marks in the air. "I really don't want to get involved, but I did tell her that I wouldn't be comfortable staying with a guy who kept secrets and wouldn't talk to me about whatever is troubling him."

"Good advice. Maybe it'll be good for her to have a distraction then."

"Yes." She didn't say more, afraid her own desires were coloring her judgment.

Zach finished the text and mere seconds after he hit Send, his phone pinged. He checked it and laughed. "Well, that was quick. We're a go. Sadie can be here as soon as tomorrow."

Try as she could to temper her reaction, Liesl was sure her smile gave her away. "I'll go start packing. Um...what is your policy on refunds for people who check out early?"

"Don't worry, I'll hold your room."

"No. I'm not sure how long I'll be staying and you may as well free up my room. Would you be willing to refund any days you're able to book it? I know it'd be short notice, so I'm not expecting—"

He waved her off. "You'll get a full refund either way. But how long will your brother be gone? I'll keep you booked for the last few days of your stay."

"No, Brad's gone for almost a week, I think, but I'll probably stay longer so I can get some time with him after he gets back. See, I would have been checking out about then anyway."

"No. You weren't checking out until the 23rd."

She eyed him, wondering if he knew all his guests' check-out dates off the top of his head.

He squirmed, looking self-conscious. "I looked it up. After I jumped the gun on the kiss."

She laughed. "Wanted to see how much you jumped it by?"

"Wanted to see how long before I could kiss you again." He shrugged one shoulder.

"Awww..." She reached up and patted his cheek. In truth, she was trying not to swoon. "That's really sweet. But don't give me any special treatment, Zach. I mean it. It won't cost me a thing to stay at my brother's and I've already paid for my whole reservation. I won't even miss the money."

"No, you'll get a full refund," he said again. "We'll talk more on the drive."

Zach only saw Liesl in passing over the next day and a half, and when his alarm went off at five on Thursday morning, he was already awake. Thankfully, after making a Walmart run yesterday for supplies to stock the guest rooms, then coming home to give the kitchen a deep cleaning, he'd forced himself to go to bed early last night. He'd gotten a solid seven hours of sleep, but it was going to be a long day. And once he got Liesl safely to her brother's, he hoped to drive at least a couple of hours toward home before he stopped for the night. It would still be late Friday afternoon before he got home, but Sadie had agreed to make coffee each morning and turn over rooms, plus be on call through Saturday so he could sleep in if necessary.

As he shaved and finished packing his bag, the adrenaline rushing through his veins surprised him. It wasn't just the thought of having Liesl all to himself, to get to know her better. He was excited just to get away from the inn for a couple of days.

He carried his bag out to the truck and tucked it on the floor in the back seat. He tidied up the cab, emptying the litter bag and shaking out the floor mats.

Curious how many miles he would put on the truck in the next twenty-four hours, he reset the trip odometer. He hadn't traveled farther than Charlotte since his honeymoon five years ago. Once Jenny opened the inn, it had tied them down. Then after her death, even if he'd found the time, traveling was the furthest thing from his mind. But although this was merely a road trip—no time to do anything except make quick stops for gas and to grab lunch and supper—he felt like he was headed to a foreign country.

And in a way, he was. The thought filled him with excitement. And dread. He had fifteen hours to win Liesl Bachman over. Or fifteen hours to discover that she was not meant to be. *They* were not meant to be.

He couldn't let himself think about that possibility.

IT WAS BARELY six a.m. and Freylan was packing the truck getting ready to leave. Watching from the cover of bushes in the alley, he slumped to the ground waiting for Sadie to arrive. She'd told him Zach was leaving her in charge of the inn for a couple of days. She claimed not to know why he was leaving. Only that he was going to Texas and the woman—the writer—was checking out of the inn today.

As if the thought had conjured her, the woman came out the front door lugging a suitcase and several other bags. But instead of going to her car, she headed toward Zach's truck. They greeted each other, smiling, and he helped her put the bags behind the seat in his truck.

They were going to Texas together? Freylan didn't strike him as the kind of guy who would go on vacations with his girlfriend. Not that he knew the man that well. But Sadie seemed to think he was some kind of saint. He wondered if she knew about this. He tried not to feel smug, but if Sadie didn't know, he'd make sure to drop that information when he saw her.

He hadn't seen her for almost a week now. Partly because they weren't getting along and she'd made excuses the last two times he suggested they do something together. But also because it was getting harder and harder to keep his secrets from her.

But with her boss gone, she wouldn't be so skittish about him hanging out with her at the inn. He could even offer to help her clean the rooms so she could justify him being there. And if he needed a key to get into the office, Sadie would have one. Although he'd have to devise a way to get it from her. She wouldn't just hand it over without him telling her why he needed it.

And why did he? He wasn't even sure. But maybe once and for all, he could know if they'd found that blasted mirror that proved he was a murderer. And whether he needed to look over his shoulder for the rest of his life.

Chapter Twenty-Three

"It looks like you're packing more than you brought with you when you checked in." Zach teased Liesl, watching her stuff a suitcase and two bags in the back seat of his truck. "You sure you're not packing out some of my valuables in those bags?"

She smiled up at him. "There are a few things in my room—I mean, the room I stayed in—that I wouldn't mind taking home with me. But never fear, your treasures are all secure. I may or may not have done a little shopping since I got here. Not that it's any of your business."

"You don't have to bring it all with you, you know. I could store some stuff inside for you if you don't want to leave it in your car." He took comfort in the fact that even if she took all her belongings to Texas, her car would still be here when he got home. And she would have to come back to get it. No matter how this trip went, he'd see her at least one more time—at least for a day or two.

"Oh, speaking of which—" She straightened and pushed the passenger seat into place. "Is my car okay parked where it is?"

He waved her off. "It's fine there." It would make him happy to see it every time he pulled into the driveway. "By the way, where is your next book set?"

"St Charles, Missouri. That'll be on my way home to Iowa."

And a whole lot farther away from him.

She fished in her purse. "Let me give you the keys in case you need to move it for some reason." She maneuvered the key from her keyring and handed it to him. "You ready?"

"I am if you are."

She climbed in the passenger side and he closed her door before walking around to get behind the wheel. Even though she'd insisted on paying for the gas on this trip, he'd filled up this morning so they could drive a few hours without stopping.

He stole a glance at her as he backed out of the driveway. Her hands were clasped over the seatbelt and she looked straight ahead, her expression somber. He kept silent until they settled into traffic on I-40. "You doing okay?"

She nodded. "Why?"

"You look...worried. Or nervous?"

She gave him a sidewise glance. "A little of both, I guess."

"Worried about the baby?"

"A little. About what I'll do if something happens while Brad is gone. I'm terrified she'll go into labor while I'm there."

"I'm sure you'll be a huge help and if anything does happen, it will be so good that you're there."

"I hope."

He reached over and gave her knee a brief pat. "You'll be a blessing. I have no doubt."

"Thanks." She managed an anemic smile.

"And what are you nervous about?"

Her smile bloomed. "The next fifteen hours. Aren't you?"

"Maybe a little. But I'm excited too."

"Really?" She seemed genuinely surprised.

"Of course. Not only do I get to spend uninterrupted time with one of my favorite people in the world, but I haven't gotten time away from the inn in forever."

"Oh." She thought for a moment, then blew out a soft sigh. "That makes me feel a lot better, Zach."

"Better? Better than what?"

"I was feeling kind of guilty for letting you talk me into this. It's such an imposition for you, and I absolutely could have driven myself."

"I know, but where's the fun in making a road trip by yourself?"

She shot him a droll look. "Did you forget what I do for a living?"

That stopped him. "Oh. I guess I hadn't thought about that."

"I don't think I've ever driven fifteen hours in one stretch but I've clocked some long days to get to my next destination."

"Well, now *I* feel guilty. Maybe you'd rather have taken this trip by yourself." He was partly teasing, partly feeling her out.

"No. I was dreading it. And not just because of a long drive by myself. I wasn't ready to leave Willowtree yet. To leave the inn."

"Oh?" He waited for her to explain.

But instead, eyeing the dashboard, she changed the subject. "You didn't tell me you had a lead foot."

He glanced at the speedometer, then reflexively tapped the brakes. "Shoot!" He'd been going almost eighty. He checked the rearview mirror for lights and sirens. "Sorry about that. I should have had the cruise on."

She grinned. "I've been known to have a lead foot myself at times. But it's been two years since my last ticket."

"Your *last* ticket? This implies there's been more than one."

"Only three."

"Three! I've never gotten a speeding ticket in my life."

She shrunk down in the seat. "I guess I won't tell you about the three I was able to wiggle out of then."

He laughed. "Please don't. What, you just bat those baby blues a few times and get off with a warning?"

"I thought you didn't want me to tell you. But if you must

know..." She shaded her eyes and turned away from him. "I cried," she mumbled.

"What! You got out of a ticket by faking tears?" He tapped the brakes. "That does it... I'm getting off at the next exit and taking you back home."

"Wait... Wait. I was *not* faking it. I promise my tears were genuine. This was back when paying a speeding ticket meant I didn't eat for a week."

"Maybe you shouldn't have been speeding in the first place then."

She rolled her eyes dramatically. "You sound like my mother."

"Well somebody has to."

Now it was her turn to laugh.

And suddenly, despite the levity of the moment, he felt tears too near for comfort. He'd completely forgotten what this felt like —this simple companionship, being with the one person you felt most at home with. The way he'd felt with Jenny. Nothing profound or earth-shattering, not conversations or highlights that would become memories for a lifetime. But simple, everyday moments. Inconsequential teasing and laughter shared because you adored the person sitting next to you in the car.

And he did.

And joy because you were getting to spend the rest of your life with that person—

But he wasn't.

He swallowed back the lump in his throat and forced the teasing back into his voice. "It's gonna be a long trip."

She seemed not to notice his emotion, and her laughter told the truth: They would be in Texas in the blink of an eye.

And then what?

AFTER THE FIRST hour of small talk, Liesl had relaxed and they naturally, gracefully drifted into deeper conversation. She found herself sharing more than she ever had about herself, the lonely time in her teens when her parents had been separated for almost two years, her breakup with her first—and only serious—boyfriend, her true feelings about her life as a writer.

Perhaps there was freedom in knowing that if things went south as they talked, she never had to see him again.

And yet, she *wanted* to see him again. In fact, with the knowledge that he'd be dropping her off in a few hours and she wouldn't see him again for at least a week, she missed him already.

Zach seemed to truly understand her. How she could love her job and want to quit all at the same time.

Now, she dared to tell him the reason why. "How can I ever have a life if I'm traveling all the time?"

"But you have a life. An interesting one. If I'm honest, I'm a little jealous."

"It's not quite as glamorous as it might seem. It gets old after a while. And how am I ever supposed to settle down and have a family this way?"

"Is that what you want?"

She only nodded, tears too close to the surface to trust her voice.

"Isn't there some other kind of writing you could do so you wouldn't have to travel?"

"I suppose I could do copywriting or even editing. I'm pretty good at that—and not all writers are. At least that's what my own editor says."

"Well, there you go. Problem solved."

"Not so fast. I'm not sure I'd love that kind of work. So then I might as well find something else I'd rather do."

"Like what? If money were no object and you could have your dream job, what would it be?"

She shot him a look. "Oh, no... Are you one of those people?"

He quirked an eyebrow at her. "One of what people?"

"The kind who love taking personality quizzes. Or worse, who love making other people take said quizzes."

He laughed. "Guilty as charged. And you can blame Jenny for that."

"Oh, yeah, blame it on somebody who—" She stopped short. She'd been about to say *somebody who can't defend themselves.* That felt cruel.

But Zach just laughed, seeming not to take offense.

"Why Jenny?"

"She loved those things. Saved links to them on her phone, and every time we went out to eat or went for a drive, she'd open one up and start asking me silly questions. *If you were a tree what kind would you be?* Stupid stuff like that."

"Exactly!" Liesl laughed. Mostly from relief that she hadn't stalled the conversation with her thoughtless comment.

"The thing was, we had some of our best conversations over those stupid little quizzes. I ended up being a fan."

"I guess that's the point. Conversation starters, I mean." She inhaled and took a risk. "What was she like? Jenny."

"Oh, no you don't." He shook a finger at her. "We'll get back to that question, but you're not ducking out of answering the one I asked first."

She laughed. "Okay, repeat the question. I forgot."

He feigned frustration. "Your dream job. If money were no object."

"Oh yeah." She sighed. "I guess I've never really let myself think about it. I mean, I guess it would be kind of a dream job if I could do the travel books internationally. I'd love to travel to Ireland or Scotland. And I suppose every writer thinks they have a novel in them. I think I mentioned I wouldn't mind trying that. But that's more like a hobby. Not much money in it unless you just happen to make it big."

"Remember, money is no object."

"Okay." She grinned. "Then I guess I'd like to have a cool office up high in a turret with a wall of bookcases and an unlimited budget to buy books. Oh, and a fancy literary agent so I don't ever have to negotiate anything. I'm a terrible negotiator."

"A turret?"

"You know—like a tower in a castle."

"I know what a turret is." His voice went up an octave. "Rapunzel, Rapunzel, let down your golden hair."

She laughed. "Exactly."

"I'm just surprised that's on your list...if money were no object."

"Well, it was more of an expression. But it seems like a turret would make a cool office."

"Maybe literally." He feigned a shiver.

"Oh, it would have a fireplace, and I'd wear ermine slippers while I worked."

"You should write fantasy," he deadpanned.

"Oh, definitely." She knew he'd been teasing, but he hadn't laughed at her dream. Even though it was a dream she'd never really dared to entertain. But she wasn't being realistic and she risked thinking out loud. "I can barely make my deadlines with these travel books so I don't know how I'd ever have time for traveling overseas or writing a novel."

"Well, if you didn't have to travel to write the travel books, you probably could. By the way, did you get the pictures you needed?"

Surprised he remembered, she smiled. "I did. As many miles as I put on my car driving all over the county yesterday, it's probably a good thing we're taking your truck. But I should have plenty to work with while I'm in Texas. I really don't like to depend on the Internet for research, but it might have to do this time. At least I'll have original photos."

"Well, if you need me to track down anything—or anybody—just let me know."

"You're sweet to offer, Zach, but you've done more than enough." Her voice broke. "Seriously, I don't know how to thank you."

"For the last time, Liesl Bachman, I'm not only doing this out of the goodness of my heart. I have ulterior motives. So you can quit feeling guilty."

"Ulterior motives?" She was fishing but she didn't care.

"Because I'm not ready for you to leave. Because we didn't get that eighteen days we were supposed to have. Because I really don't want to spend a week without you. Or more."

Her breath came fast. "I—I feel the same. I do."

"I'm glad." He reached for her hand across the console and intertwined her fingers with his. It was almost as good as that kiss they'd shared.

Chapter Twenty-Four

Four hours in, they stopped for gas and Liesl offered to drive. Zach agreed—but only after exacting a promise that she wouldn't get a speeding ticket. She solemnly swore, and they talked non-stop for the next three hours, munching on trail mix she'd brought for the trip.

When they made a quick stop for burgers and Cokes, he took the wheel again. If he hadn't been trying to get her somewhere important, he would have found a way to get lost or install a speed limiter on the vehicle—anything to slow down time. The trip was almost halfway over and he wasn't ready to deposit his passenger and drive away alone.

An hour into the next leg of the trip, her phone rang and she spent half an hour talking to her brother. From her end of the conversation, it sounded like everything was still stable with Heather and the baby. It was good to see how close Liesl and her brother were and to hear her laughter, but a selfish part of him wanted to remind them both that in a few short hours, they could talk in person to their hearts' content. He only had these last miles to spend with her.

They'd talked about Jenny—the accident specifically and all the events of that horrific night, but he hadn't yet answered Liesl's question about "what was Jenny like?" He didn't want to drop her off without having that conversation first. He dreaded it and yet he was grateful she'd asked.

Somewhere past Little Rock on Interstate 30 in Arkansas, as the sun sank behind the trees, he took Liesl's hand again. "You asked about Jenny. I'd like to tell you."

She looked up at him, questioning in her eyes. "Of course. I want to know. She must have been a special person for you to love her like you did."

"She *was* special. One in a million, and I feel blessed that I got to have her in my life as long as I did. Jenny was sweet and thoughtful. She always thought of others before herself. I don't even think she had to work at it. It was just in her nature."

"I wish I could have known her."

"I do too, except...well that would be complicated, wouldn't it?"

Liesl gave a soft smile. "Yes, I guess it would."

"You would have liked her though. And she would have liked you. But I've had to be careful that I don't...put her on a pedestal, you know?"

"I think so."

He gave her hand a squeeze before letting go. "When you lose someone, it's easy to only remember the good things about them. To forget that they were human too. Jenny wasn't perfect. She could be impatient. And a little judgmental sometimes. She had a temper, and she didn't always control it very well."

Liesl tilted her head, her brow furrowed. "From the few things you've said about her, I never would have guessed that in a million years."

"No, because those aren't the things I choose to remember. And they weren't the things that marked Jenny. She hated that temper and tried hard to keep it under wraps. And she was mostly successful. But not always. She threw a cake at me once." He felt a slow smile come with the memory.

"Oh, wow. What kind of cake?"

That made him laugh out loud. "Does it matter?"

"I guess not. I'm just trying to get a clear picture."

"Wow, you *are* a writer, aren't you?" He chuckled. "You know, I don't even remember what kind it was. It had white frosting. Sticky white frosting." He ran a hand through his hair, the memory so real he could almost feel that gooey mess. "The cake went in the trash. I remember that much. Neither of us were in the mood for eating dessert by the time the argument was over."

He glanced over to see Liesl smiling.

"I guess it's good you can laugh about it now."

"It is. And we almost always could. Jenny had a temper but she never held a grudge."

Liesl wrinkled her nose. "Ouch."

"What?"

"Grudges. That might be my Achilles heel."

"Really? You don't strike me as someone who holds a grudge."

She frowned. "I hide it well."

"Grudges against who?"

"My parents mostly. For not just bucking up and getting along for Brad's and my sake. For being so self-centered and—" She held up a hand. "See? I'm getting riled up just telling you about it. I've forgiven them. I really think I have. But that doesn't change that I wish things had been different. That they'd realized how much their fighting and the separation affected us. I'm glad they ended up staying together. But...I think my life has been scarred by their issues."

"Understandable. It's only natural that any issues our parents dealt with would affect us. We all carry scars, don't we? I don't think anyone gets through life unscathed."

"No. But I don't want to use that as a crutch. Or an excuse to act like a jerk."

"I have never seen you act like a jerk."

"Oh, yes. You have, actually."

"When?"

She shot him a coy look, her earrings bobbing. "If you don't remember, I'm not about to remind you."

"If you mean the whole thing with the gossip you overheard, I don't hold that against you. You couldn't help what you heard."

"Well, I could help how long I eavesdropped. And what I did with the information."

He waved her off. "That's all a *long* way from being a jerk."

"You're sweet to say that. But I feel really bad that I jumped to conclusions and thought you and Jenny were in the middle of an ugly divorce."

"That *was* a sad place to go. But again, a long way from being a jerk. And you didn't even know me then."

"I know. That's why it was so wrong."

He took her hand again and rubbed his thumb against the smooth skin of her palm. "I haven't given it another thought until now, so please don't lose any sleep over it."

"Thank you, Zach. I mean it." She squeezed his hand before letting go. "And speaking of losing sleep, how are you feeling? Do you want me to drive for a while?"

"I'm good. But maybe you should take a little nap in case I need you to drive later." He immediately wished he hadn't made the suggestion. They were just over three hours from Dallas, and he wasn't in remote danger of getting sleepy. And the time was flying by too quickly.

"Okay. I'll try." She scooched down in her seat and made a pillow of the folded hoodie she'd brought.

She drifted to sleep within minutes and for the next forty miles he watched her sleep, admiring the curve of her lashes against her cheek, visually tracing the contours of her face, imagining its velvety softness.

And he knew beyond a shadow of a doubt that he had fallen hard for Liesl Bachman.

Liesl woke to find Zach staring at her from behind the wheel. She sat up and rubbed her face. "Was I drooling? Or snoring?"

He laughed. "No, but if you had been, it would only make me love you more."

She stared at him wondering if he realized he'd said that aloud. And thrilled that he'd said it at all.

Zach turned back to the road, his face flushed. "I'm sorry. Maybe that was too soon?"

"Is it true? I'm not sure I trust my emotions. I've never been in love before." *Before now.*

"I have. And while I don't trust my emotions either, I know what I feel for you and I believe it's real."

"Do you think it's possible to truly fall in love in four weeks?" Liesl wanted the answer to be yes, but didn't dare to hope.

He cocked his head, thinking. "I think it's possible, but I also don't think it would be wise to rush into anything—"

"No, of course not." Heat rushed to her cheeks and she was thankful for the evening shadows that darkened the interior of his pickup. "I wasn't suggesting we elope or anything."

Her joke fell flat and for a moment, she was afraid she'd assumed too much. But he took her hand again, and there was no doubt of the current that flowed between them.

"I'm glad, because if you suggested that right now, I just might be searching for a justice of the peace."

She let that settle over her and liked the way it felt. They drove in companionable silence for a few miles. Outside the windshield, the layered peaks of the Blue Ridge Mountains had melted into rolling hills in Tennessee and now, somewhere halfway across Arkansas, they became flat plains, not dissimilar to her current address in Iowa. And yet these miles of flatlands made her feel untethered and afloat—and not in a good way.

She missed the way the mountains enfolded her in their shadows. Because it was in those mountains she'd come back to God. And suddenly it struck her that this uncomfortable feeling was the pain of being uprooted. Her apartment in Iowa was merely an address. A place to get mail and camp out between assignments. But she couldn't deny that she'd begun to put down roots in the most unlikely of places. The place where she'd grown up and thought she couldn't get out of there fast enough.

But now, for the first time in her adult life, she'd found a place where she could picture herself settling down. Picture herself being part of a town and community. She thought about Sadie and the helpful lady at the visitor center in Willowtree, the still nameless people at church who'd made her feel so welcome. When she finally let them. She wanted to know their names, to become their friends.

And Zach. Of course, Zachary Freylan was the main reason she'd begun to put down roots. And even though he was in the seat beside her for now, she was painfully aware that he wouldn't be for long.

She glanced at the GPS on the dashboard, her heart sinking. "Less than an hour to go? We're almost there. How can that be?"

"I know." He blew out a breath. "And there's so much more I want to say."

"Me too," she whispered.

"It's only for a week, Liesl."

"Maybe ten days," she reminded him. "I won't know until I get there how Heather's doing. I want to stay as long as they need me. And have some time with my brother."

"I know. But let me pretend it's only a week, okay? You can break my heart later."

She gave him a knowing smile. "So let's say it's a week. Then what?"

"Will you come back and stay at least a few days? So we can sort things out?"

It seemed she'd blinked and now the GPS said they'd be at Brad's in twenty minutes. "What if, in the meantime, you decide *this*"—she motioned between them—"isn't a good idea?"

He laughed. "Something pretty drastic would have to happen

for me to decide that." He lifted her hand in his and kissed it. "Because right now, I think *this* is a pretty great idea."

She nodded.

"I'm serious, Liesl. I want to think and pray about it, and talk things over with you more. But this trip has only convinced me more that God might be doing something between us here."

"I love my brother and Heather, but do you know how much I do not want to get out of this car in twenty minutes?"

"I do know. But maybe it's best we have a little time apart."

"I know you're right, but that doesn't mean I have to like it."

His laughter comforted her, even as she thought how she would miss hearing it.

"Let's both pray while we're apart. Ask God to show us *His* plan. So we aren't jumping the gun."

"Okay." She knew he was right, but oh, how she wanted to "jump the gun."

"And we'll talk while you're away. Every day if you can."

"Please."

He reached for her hand again, and they drove in silence for a few minutes. She checked the dashboard again. Ten minutes until they arrived at Brad and Heather's. Ten minutes until goodbye.

Chapter Twenty-Five

It was past ten o'clock when they pulled into the driveway in front of Liesl's brother's house. The cozy stone house was tucked into a cul-de-sac in a small Dallas suburb of Rockwall. Warm lights glowed in the windows and a porch light illuminated pots of flowers overflowing with bright pink and yellow blooms. Zach was thankful he'd delivered Liesl to such a welcoming place—even as loneliness overwhelmed him.

He suddenly felt drained—more from the emotions roiling inside him than from being road-weary. But he wouldn't let on to Liesl. She was already concerned about the long drive he had ahead.

He'd just stop for the night sooner than he'd planned.

"Well, here we are." He turned off the ignition, unfastened his seat belt, and opened his door. They hadn't talked about what "goodbye" would look like, but Zach changed his mind and closed the door softly. "I'd love to meet your brother and his wife someday, but I think it's best if we say goodbye here. Let's not complicate things tonight, okay? Let's wait till we have a good answer for 'Who is this dude my sister dragged all the way from North Carolina?'"

Liesl laughed softly. "I was just trying to figure out how I'd explain you to Brad. Yeah... Maybe this is best."

Liesl had only told her brother that she was catching a ride with a friend. She'd be staying in the future nursery, the former and only guest room in her brother's house. She'd offered to pay for Zach to stay in a nearby hotel, but he'd declined, wanting to get a few hours of driving under his belt tonight.

"Well, I guess this is it." He angled his body on the seat and leaned toward her, brushing his palm over her cheek. "I know it breaks my stupid rule, but...can I kiss you goodbye?"

She nodded, her eyes bright with tears.

And then they were in each other's arms, their kisses tender, yet holding an urgency he couldn't deny.

He finally pushed away, desperately needing some distance between them. "'Bye, sweet Liesl."

"Goodbye, Zach." She took his face between her hands, brushing a thumb over the lips that still held her kisses. "You sure you're awake? Please be careful on the road. I'd feel awful if anything happened..."

"I'll stop when I get tired. I promise."

He helped her carry her bags to the front porch, and once they were piled beside the door, he drew her into his arms again and held her close. "I'll see you soon," he whispered into the fragrance of her hair.

She nodded against his chest. "Thank you so much, Zach. I know it was a huge sacrifice on your part, but I loved every minute of the trip."

He affected a scowl. "It was no sacrifice. I loved every minute too. I wish I could say the same for the trip back—without you to entertain me."

Her laughter warmed him and he had to force himself to pull away.

"You'll let me know when you stop for the night?"

"I'll text you...in case you're asleep."

"I won't sleep until I hear from you. So don't forget. Besides, we'll probably be up late catching up."

"Have fun. I'll be praying for that girl baby."

He strode quickly down the driveway but waited in the car, watching to be sure she got safely inside. She waved one last time before the door opened and a man with hair the same ash brown color as Liesl's pulled her into a brotherly hug.

AT THE SOUND of Zach's truck driving away, Brad let go of Liesl and looked past her. "Your friend isn't coming in?"

"No. He—" She caught herself too late. "He wanted to drive a few more hours before stopping for the night."

"He? Where's *he* headed?"

"Back to North Carolina."

"What? I thought you caught a ride with someone coming this way. And I sure didn't know it was a he." His voice took on that sing-song teasing tone she knew so well. "You have something you want to share?"

"I want *you* to share your wife. How's Heather doing? Is she still awake?"

"She stayed up just to see you." He hefted the suitcase sitting by the door, then reached for the heavy bag on her shoulder. "Let me get that. Come on in."

Breathing a sigh of relief that she'd dodged a bullet—for now anyway—she picked up her other bag and followed him inside.

"You're still upstairs," Brad said. "We might as well go ahead and take your luggage up now. Sorry about down-sizing your bed, but I can attest that the new daybed is comfortable. How was the trip?" he asked over one shoulder.

"Long. But good. It went fast." They deposited her things on the floor of the guest room. One corner of the room was stacked with boxes of baby paraphernalia and cans of pink paint. The queen bed she'd slept in last time she visited had been replaced by a pretty daybed. "This is going to be such a cute nursery!"

"Lees? Is that you?" Heather's thin voice came from down the hall.

She and Brad exchanged smiles and headed to the bedroom at the top of the stairs.

Heather was propped up with half a dozen pillows on one side of the king bed. She wore one of Brad's old DC Talk T-shirts and her curly hair was up in a hair clip that couldn't begin to restrain it. A small table at her bedside held a wealth of snacks, novels, sudoku books, and supplement bottles.

Smiling, Liesl went to her with open arms, but hugged her gingerly, afraid of hurting her. "Look at you getting the royal treatment."

"Come here, you." Heather pulled her close. "Don't worry, I won't break. But hey, I'd trade you places in a heartbeat. It's only been a week and already I'm bored out of my gourd."

"Well, who wouldn't be bored having to spend all day with this guy." She threw Brad a wicked grin. "I promise to do my best to be more interesting than he is."

"That won't take much." Heather got into the spirit, making Liesl laugh.

"Hey you two," Brad growled, "If you want breakfast in the morning, you'd better be nice."

They all laughed. Liesl slipped her shoes off and sat Indian-style on the end of the bed the way she had the last time she'd visited and they'd talked late into the night. "You look fantastic, sis. How are you feeling?"

"Bored." Heather pulled a long face. "But better now that you're here. Thank you so much for coming. I don't know what we would have done otherwise."

"Hey, don't think a thing of it. I wouldn't have missed this for the world." She spread her palm a few inches above Heather's rounded belly. "Look at you. I didn't know if you'd be showing yet, but there's definitely a baby in there!"

Heather pulled Liesl's hand down onto her stomach and placed her own hand on top. "And the plan is to keep her in there."

"Amen." Liesl unfolded herself and slipped from the bed. "And you need your beauty sleep. We'll have plenty of time to talk after Brad leaves tomorrow."

Heather yawned. "I am getting sleepy—though I don't know how that's possible when all I've done is sleep for the past week."

Liesl patted her sister-in-law's leg. "I'll see you in the morning, okay?"

"Goodnight, Lees." She turned to her husband. "Show your sister where everything is, okay?"

Brad gave them a blank look. "Do I know where everything is?"

Heather shot him a look, then turned to Liesl. "I guess you're on your own, sis."

"I'll be fine."

She headed down the hall to the guest room feeling light-hearted and glad she'd come. Even though she missed Zach already. Maybe this time apart was just what she needed. What they both needed.

She had a sneaking suspicion that part of this crazy jumble of feelings was because she had roots now. And with roots, she could travel anywhere as long as she knew there was home waiting for her at the end.

LIESL HAD JUST TURNED out the light and plumped the pillow under her head when her phone buzzed. She lifted the phone and smiled into the darkness.

> Zach: Sorry if this wakes you up. Just wanted to let you know I'm wide awake and the trip's going good. I have lots to think about.

Liesl: I'm awake, but you had BETTER NOT be texting and driving.

Zach: Settle down! Voice texting.

Liesl: Still… Too dangerous!

Zach: Ok, mom. Bye.

When no follow-up message appeared after a few minutes, disappointment swept through her, and she wished she hadn't been so bossy. Still, if anything happened to him… She laid the phone face down on the little table by the daybed and whispered a prayer for safe travels for Zach. She closed her eyes, but sleep didn't come. Instead, she relived all their conversations on the trip. The more she got to know Zach, the more red flags fell by the wayside. Not that there'd been many flags to start with. Well, except for the fact that Zach lived in North Carolina and she lived…all over the country.

She was just drifting off when her phone buzzed again. Startled to see that her phone showed 12:47 a.m., her heart lurched. But seeing another text from Zach, she brightened.

Zach: Don't worry, I pulled over. Well, I was kind of compelled to pull over.

Liesl: Everything okay???

Zach: Speeding ticket.

Liesl: Oh, no! Seriously? I'm so sorry.

Zach: Don't be. It was well-deserved.

Liesl: How fast were you going?

Zach: Too fast.

Liesl: Zach!

Zach: 83 in a 70. Don't worry. I learned my lesson. I'll slow down. I saw signs for a hotel about 40 miles from here. I'm in Arkansas already, but I'm ready to stop for the night.

Liesl: Good! Please do. And slow down!

Zach: Did I mention I loved every minute of our trip?

Liesl: I don't think you did. ;)

Zach: Well, I did. Loved every minute.

There was a pause and for a minute she wondered if he was back on the road. Then another buzz.

Zach: I think maybe it was because you were in the car with me.

Smiling big, she scrambled for a clever reply but came up empty.

Zach: You still there?

Liesl: I'm trying to think of a clever retort.

Zach: Don't hurt yourself. And how are you ever going to write a novel If you can't come up wIth snappy repartee?

She tapped *Haha* on his comment.

Liesl: I really like you, Zach.

Zach: I really like you too, Liesl. Now go to sleep.

She sent him a smiley face with a heart and laid her phone back on the nightstand. But for a long time she stared up at the ceiling with what she knew must be a goofy grin on her face.

But as all the reasons why this couldn't work piled up in her mind, her smile faded. She and Zach lived in two different worlds and each of their livelihoods depended on them *staying* in their own separate worlds.

Chapter Twenty-Six

Zach opened the AC vent on the dashboard and directed it at his face. He wasn't sleepy yet but he didn't want to take any chances. He knew how suddenly the road could hypnotize. Still, if he could make it as far as Hot Springs, his drive tomorrow would be far more tolerable.

He'd stopped around midnight for gas and a drink the size of Texas that would probably force him to make a bathroom stop before too long.

Settling in with the easy nighttime traffic, he let his thoughts drift to the conversation he and Liesl had shared. He raked a hand through his hair. Who was he kidding? It wasn't their conversations that imprisoned his thoughts right now. He didn't think he'd imagined the electricity that arced between them in the cab of this truck a few hours ago. His lips still burned where he'd kissed her, and his fingers still tingled where they'd touched her silky skin.

He didn't like the fact that his physical attraction to Liesl was influencing him so fiercely right now. Not that it was a bad thing that he found her so appealing. But he didn't want to be swayed by the emotions that sizzled between them.

He forced himself to list the qualities that attracted him to her.

She was beautiful. She was sexy without meaning to be. She smelled good—

Good grief. Could he come up with one quality that wasn't related to her physical attributes?

Okay, he loved the way she laughed. That was still part of the "sexy" factor, he supposed, but closer to the kind of qualities he should be looking for in a woman. He loved that she was intelligent and talented. Not that her travel books were riveting, but from the little he'd read in the book he found at the library, her prose *was* well-written and even entertaining at times. And even from the few paragraphs he'd read, he could hear her voice in his head.

Still physical traits, Freylan. Cut it out.

She was kind and selfless. He'd been surprised how sweet she was with Sadie that day when his housekeeper was so upset. Liesl could have been annoyed that her work had been interrupted, but instead, she'd listened patiently and offered advice, treating Sadie with respect and compassion. It was a quality he'd always admired in Jenny—probably because it was one he sorely lacked.

And speaking of Jenny, if he was honest, he was grateful that Liesl was very different from Jenny. Not that his wife hadn't had qualities worth emulating, but he didn't ever want to confuse Liesl with Jenny or let anyone speculate that he was trying to replace her with Liesl. Jenny was irreplaceable. But Jenny was gone. And he knew now that he was ready for love again, if that's what God had in mind for him. And it was Liesl who'd awakened that desire in him once more.

As different as she was from what he'd had in Jenny, she was everything he could have wanted in a woman. And more. And Liesl loved Jesus. That, of course, was the most important thing. She'd told him how she'd drifted from her faith in recent years, but their conversations assured him that she was serious about renewing her faith in God. They'd had some iron-sharpening-iron talks on the long drive to Dallas. He looked forward to more.

But would he even get that chance? Now that he'd started falling in love with Liesl, he couldn't imagine his life without her. He dreaded going back to the inn and checking somebody else into her room. It didn't even seem right.

As he tried to imagine a future with Liesl, his thoughts turned gloomier. She had a great career, dreamed of traveling the world. Writing in a turret with a fireplace. Could she be happy living the ordinary, small-town life he lived? Running an inn and tied down to one place? Was it fair to even ask that of her? What if she ended up resenting everything she would give up to be with him?

Traffic had picked up a little as he got closer to Little Rock. He started watching the exit signs for a hotel. And maybe a hamburger.

A driver to his right laid on the horn, and Zach instinctively tapped the brakes, but when he glanced in the direction of the sound, a bright light seared through the back passenger-side window, nearly blinding him. A truck—maybe a small semi— barreled onto the highway from the exit ramp to his right crossing the merge lane as if it didn't exist. "Come on, buddy," he shouted. "Don't you know what a merge lane is for?"

Another semi in the left lane tried to pass him, so he couldn't get over. He tapped the brake pedal gently, but there was a car behind him too, so he dare not slam on the brakes. Pinned in on all sides now, with the semi on his right so close he could feel its vibrations, he laid on his horn. "Come on, come on, get over!" His voice echoed oddly in the pickup's cab.

Then he realized the truck couldn't get over. As the merge lane ended, a tall stone wall loomed to their right. Zach slowed as much as he dared, willing the truck on his left to pass him already. But the bright lights kept getting closer, the horn blaring continuously.

"What on earth is this clown up to?" he muttered. The guy's

brakes must have failed. That, or he was high on something…or having a heart attack.

The vehicle's brights blinded him so he couldn't make out any details about the truck, but it was going fast and out of control. If he'd been remotely sleepy before, he was wide awake now. "God! Help me!" He wasn't sure if he'd said the words aloud or not.

Was this what it'd been like for Jenny when she went off the road that night? He wished he knew whether she'd experienced panic like this and what her final thoughts had been before she lost consciousness.

But as he squeezed the wheel in a white-knuckle grip, he began to wonder if he might meet the same fate Jenny had that night. There was no place for any driver to go except slam against a wall or ram into another vehicle. He could only go forward and try to avoid crashing into one of them or being wedged against the wall himself.

Surely the semi driver on his left could hear the horns blasting, but Zach doubted he could see the trouble he was in. Not that there was any place for him to go with traffic thick on one side and a concrete barrier on the other. *Please, Lord. Get me out of this mess…*

Something slammed into his rear bumper and the front of his truck swerved dangerously close to the semi. The steering wheel was unresponsive as he fought to straighten out again. Another bump and then a horrific screeching sound pierced his ears. Sparks popped up from the road's surface and landed on the hood of his pickup. Then he was slammed from behind again.

The breath seeped from his lungs and he fought for air. He wasn't going to get out of this. Not in one piece. *Lord, please be with Liesl. If anything happens to me, don't let her blame herself. Let her somehow know that I didn't fall asleep. I wasn't—*

He had the sensation of falling…falling… He thought of Jenny and wondered if he'd see her this very day. But then he thought of Liesl and—

Everything went black.

Taking a deep breath, Liesl tapped out a text then hesitated a moment before hitting Send.

> Liesl: Good morning, sleepyhead. Are you on the road yet? If not, I hope this didn't wake you.

She'd hesitated to text Zach before he texted her. She was old-fashioned that way, but it was the twenty-first century, after all, and she would worry until she heard from him.

Now it was almost ten o'clock. She'd expected him to get on the road long before this. But maybe he hadn't slept well and decided to sleep in. He hadn't texted to let her know when he got to his hotel last night either, but he'd told her he was ready to stop for the night before she fell asleep, and knowing him, he didn't want to wake her with another text.

Five minutes went by and no reply. Well, she *had* chewed him out for texting while driving. He must already be on the road. Or maybe he was in the shower. She'd give him another hour and if he didn't respond, then she'd worry.

She'd made breakfast for Heather earlier and the three of them ate together leaning against the headboard in Brad and Heather's bed. Sharing that time, realizing that Heather was doing well and there was strong hope for the baby, made Liesl so grateful she'd come. But that didn't change how much she missed Zach already.

She did a load of laundry and straightened the house while Brad packed his bags. Heather was resting, and Liesl used the time to get some writing done before she had to take her brother to the airport.

She poured a second cup of coffee and settled in at the table in the kitchen's breakfast nook. Her view into their backyard reminded her of the one from Zach's covered back porch. A sprawling lawn that Brad had mowed early this morning, and flowerpots overflowing with geraniums and petunias and a pretty pink blossom she couldn't identify. Along with helping Heather, those flowers would be her responsibility to tend while she was here. Too bad it was already blazing hot in Texas. Her days of sitting outside to work were likely over, and she would miss the cool mornings and evenings of North Carolina, but this would be a pleasant and private office while she was here since Heather was confined upstairs.

Liesl checked her phone again before opening her laptop. Still nothing from Zach. She wasn't worried yet. He knew she'd be busy with Heather and with getting her brother off to the airport today. Zach was just being his thoughtful self. Still, if she hadn't heard from him by noon, she would call.

She opened her Photos program and selected a dozen of the photos she'd hurriedly shot last week. She enlarged several, relieved to find they were better than she'd thought while she was shooting them. Some minor color corrections and enhancing the light on a few and she definitely had something she could work with. Editing photos wasn't really her strength, and sometimes the publisher made further corrections before they went to press, but the photographs were what inspired her writing.

She enlarged a picture of the lake at Willowtree—Sourwood Lake. It was more like a large pond, really, but the walking trail around it was the feature she would highlight for the book. That and the views of the Blue Ridge Mountains, and the miles-long range in the distance known locally as The Seven Sisters. The woman at the visitor center had told her about a marked hiking trail that led from the second "sister" to Graybeard Mountain, which some called the "father" to the sisters mountain range.

She made some preliminary notes with highlights about what to research to fill in the blanks. She doubted she'd get a chance to hike that trail now, but there was plenty of info to glean from online, and Zach might be able to provide the kind of details the Internet couldn't. Like what scents might be on the breeze or the flora and fauna one could see along the way. She'd ask him when she talked to him.

She checked her phone again and was startled to see it was almost noon. Now she was starting to be annoyed that he hadn't texted yet. A simple "I'm on the road." would have been nice.

She dialed him, praying she didn't distract him while he was driving. His phone went to voicemail and she hung up, not knowing what to say. She'd already played the mother hen too much.

Before she could overthink it, she dialed his number again. It went to voicemail, but at least he would see that she'd called and maybe take the hint.

She made sandwiches for the three of them, but took hers to the table, giving Brad and Heather a chance to say goodbye. She wrote for another hour before Brad called her to the garage to go over the trash and recycling schedule.

Back at her "desk" she checked her messages again. A couple of questions from her editor but nothing from Zach. Worry niggled at her now. Trying to tamp down the annoyance she felt, she tried his number again.

Same result. Straight to voicemail. She hung up quickly, not wanting to leave a message while she was irked.

If she got too analytical, it would be easy to imagine that he'd had a change of heart and realized there was no way their relationship could work, so why bother? Common sense told her that Zach wasn't the type to just let her wonder. If he really was rethinking things, he would tell her so. Let her down easy.

Stop it, Bachman. You're acting like a seventh grader with a crush.

Besides, when she thought of the kisses they'd shared, she knew in her heart that he wasn't having second thoughts.

The heart is deceitful above all things and desperately wicked. The Scripture from the book of Jeremiah appeared in her mind's eye. She'd seen it just this week in an online daily devotional she'd been reading. Okay, so maybe it wasn't good theology to think in terms of "knowing in her heart." But still, even thinking with a—

mostly—sound mind, she didn't think Zach had changed his mind about her.

She dialed him again, and this time left a brief voice message: *Hey, just wondering if everything is going okay. I've been praying for you. Hope you're getting close to home.*

Even if he'd left at six this morning, he probably wouldn't be home till this afternoon. But she'd already said it. She hung up, feeling a little foolish. But that was his fault. He should have called her.

Chapter Twenty-Seven

"Hurry home, bro." Liesl gave her brother a quick hug as they stood beside his car at the airport. "But don't worry about us. Heather and I are going to have one big fun, girlie sleepover."

"Oh brother." Brad gave her a droll grin. But popping up the handle on his suitcase and hoisting his backpack over one shoulder, his expression turned serious. "Take good care of my girls."

"You know I will, Brad."

"Thank you for coming. I know Heather's in good hands. And the baby too." He stepped back and eyed her. "Everything okay? You look worried."

"I'm fine. I'm just a little worried that I haven't heard from Zach—the friend that drove me here."

"He was supposed to be home by now?"

"Not necessarily. It's just not like him not to let me know."

"You never answered my question."

"What question is that?"

"Is this guy someone special?"

She shrugged. "I don't know. Maybe." She really didn't know now.

"Well, I hope he deserves you."

Tears welled unexpectedly.

Brad cocked his head. "And if he's being a jerk to you, I'm gonna give him what for."

She forced a smile. "He's not a jerk. Unlike my brother."

"Hey, watch it!" He socked her arm playfully, then checked his phone. "I probably better get going. Be careful."

"Be careful with your car, you mean?"

"No, I mean be careful with my favorite sister."

"Awww. I take back what I said about you being a jerk."

"That's more like it." Another quick hug and Brad hurried to check his luggage curbside.

She merged into the exit lane and instructed Siri to get directions back to Brad and Heather's house. She'd just turned onto their street when her phone dinged. A notification from the B&B app. A reminder probably. Her check-out date for The Inn at Rosebud Lane was a week from today.

She tapped the garage door opener on the visor of Brad's car and waited for the door to rise. She pulled in and turned off the ignition, but before she went inside, she checked her phone. The B&B app said she had a message. Probably just an automated reminder about her check-out date, but maybe it was from Zach.

She opened the app and accessed her messages. Zach's photo appeared in the sidebar with a message from The Inn at Rosebud Lane:

> The Inn at Rosebud Lane: This is Sadie from the inn. Zach wanted me to contact you and let you know he was in an accident last night and lost his phone. He's okay, and he said to tell you he's sorry he didn't let you know sooner, but he didn't have access to a computer in the hospital.

Hospital? What on earth?

She opened her car door to let in some air, but the action only ushered in a blast of furnace-hot air from the garage. She grabbed her purse and exited the car, letting herself into the house as quietly as possible, hoping to avoid having to explain what was going on to Heather.

She tried to call Zach again, then huffed in frustration when she remembered that Sadie had said he'd lost his phone.

Trying to steady her fingers, she typed a brief message back to Sadie.

> Liesl: What happened? Is Zach okay?

It felt like an eternity before a reply finally lit her screen.

> The Inn at Rosebud Lane: He's still in the hospital. He broke his wrist and is supposed to have surgery on it sometime next week. Something about waiting to see a specialist before they could do the surgery.

With trembling fingers, she typed words she couldn't have spoken aloud:

> Liesl: Did he fall asleep at the wheel?

> The Inn at Rosebud Lane: I don't think so. Why?

Oh, thank you, Jesus. She typed the same thought—a prayer, really—to Sadie, ending with:

> Liesl: How did it happen?

> The Inn at Rosebud Lane: I don't know many details, but he apparently got sideswiped by a semi and his pickup is totaled.

Liesl's heart hammered in her chest and she fought to still her fingers enough to type.

> Liesl: But he's going to be okay? No other injuries?

> The Inn at Rosebud Lane: He said he has two black eyes, and they're watching him for a concussion, but other than that, he sounded good.

Concussion?

> Liesl: What hospital is he in?

A long pause, then finally:

> The Inn at Rosebud Lane: I'm so sorry. I didn't ask. I think he said he was in Arkansas. Springfield, maybe? Is there a Springfield in Arkansas? Sorry!

Liesl googled quickly. There was but it wasn't even a real town, and she couldn't seem to find any hospital there.

> Liesl: Do you have the phone number he called you from?

> The Inn at Rosebud Lane: Hang on. I'll see if I can find it.

She wanted to scream, but instead she typed her phone number.

> Liesl: Can you please call me at this number, Sadie?

Her phone rang a few seconds later displaying an unfamiliar number with a North Carolina prefix. She hit Answer. "Sadie?"

"Hi Liesl. I'm so sorry I don't have the hospital information for you. Zach called me on the inn's landline. It's old-school, so I don't have any way to get the number he called from."

"Can you contact him through the inn's app?"

"I don't think he has a computer or anything in the hospital."

"Oh, of course. Dumb question. You don't know how the accident happened?"

"Not really. He just said he got sideswiped and his pickup was totaled. And that he was in the hospital waiting to have surgery on his wrist."

"Okay." Nothing more than the girl had already told her. "Well... I really need to talk to him, Sadie. If he calls you again, can you please give him that number I just gave you and ask him to call me?"

"Yes, of course. I will. And I'm so sorry I didn't get any other information."

"It's okay. Just have him call me. Did...did he sound okay?"

"I guess. He sounded...I don't know...sleepy."

A chill went through her. "Would you please call me the minute you hear anything else from him."

"I will."

"Tell him I'm trying to get in touch with him. It's important. Is...is everything going okay with the inn?"

"Yeah. We had one cancellation, but everyone else checked in and out when they were supposed to."

Liesl heard muffled voices in the background, then the line went quiet. "Sadie? Are you still there?"

An extended silence before she came back on the line. "Um...I see a lot of messages and reservation requests in the app, and I don't really know what to do about those. Zach said to just check for messages and let him know if there was anything urgent. But then, he was supposed to be back by now."

"Well, hopefully those can wait until he returns."

"Davis, stop it!" Sadie's whisper came through clearly. "Davis...I'm on the phone!"

Davis? Her boyfriend was there? "Sadie? Is everything okay?"

"Um, yes. Sorry. I'll let Zach know you're waiting to hear from him."

"Okay. Well, thanks for holding down the fort." It felt like a silly thing to say since she had nothing to do with the inn and certainly no authority over Sadie, but the uncertainty in the girl's voice made her feel like she needed to offer some encouragement. "I'm not sure how I can help, but feel free to call me at the number I gave you if there's anything at all I can do from afar. I'm in Texas at my brother's house. I'm not sure if Zach told you."

"Yeah, I think he did. Um…I'd better hang up now."

"Oh. Okay. Well, let me know if—"

The phone went quiet. Liesl stared at the screen. She had an odd feeling about the call. It was probably nothing. Sadie was probably just nervous that Zach might find out she'd allowed her boyfriend at the inn while she was working. And it was almost five o'clock in North Carolina so maybe Davis was just there to pick her up.

She heard the TV come on in Heather's room upstairs. She needed to go see if she needed anything and let her know that Brad had been safely delivered to the airport. But before she started up the stairs, she stood at the stair rail and whispered a prayer for Zach.

HE FELT like he was floating in the bed. Staving off nausea, Zach groped at his right side for the call button. His fingers wouldn't cooperate and a sharp pain zinged up his forearm. Then he remembered they'd put the call button on his left side since it was his right wrist he'd broken. Multiple fractures and one bone whose name he'd forgotten, was nearly shattered, according to the specialist he'd seen this morning. Dr. Morrow, he thought the name was.

Since the accident had happened on the weekend, and he had considerable swelling, they wouldn't do the surgery until Monday morning.

For now, they had him on pain medicine that made him feel groggy and nauseous, and all he'd done was sleep.

He wondered if Sadie had been able to get hold of Liesl yet. He'd never been one to be glued to his phone, but right now, he would give his right arm to have his phone back. It was frightening to realize that he could not call one person from the hospital phone because he didn't know anyone's phone number except his own. Fortunately, he did know the number of the landline at the inn, and he was grateful Sadie had answered right away.

According to the nurse—Dory Schmidt, her name tag said—the police had his "personal effects" in their possession—including, hopefully, his cell phone—and would return them to him on Monday, but a lot of good that did him now. And on Monday he'd be in surgery.

He wanted to hear Liesl's voice. He worried she would blame herself for his accident and he wanted to reassure her that was not the case. He should have asked Sadie to tell her, but at the time, he'd been in shock and doing well just to figure out how to call out from the phone in his hospital room.

He should have had Sadie look up Liesl's number on the inn's app, too. He would ask her next time he called.

But he couldn't ask her to come to the hospital. He wasn't even sure how far this hospital was from where the crash had happened, but he'd been on the road almost four hours when it happened. That was a good day's drive round-trip. And besides, she was with family, with her sister-in-law where she needed to be.

And even if she hadn't been needed in Texas, he had no claims on her.

Chapter Twenty-Eight

Liesl crawled out of the daybed in the nursery, groggy from a sleepless night, and trudged down the hall to the bathroom. After explaining to Heather about the accident, the two of them talked late into the night, and Liesl confessed that she thought she was falling in love with Zachary Freylan.

She smiled over her toothbrush now, remembering.

"My little sissy is in love," Heather had cooed.

"That's not what I said. And don't you dare tell Brad that. I said I *think* I'm *falling* in love."

"Girl, I can tell just looking at you that you've done falled. I *thought* something was different about you."

Liesl laughed at her grammar-nazi sister-in-law's silly phrasing. But she'd felt compelled to set the record straight. "I really don't believe in love at first sight. I don't want you—or Brad—to think I'm being impulsive or reckless—"

"But sometimes when you know, you know." Heather looked up at her from the cocoon of pillows on her bed. "That's how it was for Brad and me. And we weren't wrong. Gosh, I miss him already."

"How long did you know Brad before you were sure, absolutely sure, he was the one?"

She thought for a moment. "I'm going to say six weeks. But I was *almost* sure a few weeks before that. Don't get me wrong, sis, I don't want you to rush into something that isn't in God's plans for you. But don't think there's some magic number to put on the timeline. Our pastor and his wife knew each other for two weeks before they got engaged."

"Oh wow. That's just crazy."

"Yeah, that's what their parents thought. And to be completely transparent, they had some struggles early in their marriage. But they are committed to each other. So they made it work and now they have one of the best marriages I know—next to mine and Brad's, of course."

Liesl rinsed and spit in the sink, still smiling at the memory. But she sobered quickly thinking of Zach and what he must be going through right now. She worried that Sadie had played down what really happened to him. Otherwise, why was he in the hospital? They didn't usually admit you with broken bones, did they? But maybe it was the concussion they were watching. Concussions could be serious. She knew that from Brad's football days. *Oh, Lord, be with Zach. Please let him be okay...*

She gave a little moan as she dried her face. She just wished she could talk to him and hear that he was okay in his own words.

She finished getting ready and hurried to Heather's room. That's why she was here and she didn't want to let Zach's situation overshadow Heather's needs. She knocked softly on the door before pushing it open a few inches.

Heather was sitting up in bed brushing her hair.

"Good morning, sunshine. Are you about ready for breakfast?"

"Whenever you are. I really, really want a shower today. Do you think we could make that happen? And wash my hair?"

"You're feeling good? No contractions? No bleeding?" The weight of responsibility felt heavy. If anything happened to this baby on her watch, she would never forgive herself.

"Nothing more than I've been feeling. You know my doctor said I could shower twice a week."

"I know. I just want to be sure."

"Thank you, Liesl. I know this isn't easy."

"No, I didn't mean that. I feel honored you guys trust me to stay with you. I just don't want to do anything to…"

"Come here." Heather held out a hand. "It'll be okay. And if anything happens, it will *not* be your fault. Understand?"

Liesl sat on the bed beside her. "We'll figure out a shower and a hair wash, okay?"

"Bless you, my sister," Heather said dramatically. "I shall be forever indebted to you."

They giggled and the mood was broken. "Bacon and eggs?"

"I'll eat whatever you bring me."

Liesl hopped off the bed. "As if you had a choice."

Heather rolled her eyes. "Tell me about it. But bacon and eggs does sound good. And maybe some yogurt? I think Brad said he bought some."

She nodded. "I saw it in the fridge last night."

"Have you heard anything more from your guy?"

"He's not my guy…" She winked. "Yet. And no news. If I haven't heard anything by noon, I'm going to try to track him down."

"So you don't even know what hospital he's in?"

She shook her head. "I don't even know what town he's in. Sadie didn't ask. I don't blame her. I'm sure I wouldn't have thought to ask either—in her shoes. But it sure is frustrating." She gathered up some laundry from the hamper and started out of the room. "You need anything before I go down?"

"I'm good."

"Okay, I'll be back with breakfast in a few."

"Thanks, sis."

She was dishing scrambled eggs onto plates when her phone buzzed in her jeans pocket. She made sure the burner was off, then checked her screen. Her pulse raced. *Regional Medical Center.*

"Hello?" Her voice trembled.

"Hey there."

"Zach! Finally!" Relief coursed through her at the timbre of his voice.

He laughed softly into the phone and she didn't think she'd ever heard a more beautiful sound.

"Are you okay?"

"I'm okay. And if I sound drunk, it's because they have me hopped up on some weird pain meds."

"So you're still in the hospital? I'm so sorry!"

"Stop. I'm going to be okay. Did Sadie tell you what happened?"

"Yes, but I want to hear it from you."

"Not much to hear. I got sideswiped by a semi. That's the part I remember. I don't know if the guy didn't see me or if he just didn't have any place to get over. I still haven't been able to find out what happened, but apparently, my little pickup ended up pinned between two semis. The next thing I knew I was waking up in a strange hospital."

"Where *are* you? Sadie didn't know. I would have called you otherwise."

"Yeah, she felt really bad that she didn't know where I was...to tell you. I'm in Hot Springs. In Arkansas. I guess they took me to the closest hospital."

"Sadie said you broke your wrist."

"Uh-huh. I'm pretty helpless. But I'm getting a little better at doing everything left-handed."

"Oh no. It was your right wrist you broke?"

"Naturally." He didn't sound drunk. He sounded just like himself. And she missed him like crazy.

She looked at the eggs and bacon starting to congeal on the plates. Heather was waiting. But she couldn't tell Zach she had to go.

She could heat her own breakfast up later. She lifted one of the plates, grabbed a fork and a napkin and started up the stairs with her phone tucked between her shoulder and her chin. "So are you in a cast?"

"From my fingertips to my shoulder. They're doing surgery on Monday and I think the cast I get after that won't be quite so restrictive. At least that's what the ER doc said."

"Oh wow. Zach, I'm so sorry. Is anybody there with you?"

"No. And I still don't have my phone back. Apparently it was thrown out of the truck."

She shuddered, imagining the horror of the accident. "Can I call anybody for you?" But who could she call? Sadie was holding down the fort at the inn and there really wasn't anyone else close enough to ask. Jenny's mom maybe? Or the pastor of the church they'd been attending? For the first time, she realized how alone Zach had been. Her heart broke for him. How isolated he must feel now, trapped in an unfamiliar hospital without any way to reach out.

"I'm fine, Liesl. Bored out of my mind. If I see one more rerun of Mayberry RFD... But I'll be okay once the surgery is over. It might be a while before I can drive though. Not that I have anything *to* drive."

"Oh. Your truck..."

"Totalled."

"Oh wow. I'm sorry, Zach. I was so afraid something like this would happen. I should—"

"Liesl, stop. This wasn't your fault and it wasn't mine. It just happened. Things just happen sometimes."

She knew by his tone that he was thinking of Jenny's accident. And he sounded resigned. To what, she wasn't sure.

She carried the plate into Heather's room and placed it on the little overbed table they'd rented for the duration. "Zach!" she mouthed, pointing to her phone.

"Yay!" Heather mouthed back. "He's okay?"

She nodded.

Heather gave a relieved sigh then waved her away.

Grateful, Liesl took her phone back downstairs, listening as Zach regaled her with funny stories of his hospital stay—what he remembered of it anyway. He seemed to be in surprisingly good spirits considering all he'd just been through.

"So when do you think you'll get your phone back?"

"Probably not until Monday. And then I might be too out of it after the surgery to use a phone."

"That stinks. I'm glad you at least have the hospital phone."

"Well, besides the inn, you are the only phone number I have so you're probably going to be sick of talking to me before this is all over."

"No, I won't be. I promise." An unexpected lump formed in her throat. "I'm just glad you're okay."

"I'm not sure what I'm going to do about the truck. I don't really want to buy a new one in Hot Springs, Arkansas. But I guess my insurance company will pay for a rental, so I can wait till I get home to worry about that."

"But how will you drive with a broken wrist? Especially your right one?"

"Not sure about that. One day at a time. I guess I'll ask my doctor what he thinks."

"Oh, Zach... I wish I could come and drive you home. After all you did for me—"

"No. You are right where you're supposed to be. Don't think another thing of it. It'll all work out. And it seems like Sadie is handling everything at the inn, so that's good."

"Yeah, she sounded like everything was under control." She wouldn't tell him about her suspicion that Davis had been at the inn when Sadie called her. It was probably nothing, and Zach couldn't do anything about it yet anyway. "Are they feeding you okay there? I hear hospital food leaves a lot to be desired."

"It's okay. I haven't had much of an appetite, and I know I won't be able to eat anything for a while before the surgery, so that's okay."

"You have a better attitude than I would."

"Yeah, well, you didn't hear me bark at the nurse in the middle of the night. You know that joke about them waking you up to give you a sleeping pill? Totally true." A commotion muffled his voice before he came back on. "And speaking of nazi nurses, mine is here now wanting to take the rest of my blood."

She giggled. "I'm just glad I finally heard from you. I'll be praying for you, Zach."

"Hey, I appreciate that. Seriously."

"Then I'll pray seriously."

"I'll call you later... If that's okay?"

"Of course. Please. I— I'd better let you go." She'd been so close to blurting out *I love you*, it scared her.

Chapter Twenty-Nine

"Okay, Mr. Freylan, we're taking you back now. Are you ready?"

Zach scooted up on the narrow bed. "Do I have a choice?" He was already growing drowsy from whatever they'd given him earlier.

The nurse laughed and unlocked the wheels on the gurney they'd transferred him to a few minutes ago.

He felt like all he'd done was sleep for the last three days. No doubt the effects of the painkillers they had him on. He'd be glad when this was over and he could get out of this hospital gown and out of this hospital, period. He would never again complain about cleaning toilets at the inn.

"Is anyone in the waiting room for you that we should let know once you're out of surgery."

He shook his head.

The door opened wider and Dory, the young, blond nurse who'd been on duty when he first woke up in the hospital, walked in. "Are you ever going to be happy to see me," she chirped. She held up a cell phone, familiar except for the long, diagonal crack across the screen—hopefully only the screen protector. "They dropped off your personal effects from your vehicle just a few minutes ago. I'll put everything in your dresser here, since you'll be coming back to this room for recovery."

"Hey…" He struggled to sit up in the bed, the bulky bandage and splint on his arm making it difficult.

Both nurses intervened, pushing him gently back onto the pillow. "You don't want to be sitting upright right now," Dory said.

"Okay, but… I need to call someone real quick before you put my phone away."

The two exchanged looks and Dory shrugged and handed him his phone. "Make it speedy. We'll be back in five minutes."

"I will. Thanks."

LIESL AWOKE with Zach's surgery on her mind. She wished she could at least send him a text message to let him know she was praying for him, but he probably wouldn't get his phone until later today. If they'd even found it in the wreckage. She shuddered to think of the accident and sent up a prayer that the surgery would go smoothly.

She and Heather already had a nice routine going, and she'd even been able to get some writing done this weekend.

After talking to Zach yesterday, she'd poured her heart out to Heather and told her every detail about her time with Zach at the inn. She'd confessed how heartbroken she was that he would be alone during the surgery and that there'd be no one with him when he woke from the surgery or after, during the recovery time.

Heather's forehead had wrinkled. "Isn't there anyone who could come and be with him?"

"Not really. He's still pretty close to Jenny's mom, but his parents are both gone and he doesn't have any siblings. I mean, everybody in town loves him, but it's not like you can ask someone to drive nine hours to sit with you in the hospital."

"I'm so sorry, Lees. He sounds like a great guy," Heather said.

"He is. He really is."

"How long did you say it's been since his wife died?"

"Two years."

"And has he dated before? Since she died?"

"No. He said I'm the first one he's ever been interested in since Jenny. Why? Does that...concern you?"

Heather shrugged. "Maybe a little. It would a lot if it had only been a year or something. But two years is a long time when he's so young. And they had a good marriage? He and Jenny?"

"Yes, very good. He loved her a lot. But I also respect that he doesn't want to put her on a pedestal." She'd told Heather about that conversation she'd had with Zach.

"That's a good thing, I think," Heather said. "It sounds like he has a good head on his shoulders. Of course, if he's in love with you, that just proves it."

She smiled at the memory. Heather had always been a dear friend, but this time they spent together had sealed their friendship and made Liesl love her brother's wife even more.

She started for the bathroom when her phone chimed. Probably Brad texting to see how they were getting along.

Zach's photo appeared on her screen.

Zach: Hey you! Can I call you?

Liesl: Of course! You must have your phone back! Yay!

Her phone rang and she quickly answered. "Zach? How *are* you? Are you out of surgery already?"

"No. Just going in. I'm pretty groggy and they won't let me talk long, but I just wanted to tell you something before I go in."

"Okay..."

"I...I think I love you. I mean, really, *really* love you. I kind of skirted around it before, but—"

"How about you get through this surgery, get sobered up, and then we'll see if you remember what you just said." Her heart raced but in the best kind of way.

"I'll remember." His words were a little slurred, but she thought he was coherent. "I'll remember, Liesl-rhymes-with-Cecil."

She laughed. "If you remember *that*, I have high hopes." She turned serious. "Oh Zach, I'm so sorry you're all alone there. But I'll be praying for you every minute. Call me as soon as you can, okay?"

"I will. Oh. Gotta go. They're taking my phone away from me."

"Zach?" She couldn't tell if he'd hung up or not. "I think I love you too," she whispered before she pressed End.

The phone rang again, startling her.

Brad's photo appeared on the screen. "Sis? Where are you right now?"

She frowned. "In my room—the nursery," she corrected. "Getting ready. Why? Is everything okay?"

"Yeah, fine. But listen. You need to finish getting ready, then hop in the car and drive to Hot Springs."

"What? No, Brad. I can't leave Heather."

"Two of her friends from church are coming over to stay with her until late tonight. Heather worked out all the details. She seems to think you need to be with that guy."

"Heather said that?"

"Yes, and don't you disappoint her, you hear?"

"Oh, Brad. Are you sure?"

"I'm not sure at all. But I trust my wife in matters of love, and she seems to think you are in love with this yahoo."

She laughed. "Nobody says *yahoo* anymore, Bradley."

"And nobody calls me Bradley and lives to tell the tale. Now get your butt in the car. Don't you dare speed, but if you hustle, I bet you can be at the hospital by the time he wakes up."

"Oh, Brad..." Her heart soared. "You are the best brother in the whole wide—"

"I know, I know... Now get a move on!"

Laughing, heart full, she hung up and ran down the hall to Heather's room.

Her sister-in-law sat upright in the bed beaming. "You talked to Brad. I can see it in your face."

"Heather, you are absolutely *the* best! Are you sure? Absolutely positive?"

"Of course, I'm sure."

"I won't leave until your friends get here, but I can't thank—"

The doorbell rang downstairs and Heather's phone confirmed with a ringtone. "That's them now," she said, waving Liesl off. "Now hurry up and get on the road. You know which hospital, right? Do you need gas before you go?"

"No... No, Brad filled up his car before I took him to the airport. And I know the name of the hospital. But—"

"Good. Now go!"

She pulled Heather into a tight hug, then raced downstairs to answer the door.

ONCE SHE GOT on the Interstate, Liesl set the cruise control on exactly seventy miles per hour, but she felt like she was flying. I-30 stretched out like a ribbon under a crystal blue sky and the miles ticked off on the odometer of Brad's Volvo.

She hadn't thought to ask if they'd told Zach she was coming, but unless they'd called the hospital, they wouldn't have known how to reach him. She didn't remember even mentioning his last name to Heather. She smiled at the thought of Brad and Heather conspiring to get her to Zach in Hot Springs. She'd never felt more loved—especially given her conversation with Zach this morning.

She was curious if he would actually remember talking to her. But something inside her told her he would. And this time, she wouldn't whisper her response.

Chapter Thirty

"Mr. Freylan? Mr. Freylan, can you hear me? You need to wake up."

The unfamiliar voice came from somewhere above him. He struggled to open his eyes, but had to squint against the bright lights overhead.

"Mr. Freylan? Zachary?"

He grimaced, feeling like an old man. "It's Zach."

"Good. You haven't forgotten your name."

"Why? How long was I under?"

"Almost four hours. And we've been trying to wake you up for the past thirty minutes."

"Four hours. How bad was it?" He looked down at his bent arm but the gauze covered splint didn't provide any answers.

"The doctor will be in to talk to you shortly. He'll explain everything."

Zach remembered the specialist telling him surgery would likely last "a couple hours." What had made it take four hours to fix a broken wrist? It couldn't be good.

"Once you've talked to the doctor you have a visitor in the waiting room."

"A visitor?" He hadn't told anyone back home, except for

Sadie that he was here. And it had better not be her in that waiting room because the inn wouldn't run itself. Maybe Glory had somehow heard about his accident. It would be just like Jenny's mom to come to be with him. An unexpected wave of nausea came over him. "I think I'm going to be sick," he told the nurse.

She quickly thrust a small, kidney-shaped basin under his chin. "That sometimes happens coming out of the anesthesia. Here—" She pushed a button, and the head of his bed rose slowly. "Sometimes that helps." She waited a minute, watching him closely. "Better?"

He closed his eyes and waited for the sensation to pass. Thankfully it did. Just in time for his doctor to appear in the doorway to the recovery room.

"So you finally decided to wake up for us, did you?"

In no mood for small talk, he managed a wan nod.

"Well, the bad news is, you're going to be setting off the alarms in airports for the rest of your life. Unfortunately, the type of fractures you sustained require some hardware to put you back together." He went into more detail than Zach had the stomach for about the pins and screws and plates required to repair the multiple fractures. "The better news is, you should be almost as good as new once those bones have a chance to heal."

"Almost?" He didn't like the sound of that.

The doctor frowned. "We have you in a splint now because of the swelling. We'll put a cast on the arm in a day or two to keep everything immobile. I'll want you to wear that for six to eight weeks and then you're probably looking at some physical therapy once the bones are healed. But you're young enough that you should make a full recovery. Patience will be the name of the game."

Zach shook his head. "Not my favorite game, doc."

"No, I don't imagine it is." The man didn't sound the least bit sympathetic. "We'll observe you for another hour or two and then send you home with something to keep the pain manageable. Do you have a ride home?"

The nurse answered for him. "Home is North Carolina, Dr. Morrow. And Mr. Freylan's vehicle was totaled in the accident."

"Oh, that's right. Sorry, I probably knew that." He blew out a breath. "Well, regardless, you're not driving anywhere for at least a day or two with the meds you'll be on. And I'm not crazy about you driving that distance any time soon. Especially with this being your dominant hand. What is it...seven or eight hours to home?"

"Closer to eleven."

"Okay. No. That's not happening. We'll have to work something else out."

We? Zach suddenly hoped it *was* Glory in the waiting room down the hall, because he did not want to be stuck in Hot Springs, Arkansas one minute longer than necessary.

Dr. Morrow turned to the nurse. "Let's get an appointment scheduled for Wednesday for the cast. And maybe we can look at a cab to DoubleTree later today?"

Zach waited till the doctor's attention turned back to him before asking, "If I can get home, can you refer me to somebody there? In Willowtree. North Carolina. Or Charlotte if there's nothing closer."

"I'm sure we can. But you're not driving that far. At least not for a few days. We can work something out, I'm sure. Any other questions?"

Zach shook his head even though he had a million of them swirling through his head.

The doctor left the room and he turned to the nurse. "You said I had a visitor? It might be a ride." He prayed that somehow Glory had found out about his accident. But he also hated that she'd had to drive all the way from Charlotte. She was sixty-something—maybe closer to seventy by now—and had health issues of her own.

"Shall I tell her she can come in?"

"Yes. Please." He probably looked like death warmed over, but if Glory was his ticket out of here, he didn't care.

The nurse left the room and a few minutes later there was a soft knock on the door.

"Yeah, come in." He hadn't even thought to check a mirror but ran a hand through his hair, feeling instantly that it was a disheveled mop.

The door opened slowly, and Liesl's smiling face appeared around the corner.

He sat up quickly, wincing at the sharp pain that seared his arm.

She hurried to his bedside and tentatively touched the shoulder of his injured arm before gripping the bed rail. "Are you okay?"

"I'm fine. I'm just...surprised to see you. How did you get here?"

"I drove...Brad's car."

"But your sister-in-law? I thought—"

"Some friends are staying with her until tonight. Brad and Heather arranged everything. So I could come and see you." She studied him, cringing. "Those are quite the shiners you've got there. Sadie said you had two black eyes, but wow..."

"Well, I know you can't say the same for me, but you are a sight for these sore eyes." He ran his fingers through his hair again, knowing it was useless.

"Don't be so sure." She rested her hand on his shoulder. "They said you just got out of surgery a little while ago."

"Yeah. I'm still a little out of it. I thought maybe I was seeing things when you walked through that door."

"Nope." She grinned. "It's really me." She told him about the surprise that had met her this morning and the unexpected four-hour drive she'd made.

"You have no idea what a gift it is that you're here." He glanced past her to the uncomfortable looking vinyl chair in the corner under the television. "Pull up a chair, please."

She did as he bid, and he tried to turn on his side so he could see her better. Even though it had only been a couple of days since he'd dropped her off at her brother's, it felt like he was seeing her for the first time in months, and her very presence in the room was better than any medicine they'd prescribed for what ailed him.

"So what happened? The accident... Or is it too soon to talk about it?"

"It's not my favorite subject but you deserve—"

"No, it's okay. You can tell me later. I'm just glad you're okay." She nodded at his wrist. "You didn't have to get a cast. That's good."

He frowned. "That happens in a couple days. Too much swelling now."

"Oh. Bummer. A couple days? So you'll be in the hospital for a while?"

"A hotel, I guess."

"Oh, Zach. That stinks."

"But slightly better than being stuck in this hospital."

"So when do you get out?"

"I think I can leave as soon as I can prove I'm not going to faint on them. But I'm not leaving as long as you're here."

"I probably need to leave by four. Heather's friends are only there till I get back. And I don't want to drive in the dark too long."

"No. I don't want you to either." He shuddered involuntarily, thinking about his accident. "What time is it now?"

"Lunchtime. Can you eat?"

"I hope so. They starved me half to death before this stupid surgery. You must be good for me though. I felt kind of sick when I came out of the anesthesia, but I'm famished now."

"Then let's find you something to eat. If they'll let me spring you out of here, I can take you to your hotel." Her brow wrinkled. "Had you already checked in someplace?"

"No. I was going to stop here that night—in Hot Springs— but took this stupid detour instead." He lifted his splinted arm and winced again. "The doctor mentioned a DoubleTree hotel. It must be close by."

"How about you rest, and I'll call and reserve a room. We can find some lunch and then I'll drop you off at the hotel before I have to leave?"

"That sounds like the next best thing to you just taking me on home."

"Oh, I wish I could, Zach. I really do. I'm sorry—"

"No..." He shook his head. "I didn't mean that to make you feel bad."

"I know. But I still wish I could take you home."

He reached for her hand with his good arm and she took it as if they'd been holding hands for half their lives. Maybe someday— he did a quick calculation—if they both lived to see their sixties, that could be true.

Chapter Thirty-One

iesl brought the car around to where the hospital staff had instructed and waited for them to bring Zach out. Judging by the reluctance in his expression, he was embarrassed that they'd insisted on bringing him out in a wheelchair, but she was glad for it when she saw how pale he looked.

When the door opened and his wheelchair appeared, she jumped out and ran around to open the passenger door of Brad's car.

The young orderly helped Zach stand and slide into the car while Liesl stood by feeling a little helpless.

The orderly folded the chair and gave her a questioning look. "You got it from here, ma'am?"

"Yes sir. Thanks for your help." She turned to find Zach looking up at her, that same veiled dismay on his face. It registered that he couldn't reach the door handle with his left hand. She started to close the door for him, then realized he wasn't buckled in.

Taking a deep breath, she pulled the seatbelt out and around him. "Don't let me hurt you, okay?"

As soon as she snapped the belt into place, she felt a strong arm come around her shoulder and cradle her head.

"Hey you."

She looked into eyes full of affection and gratitude.

"Hey you," she echoed.

He didn't kiss her like she thought he might but instead cupped her cheek with his palm. "Thank you. I truly don't know what I would have done if you hadn't come today."

"You would have figured it out. And it's Heather—and Brad —you should thank. They arranged the whole thing."

"But you didn't have to agree to it."

"Zach..." She squatted down beside the car so she could look him in the eye. His left hand never left her face. "You have no idea how badly I wanted to be here for you. I know I committed to be with Heather and she *does* need me, but this is where I wanted to be most." She motioned between them.

"Really?"

"Of course really. I'm so thankful they made it happen."

"Me too."

"Especially after you went to the trouble to bring me all the way to Texas."

"Right now I'm thinking that's the best decision I've ever made."

"What? Even after this?" She pointed to the splint and his swollen hand. "Why?"

"Because I fell head over heels for you on that drive." He pulled her closer and started to lean in to kiss her, but grimaced with pain. "Come here. You're going to have to meet me halfway."

She rose to meet his kiss. It was as sweet as she remembered. "Well, that makes two of us head over heels. I love you, Zach. I should have said it on the phone. When you called this morning."

"Was that just this morning?"

She nodded.

"Wow. Time *doesn't* fly when you're woozy from surgery."

"No, and I'm still waiting until you aren't under the influence before I—" She stopped mid-sentence. She really did want to be sure he knew full well what he was saying.

"Before what?"

"Before we talk about what you said this morning. And what you said just now."

"About being in love with you? About being head over heels? Liesl, I'm fully cognizant of what I'm saying."

She shook her head, grinning. "We'll see. I want to get it in writing—when I know you're not on drugs."

She jumped to her feet, carefully closed the passenger door, and went around to slide behind the wheel.

She looked over at Zach. "You doing okay?"

He looked surprisingly good for just coming out of a four-hour-long surgery. A little pale, but that was to be expected after all he'd been through. Liesl fastened her own seatbelt and drove with extra care, not daring to take her eyes off the street for more than a cursory glance at him in the passenger seat beside her.

The hotel was less than five minutes from the hospital but Zach had requested Chipotle after being "starved" at the hospital. She'd ordered burrito bowls online and they were headed to the drive-through pickup.

"That's what Glory brings me from Charlotte when she comes to visit. She's who I thought you were when they first told me I had a visitor."

"Glory? You think I look like an old lady?"

He laughed. "No, although Glory looks pretty good for her age. But I hadn't seen you yet. I just couldn't think who else would have driven so far to visit me."

She smiled without turning his way. "That would be me."

"Well, I love you for it."

"Seems like turnabout is fair play. You drove me quite a ways, as I recall."

"In that case, you owe me big-time." The Chipotle appeared on their right and she pulled into the drive-through.

Zach started to reach for his wallet, then made a face and held up his splinted arm.

She plucked her wallet out of her purse. "Nope, this one is on me."

At the hotel she left him in the car and went to check him in. The colorful, homey lobby made her feel better about leaving him alone here. At the front desk, she explained that Zach had just been released from the hospital and would probably be staying until after his appointment to get the cast on.

"Will your husband need transportation to appointments during his stay?"

"Um...he can arrange that later if he does." She felt a little guilty not correcting the agent, but it seemed simpler. And she didn't mind the sound of that—*your husband*.

After giving her the keys and explaining where the room was, the front desk offered her fresh-from-the-oven chocolate chip cookies. She thanked them and wrapped a couple in a napkin. They'd be a fun surprise for Zach, and he wouldn't have to retrieve them himself later. She worried how he'd handle the breakfast buffet in the morning. Oh, how she wished she could stay and help him navigate everything. But she would just be grateful she got to be here for him at all. And he was a grown man. He could probably figure out how to manage breakfast with one hand.

WITH THE CHIPOTLE bag hooked on one arm—with the cookies tucked inside—and Zach's duffel bag, plus her purse on one shoulder, Liesl waved the keycard and opened the door wide. She turned back to look at him. "You good? You're not going to faint on me or anything, are you?"

"I'm good, but I wouldn't mind sitting down in the next thirty seconds or so."

She hurried into the room and deposited the bags on the desk, pulling out the rolling desk chair. When Zach was settled, she opened the curtains wide. "Look, you've got a little lake down here." The view behind the second set of sheer curtains—a blue lake with boat slips and docks—made her open those too.

He swiveled his chair to look. "Nice. I wish you could stay."

Her expression must have made him realize the implications of what he'd said. "In the room next door," he added quickly.

She laughed. "I knew what you meant. I wish I could stay too." And if she was honest, she didn't want to be next door either. But she was grateful she knew where Zach stood on that subject, as difficult as it might be for both of them to wait. Probably him especially, since he'd already known the love of a wife.

Not trusting her thoughts, she went to get their food and arranged it on the tiny end table in one corner. A delicious aroma rose when she took off the lids.

Zach shuffled his feet and rolled his chair over to the table. He patted the chair arm with his good hand. "This thing is going to come in handy."

"Can you eat left-handed?"

"Oh, believe me, I've mastered broth and Jell-o. We'll see how I do with a burrito."

She laughed, watching him wolf down the food. "Maybe you should pace yourself there, buddy."

"Mmmm," was his only reply.

She joined him, enjoying the savory food almost as much as he seemed to.

While they ate, they watched ducks on the water and Liesl checked a map of the area on her phone. "Oh. This isn't a little lake. It's huge. Lake Hamilton. And there's a casino just a couple miles up the road from here."

"Just what I need. A one-armed bandit." He held up his splinted arm and gave her a goofy look. "Get it?" Just as quickly, he grimaced and lowered it. "Man, I've got to quit doing that."

She laughed, shaking her head "Do you need to take some pain meds?"

"I'm okay. I'm going to try to only take them at night. We'll see. But I don't want you thinking everything I say is—" he chalked quote marks in the air—"under the influence."

She waved off the comment. "I can't honestly say I was teasing about that. But seriously, Zach, I don't want to be responsible for you being in pain. Please take whatever pills you need. We can always talk later."

He nodded and pushed his empty bowl away.

She stood and started gathering the take-out containers.

But he tenderly touched her arm. "Hey, sit down for a minute, will you? I want to tell you something, Liesl. And please don't think I'm trying to pressure you or force you to make some kind of decision, but...something significant happened during the crash."

Reading the seriousness in his gaze, she sat back down. "Significant?"

"First, I have to back up and tell you another story."

"Okay." She leaned forward, her curiosity deepening.

"About a year after Jenny's accident, I almost had a wreck myself. A car was passing in a no-passing zone and we almost had a head-on collision. It ended up just being a close call, but in those few split-seconds when I thought I was going to die, I realized I was kind of disappointed that I didn't. I wasn't suicidal or anything, but in those few brief seconds, I was so excited and happy that I was going to be with Jenny again."

She could understand that on some level. But she wasn't sure where he was going with this, so she simply waited.

He reached for her hand. "I'll be honest, Liesl, I was a little depressed after that. Because now I had no choice but to figure out how to go on without her. And I did. I have. But here's the thing. The other night, in those harrowing seconds before I lost consciousness, I did think of Jenny and wondered what it must have been like for her, just before the crash. But mostly I thought of you. And I didn't want to die. More than anything, I wanted to get back to you. To have a life with you. And when I came to in the hospital, I was grateful and...excited even. Because it meant God must have more for me. And I hope more for...us."

She tried to stem the tears that threatened, but they came in silent sobs. But when she saw the distress on Zach's face, her tears turned to awkward laughter. "Don't worry, these are happy tears. I promise. And oh, Zach, I hope he has more in store for us too."

"We'll make a way. If it's supposed to be, God will make a way."

Chapter Thirty-Two

"I'll walk you to the car." He supported the splint with his left hand, preparing for the pain he knew would come when he rose.

"No, Zach. I'm fine. Please..." She pointed in the general direction of the hotel parking lot. "I'm parked just out here and I'd feel better if I was sure you were safely tucked in this room when I drive away."

"What? You think I'm going to faint and lie on the ground outside the hotel all night?"

"Something like that. Just please humor me, okay?" The affection in her smile persuaded him.

"Okay." But after she slung her bag over one shoulder, he got up and followed her to the door, trying to hide a grimace of pain. "I'll miss you."

"And I'll miss you."

"Call me when you get back."

"Oh?" She studied him, a spark of mischief in her eyes. "Like you called me?"

"Hey, that's not fair. I was slightly unconscious."

"Exactly."

He moved closer and tucked a stray strand of hair behind her ear, desperate to touch her, to kiss her.

She must have sensed it because she turned her face up, giving him that coy smile he loved.

He drew her close with his good arm and kissed the crown of her head, then her forehead.

She put her arms around him and leaned closer, meeting his lips. But after a much-too-short kiss, she put the palm of her hand on his chest and pushed away. "I need to go."

"Yes, you do." He gave her another quick kiss, then took a step back and met her gaze. "To be continued."

"Definitely."

When she closed the door behind her, it felt like she took the sunshine with her.

Sighing, he went back to the desk and tried to get comfortable with an arm that was beginning to throb again.

He had plenty to do to take his mind off the pain. He needed to call his insurance guy to be sure he could rent a car to get home, and he needed to call Sadie and make sure things were going okay at the inn. Thankfully, this time of year the inn was usually booked for multiple-night guests so she wouldn't have to do a complete turnover of very many rooms. Not that Sadie wasn't capable, but she had a couple of other part-time jobs and was going far above and beyond for him this week. He didn't want to take advantage of her generosity.

Twenty minutes later, he'd arranged to pick up a car Wednesday afternoon after he got the cast on. He'd catch a cab to the rental place and get a few hours down the road before stopping for the night. He'd see how it went from there.

Now, to call Sadie. He texted her to make sure she was available. Her reply came within seconds.

> Sadie: Hi Zach. Yes, I can talk. I'm at the inn, in fact. I'll wait for your call.

He dialed the inn, then, feeling a little light-headed, went to lie on the bed while he waited for her to answer.

"Hi Zach. How are you doing?"

"I'm good, Sadie. Thank you again for handling everything while I'm gone."

"It's no problem. Everything is going good. Nobody has complained about the granola bars yet. And apparently I make good coffee because nobody has complained about that either."

He laughed. "You're killing it then."

Sadie laughed in return. "When will you be back? Not that I'm rushing you or anything," she added quickly.

"The doc says they have to wait for the swelling to go down, so I don't get my cast on until Wednesday, so I probably won't be back until late Friday. You okay with that?" He wasn't sure how much help he'd be come Friday either. With a stupid cast on his right arm, it was going to be challenging just getting himself clean, let alone a room at the inn.

"Sure."

He put Sadie on speaker and scrolled to the inn's app. "Let's see... From what I can tell, there's only one new party checking in before Friday, so you'd only have to turn over #5. Just do the minimum on the other rooms."

"Yes, that's what I saw too. But, um...the couple who checked in to #3 after you left asked me to do the bedding every day. Wash all the sheets and stuff, I mean."

"No. Let me contact them. That is not necessary, and they'll understand under the circumstan—"

"I really don't mind, Zach. And, um... I hope you're okay with this, but my boyfriend has been helping me out for about an hour each evening when he gets off work. Don't worry—he doesn't expect to be paid or anything. But he's really been a big help."

Davis. Zach felt a check in his spirit. For one thing, he didn't like the idea of Sadie in his house with a boyfriend. Any boyfriend.

But given Liesl's suspicions about Davis Simmons, he felt even more wary. But he was already asking a lot of Sadie. Beggars couldn't be choosers, right? "I guess that's okay. Just for this week."

But what was he going to do next week and the week after that?

He pretended to be intent on the dusting Sadie had assigned him, but Davis strained to hear her end of the conversation with Zach Freylan on the landline phone in the inn's office. Zach was apparently still in the hospital after the car accident. The poor guy couldn't seem to catch a break. At least this one wasn't his fault, though Davis would have traded being responsible for a mere broken wrist—instead of a life—*in a heartbeat.*

Sadie was asking her boss if it was okay if her boyfriend helped out. Apparently Zach said yes. It would have been a very different answer if Zach knew who he really was. What he'd done. But being Sadie's boyfriend apparently gave him special privileges in her boss's eyes.

Boyfriend. *Sadie had finally agreed to make it official just last night. They weren't engaged or anything, but they'd talked about it. Even about marriage. He felt bad leading Sadie on that way. It wasn't fair to her. She deserved better. And he wouldn't let her go on believing in the dreams they'd entertained. He wasn't cruel. But he couldn't tell her everything until he was sure she really loved him. Was committed to him.*

And he did plan to tell her everything. Maybe even tonight.

But once she knew the truth, it would all be over. He'd already made up his mind that he would turn himself in. And he'd make sure she knew his intentions. He didn't want to risk that she would feel obligated to turn him in herself. Or tell Zach what he'd done.

If it meant spending his life behind bars, so be it. It couldn't be any worse than this self-imposed prison he'd been living in for two years now.

Chapter Thirty-Three

Liesl woke with a start on Wednesday morning. She rubbed her eyes and checked her phone. Six a.m. Zach would be getting the cast on in a couple of hours. The procedure wouldn't be nearly as bad as the surgery, but she whispered a prayer for him nevertheless. She prayed, too, that God would show them both if this love growing between them was part of His plan for them.

She didn't want to make a mistake. But she knew where this was going and that if she and Zach continued to spend time together, it was inevitable they would fall deeply in love. She sighed and crawled out of bed. Who was she kidding? Already, she couldn't possibly love the man more. And if God said no, it was going to be excruciating to say goodbye to Zach.

A few minutes before eight, she texted him.

Liesl: Praying for you right now. Hope it goes even better than you expect.

Immediately, dots appeared on the screen and she smiled, anticipating his reply.

Zach: Thanks. Good timing. My Uber just pulled into the hospital parking lot. It should all be over in an hour or so.

Liesl: Good. I'll be glad when it's done. Call me when you're finished, will you? Better yet, send me a picture of that bad boy.

He sent a goofy smiley face in reply.

Wearing her own goofy smile, she went to get dressed.

A few minutes later, she checked her phone again.

Zach: Here's the plan: I'll stay at the hotel one more night, practice with my arm, and see if I can get by without any meds. Then I'll decide about starting home in the morning.

Liesl: Sounds like a plan. I'm praying for you.

That earned her a heart emoji.

Liesl knew he was eager to get home, but she wished he could wait just two more days. Brad would be home tomorrow, and maybe she could talk Zach into waiting until she was ready to leave. She'd considered renting a car and driving to Hot Springs so she could help Zach drive back to Willowtree. But it really wasn't her place to make arrangements for him. And she would feel guilty ditching and leaving as soon as Brad got home.

She was behind on the Willowtree book but her publisher had given her grace. She could probably stay at the inn a couple more days to finish the book, but the truth was she had all the photos and information she needed. Now it was just a matter of finishing the writing. And she needed to go back to her apartment in Iowa before she headed to St. Charles in Missouri to start work on the next book.

She sighed, thinking of the verses she'd read in the book of Matthew just last night before she fell asleep. The Bible said not to worry about tomorrow, because tomorrow "will worry about itself. Each day has enough trouble of its own." Well, that much was certainly true.

She slipped her phone in the back pocket of her shorts and hurried downstairs. She had a special breakfast planned for Heather. She'd been trying to make it up to her sister-in-law for leaving her in the lurch last week. Even though Heather insisted she didn't mind, and in fact, claimed she'd had a wonderful time with her friends. "It was like a slumber party back when we were in school. Never mind we were all ready to zonk by sunset."

Liesl had laughed at that, but it made her feel a little envious too. She missed having close friendships like Heather's.

She made muffins and a Denver omelet and took their plates up to Heather's room on a tray. Heather was in the shower—her one excuse to get out of the bed she'd been in for more than a week now—and Liesl opened the French doors that led to the balcony and knotted the curtain panels so they wouldn't block the unseasonably cool morning breeze that had come on the tail of last night's rain. It would be in the nineties by noon, but for now, it truly felt like spring. It reminded Liesl of the North Carolina she'd left, and she ached for the sultry mountain air and the grape-soda scent of mountain laurel.

On a whim, she pulled Heather's bed away from the wall and angled it closer to the window so she could catch the breeze better. She smoothed the sheets and turned down the bed, tidied the nightstand, and cleared off the overbed table where Heather ate her meals. Then she quickly rearranged the bouquet of grocery store flowers Brad had bought before he left and set it beside Heather's plate.

When her sister-in-law emerged from the bathroom, she took in the scene and eased back into the bed with a sigh. "I was just in there washing my hair and thinking I wasn't sure I could stand to be in this room for another day, let alone the weeks I probably have to go. And look at you! I come out to my own pretty little Airbnb vibe."

"I'll put the bed back whenever you want, but I thought it would be nice to open the windows at least until it gets too hot."

"I love it. How about we rearrange the furniture every day?"

"Ah, trick you into thinking you're in a different room each day. Good idea. But don't *you* dare move so much as a throw pillow."

"Don't worry. I promised Brad."

She studied her sister-in-law. "You still feeling okay? No contractions?"

"Everything's good. Not so much as a cramp." Heather picked up her fork and studied her plate. "This looks great. Brad never mentioned what a good cook you are."

"Ha! Thanks for the compliment. I actually love cooking. I'm just rarely home long enough to do it. Brad probably has no idea. But I've really enjoyed this. It's nice when somebody else is making the shopping lists and menus, and all I have to do is hop in the car and go pick up the ingredients."

Heather reached across the table and patted her hand. "Let's pray so we can eat before it gets cold." She bowed her head and said a short blessing over their breakfast. When she looked up, she caught Liesl's eye. "I hope you know how much I appreciate everything you've been doing for me, Lees."

"I just hope Brad picks up the slack when I have to leave."

"He will." Heather looked confident. "He's been a rock star. He really has."

Liesl smirked. "Yeah, for two days before he left you to go to the conference. I'm talking about the long haul."

"I'm not worried," Heather said over a bite of muffin. "Your brother always rises to the occasion."

"Brad *is* one of the good ones, isn't he."

"The best. I hope your guy is just like him."

She hesitated, not sure how much she was ready to share. But before she could respond, her phone buzzed from her pocket.

Her expression must have given her away because Heather laughed. "Speak of the devil."

"Sorry, I'll just be a minute. Zach is getting his cast on today." She opened the text message and started laughing. Turning her phone toward Heather, she showed her the bright purple cast on Zach's upraised arm. He was grinning like a little kid in the picture.

"Is that *purple*?"

"Looks like it to me. He didn't tell me he was going to go crazy." She texted an LOL emoji and typed:

> Liesl: I'd ask if everything went okay, except I can see that something went horribly wrong.

"You didn't tell me he was drop-dead gorgeous," Heather whispered. "My goodness. No wonder you're crazy about the man."

She laughed. "You don't have to whisper. And yeah, even with two black eyes, he is pretty cute, isn't he?"

Heather feigned a swoon then quickly sobered. "But looks aren't what's important."

"I know that. But he's as nice as he is nice to look at."

Her phone pinged.

> Zach: Hey, what's the problem? You don't like purple?

> Liesl: Did you get that to match your shiners? You do know they won't still be purple in eight weeks, right?

> Zach: Six weeks. Maybe only five. Please don't make it longer than it has to be.

> Liesl: Sorry. Glad that's over. You feeling okay?

> Zach: I'd feel better if I was home. But yeah. Doing good.

She texted a heart, set her phone on the nightstand, and turned to face Heather.

"Sorry about that—"

Her sister-in-law was eyeing her with an enigmatic grin.

"What?"

"Girl, you are so in love, it's not even funny."

"What? Why did you say that?"

"Your face. Look at you! You're practically glowing. The whole time you were talking to him—or typing or whatever."

She felt her cheeks heat and made a face at Heather, secretly wishing she could go look in a mirror and see what "in love" looked like on her.

"Hey! Anybody home?" Brad's voice came from the bottom of the stairway.

"Brad!" They shouted in unison.

Heather started to get out of bed, but Liesl gently pushed her back. Laughing, she pointed at Heather's flushed face and knew then exactly how her own must have looked. "Now look who's glowing."

Heavy footfalls sounded on the stairs and Brad appeared in the doorway. He hurried to kiss his wife, plopping down on the bed beside her.

"What are you doing here?" Heather scooted closer until she was practically in Brad's lap. "You weren't supposed to get home until tomorrow."

"The boss had mercy on us. Actually, I was done with my presentations and things were super slow at the show, so he sent Marcus and me home. We were able to catch a flight at six this morning, and Marcus dropped me off on his way home." A gleam came to his eye and he acted like he was going to get up. "I can go back if you want me to."

But Liesl noticed he didn't let go of his wife's hand.

"Oh no you don't." Heather pulled him closer.

Liesl warmed at their affection, and a wave of unrestrained hope swept through her.

Chapter Thirty-Four

Brad helped Liesl scoot the living room recliner into the breakfast nook, then he carried Heather downstairs so she could watch while he and Liesl made lunch.

"I can't tell you how good it is to get out of that bedroom." Heather stretched out in the chair, turning her head toward the kitchen.

"Yeah, well, you're going right back in that bedroom after dinner." He resumed chopping onions for the guacamole they were making to go with the tacos.

Heather groaned good-naturedly and looked around the space. "The only bad thing about being down here is I see all the dust that's accumulated while I've been lounging in bed.

"Don't you worry about the dust. I'll dust tonight," Liesl told her.

"You'll do no such thing," Brad said. "A little dust never hurt anybody. Besides, you need to call that boyfriend of yours. How's he doing?"

Liesl told him about the purple cast and Zach's plans to start driving back tomorrow.

"Why don't you rent a car and go help him drive home?"

"I thought about that, but then I wouldn't have any time with you."

He motioned between them with the knife he was using. "What do you call this?"

"This is great, but I'd have to leave this afternoon if I'm going to get there before Zach leaves early in the morning. I'd have to arrange for a rental car and get a hotel room... I think it's just too short of notice."

Her brother thought for a minute, then lifted a finger as if testing the direction of the wind. "How about this? If Heather's friends can come and stay with her during the day tomorrow, I'll drive you to Arkansas and then you can help Zach drive back. Didn't you say he was renting a car?"

She nodded, excitement growing at the possibility.

"If we left super early, maybe six, we'd be there by 10. That way, between the two of you, you could drive it straight through like you did to get here. And he won't have to spend two or three days getting home. And"—Brad winked—"then I can meet this yahoo and see if he's worthy of my sister."

Laughing, Liesl smacked his arm. "And you and I will have four whole hours to yak."

"Oh." Brad's shoulders slumped as if he hadn't yet thought of that aspect. "Never mind. Deal's off."

"I'll be quiet, I promise. But—" She brushed off his teasing and turned to her sister-in-law. "This isn't really fair to you, Heather. Brad just got home. I can't do that to you..."

"You can and you will. I'll have all night with him, and I wasn't expecting him to get home until tomorrow anyway. Please say yes, Lees! I'm just jealous I won't get to meet this guy."

"Oh, I wish you could. Are you *sure* about this, you guys?" She wanted to cry at their kindness. But even as selfish as she felt putting them both out like this, it felt like the perfect solution.

"Listen here, sister!" Brad laid down the knife, wiped his hands, and took her by the shoulders. "Do you want to be with this guy or not? He needs your help. You need to be with him.

God is handing you this opportunity on a silver platter. Take it!"

She gave him a sidewise glance. "God seems to be getting an awful lot of help from Brad and Heather."

Brad and Heather laughed, and her brother pulled her into a one-armed embrace. "You can come and see us again when your niece gets here."

"I can't wait for that!" She gave him a full-on hug, reaching out a hand to the recliner to include Heather. "I love you guys so much. How can I ever thank you?"

Brad pushed her away. "Now don't get all sappy on me."

She leaned back and looked at him. "Are you *crying*?"

"Of course not. It's those stupid onions." He hooked a thumb toward the offending vegetables.

She laughed. "Okay. It's a deal. If Zach agrees, I'm going. Thank you!"

Heather scooted up in the chair. "You can thank us by getting your butt up to your room and packing. Right after you make me a taco, that is."

ZACH YAWNED and waited for a mild wave of nausea to pass. Either he'd picked up some bug in the hospital or this was a reaction to getting off the pain meds. He'd only taken four or five doses of the prescription drugs since the accident, and nothing but ibuprofen since Monday. He wouldn't drive until he was sure it was safe, but he would go stir-crazy if he had to stay in this hotel another day.

When he talked to Sadie this morning, even though she assured him everything was going okay, he sensed she was getting antsy. And he couldn't risk her quitting on him. He was going to need her help more than ever when he got back to the inn since he needed to start looking for a truck to replace the one he'd totaled, plus he'd have all the insurance stuff to deal with.

As much as he hated the thought, maybe it was a good thing Liesl wouldn't be there when he got back to the inn because he wasn't going to have time for one extra thing.

His phone rang and he picked it up, smiling. *Liesl.*

He tapped Accept. "Hey you."

"Hi. How are you feeling?"

"Pretty good. Not a fan of lugging this stupid cast around, but it went okay, I guess. My doctor seems pretty happy with how it's healing."

"Good. Does it hurt?"

"Not too much. Ibuprofen helps. And it's better when I don't think about it."

"I bet. So..." Hesitance laced her voice. "What's the plan? For going home, I mean."

"I had the Uber driver drop me off at the rental place this morning, so my car is here at the hotel ready to go. It wasn't as bad as I thought it might be, driving left-handed. I was hoping to leave first thing in the morning, but I'm not sure. Right now I'm feeling a little queasy, so I guess I'll just wait and see how I feel in the morning. To tell you the truth, I'm going a little stir-crazy."

"Okay... Let me run something by you."

"What's that?"

"You can say no... I don't want to be pushy, but what if I came tomorrow and helped you drive back?"

"Came here? But how would you get here?"

She told him that her brother had come home early and offered to drive her to Hot Springs. "We'd leave early in the morning, but we still wouldn't probably get there till ten, so I understand if you wanted to be on the road sooner. But this way, you'd have help driving so we could drive straight through. I could get my car and..." Her voice trailed off.

He wished she would have finished the sentence. Since she'd left here on Monday, he was in the dark about what she'd been thinking about their future. But the idea of seeing her again cheered him considerably and made him forget about the nausea and pain. "You're not just doing this to return a favor?"

"No. I promise. But what if I was? Would that be so bad? Honestly, Zach, I wish I could say it was my idea but it was Brad's. But it does solve my problem of getting my car back too. So it's win/win. What do you think?"

He thought for a minute before answering. "I think it sounds like the best offer I've had since you walked in the door of The Inn at Rosebud Lane."

"Awww. I bet you say that to all your guests."

"I guarantee you I do not." He grinned into the phone. "But if I get help driving home and I get to spend time with you again, what's not to like?"

"Well...about that..." That hesitation again. "I should probably warn you that my brother is looking at this as a chance to interrogate— Er, I mean to *meet* my new boyfriend."

He laughed. "I don't blame him. If you were my sister, I'd be looking out for you too."

"Brad's a big teddy bear, but he might give you the third degree."

"We'll see if I pass the test. I guess if I don't, that might give us our answer."

"Our answer about what?"

"Whether we are 'meant to be.'"

She huffed "My brother is not going to pick out my boyfriends. But I'm not worried. How could he help but love you."

"Wait a minute. Boyfriends? Plural?"

She laughed. "Figure of speech. So you're good with this plan?"

"Golden."

"Yay!" She sounded a little giddy.

Which was exactly how he felt. "Okay then, I'll see you tomorrow. You and Detective Brad."

"I'll tell him you said that," she said wryly. "Now I'd better go pack."

Chapter Thirty-Five

After a tearful goodbye to Heather, Liesl and Brad got on the road before sunrise the next morning. They sipped too-strong coffee from Dallas Cowboys travel mugs and made small talk.

Somewhere past Greenville, the sun popped over the horizon, and for the next hour, she apologized to her brother every ten minutes for making him drive with the sun in his eyes.

"You don't *make* me do anything, little sister."

He drove on with the visor down and eyes on the road, but a while later, when a cloud graciously hid the sun, he turned to her and got down to business. "So you think this guy's the one, huh?"

She laughed. "I wondered when you were going to get around to this conversation. And after all you've done to get me to him, I'll feel terrible if he's *not* the one." But she turned serious, not wanting to waste a chance to get her big brother's opinion. "I really do think he might be, Brad."

"Well, if he's not, don't keep hanging out with him just because we've invested half our lives in this deal."

She reached across the console and gave him a sisterly punch. But sobering again, she added, "What if he's *not* the one. And how do you even know? When were you absolutely one hundred percent positive that Heather was the one?"

"The second after we said 'I do.'" Brad didn't sound like he was joking.

"No, really. I'm serious, Brad."

"So am I. I loved Heather and more importantly, I genuinely liked her. But I couldn't be positive she was 'the one' until I promised to love, honor, and cherish her in front of God and a whole bunch of people."

"Wait. So you married her not knowing for sure she *was* the one?"

"Not exactly. I was pretty sure. But once we said 'I do,' after that if I ever thought maybe I'd been wrong and she *wasn't* the one, I was stuck with her anyway. Neither of us believe in divorce and so that was our ground rule: We don't even bring up the D-word. We're in this for the long haul. No matter what."

"*You* might not believe in divorce, but that doesn't mean it doesn't happen. To a lot of people. It almost happened to Mom and Dad."

"But it didn't. They stuck it out. And I think they're both glad now."

She nodded. Yes, Mom and Dad had stuck it out, but only after they'd inflicted a lot of damage on her and Brad.

He went on. "But as far as it depends on you, you can choose not to let it happen. I wish people would worry less about *finding* the right person and worry more about *being* the right one."

She thought about that for a long time. And prayed she could somehow figure out the secret to being the right one for Zachary Freylan.

As if he'd read her thoughts, Brad spoke quietly. "It's one day at a time, sis. It's a marathon. And it means being competitive. Super competitive."

"What?" She looked askance at him. "You and Heather aren't competitive. At least not with each other. Well, except maybe when we're playing Uno."

He grinned. "Not that kind of competitive. We decided a long time ago to try to outdo each other in kindness and little favors and selflessness. Heather's pretty good at it too." He tossed her a smirk.

"Yeah, I was gonna say…" She laughed and her heart swelled with a new admiration for this brother of hers and for a marriage she wanted to emulate.

They talked the rest of the trip. Brad shared wisdom she'd never expected to hear from her big brother and her admiration for him grew.

When they got close to the hotel, she texted Zach.

> Liesl: We're about five minutes out. Shall we come to your room?

> Zach: I'm all packed, so I'm going to go ahead and check out, but we can talk in the lobby if you want to. Or better yet, I'll meet you by the pool. It's not too hot yet and nobody's out there right now. This way, if your brother gets out of hand, I can dunk him. :)

She laughed.

"What?" Brad peered across the console at her phone.

"Zach's plotting to throw you in the pool if you get out of hand."

"Tell him that is not a good way to start off a relationship with your future brother-in-law."

"Brad! We're not engaged or anything."

"Yeah…we'll see about that."

"Don't you dare say anything to him about that. We've only known each other for a month."

"Yeah, but you've been living with him that whole time." He winked.

"Brad! I have not! Cut it out."

He laughed and reach over to pat her knee. "Don't worry. I'll be on my best behavior."

And he was.

Liesl had been more nervous than she expected about having Zach and her brother meet, but the two of them hit it off immediately, and after a few minutes it was as if they'd completely forgotten she was even there.

She loved watching them talk and sat there with a beautiful view of the lake, listening quietly to their conversation, and falling more in love with Zach by the minute. She couldn't help but entertain visions of him being part of their family, visiting in Dallas with Brad and Heather and the baby...and maybe with a baby of their own some day.

Heat rose to her cheeks at her thoughts. She was getting way ahead of herself. But the two men seemed not to notice.

Finally, after almost forty minutes, Brad rose and extended his right hand, then quickly switched to his left. "I should probably let you two get on the road."

Zach shook his hand, then pulled Brad into a brotherly hug. They clapped each other's backs and called each other bro, and Liesl's heart soared.

Brad hugged her and the wink he gave her clearly said he approved. "Let me know when you get back, okay, kiddo?"

"I will. Keep me posted about Heather."

"I will. You keep me posted on"—he cleared his throat and shot her a pointed look—"other stuff too, huh?"

She gave him a playful shove, hoping Zach hadn't heard. "Now, get outta here."

As happy as she was to be with Zach again, a heaviness seemed to hang in the air between them. Liesl looked over at him from her place behind the wheel. She thought he was feeling it too. But maybe he was just feeling off because of his arm and the unfamiliar cast.

She'd offered to drive the first shift, since he'd said he was feeling a little queasy. She'd driven for almost five hours before he offered to take over. Now they were two hours from home and she was driving again. She didn't mind. She was just thankful he was here beside her. And the hours had gone too fast as it was.

Except for when Zach fell asleep for a few minutes, they'd talked the whole time. Just not about what was foremost on her mind. Not about what came next for them.

They drove another hour in silence. He was so quiet, she'd started to worry that something was wrong. She was relieved when he reached across the console and took her hand.

"Thank you for doing this. It was a really good idea."

"It was. Brad gets the credit though."

"I like your brother. I can see why you speak so highly of him."

"He's the best. It was really good to spend time with him and Heather."

"I'm sorry it got cut short on my account."

"It really didn't, Zach. In fact, I probably had the best visit I've ever had with Brad on the way here." She didn't tell him that she and Brad had mostly talked about Zach. And about marriage. "And I'll be coming back in a few months when the baby is born."

"That'll be good. A few months. So..." He squeezed her hand. "Where do you see yourself in a few months?"

"I'm not sure." She trained her eyes on the road, not trusting her voice. "The next book—after St. Charles—is set in Iowa. Figured I should do something on my home turf."

"You have a contract for that one already?"

She nodded. "That's the last one in this current contract, but I think I can write for this publisher as long as my books keep selling."

"So, I've been thinking." He loosened his seatbelt and shifted in his seat, angling in her direction. "How would you feel about relocating your home turf?"

"Relocating? To where?" She held her breath, not sure she was ready for what he might be proposing.

"Where do you think, silly?"

She shrugged, not willing to guess wrong.

"How would you feel about making the inn your home base? I don't know what you pay for rent on your apartment, but I could rent your room to you for what you're paying now, and you could come home—to the inn, I mean—as often as possible while we make sure this is what we both want. Unless you've had second thoughts—"

"Zach... No, I'm not having second thoughts about us. No." She was as relieved as she was disappointed that he wasn't proposing. And yet, his solution felt altogether possible and, for now anyway, it was a kind of pre-proposal. "I—"

"Shh." He untangled his fingers from hers, but kept hold of her hand, his thumb making aimless circles on the inside of her wrist. "You don't have to decide now, but I just want you to know that I'm not willing to let you go so easily. Maybe I'm wrong, but I think you feel the same."

"You know I do. But my lease isn't up until January."

"You don't think you could get out of it?"

"I'm not sure. But I could—"

His phone rang. He let go of her hand, fished his phone from his pocket, and checked the screen. "It's Sadie. Sorry, but I should probably take this." He raised her hand to his lips and kissed it. "To be continued."

"Of course." She was grateful for a reprieve. To consider what he'd suggested.

"Hey, Sadie. How's it going?"

Liesl couldn't understand what Sadie was saying, but alarm rose in her at the shrill tones coming through the phone.

"Sadie. Sadie, calm down," Zach said. "I can't understand what you're saying."

More panicked cries. Liesl slowed the car and let traffic pass her.

Zach's brow furrowed and he leaned forward, straining to listen.

"No, I'm on the road home now, but it's going to be almost an hour before we get there." A pause, and Zach's expression grew more concerned by the second. "Are you sure? Okay, Sadie. Listen to me. You need to call 911."

Chapter Thirty-Six

Zach gripped his phone, his heart pounding. "Where are you right now, Sadie?"

"I...I'm at the inn. I came to clean and he was here... waiting for me."

"He's there right now? At the inn?"

"Yes!" The word came on a wail.

"Is he right there beside you?"

"He—he's in your office. He locked himself in." He turned to Liesl and mouthed, "Davis."

She gave him a questioning look, but he didn't dare stop to explain.

"And where are you, Sadie?"

"I'm at the inn!"

"No, I mean what room are you in?"

"Oh... The kitchen. I'm in the kitchen."

"Okay. Sadie, I need you to stay on the line with me, okay?"

"Okay." Her voice trembled and he could almost picture her cowering in fear.

"I want you to go in the powder room and lock yourself in there, do you hear?"

"Okay."

"Now, hang on just a minute, okay. Don't hang up." He tapped Mute and turned to Liesl. "I need you to call 911 and have them send a deputy to the inn. You'll need to tell them it's in Buncombe County and give the address."

"What on earth?" Her panicked expression must have mirrored his own, but she did as he asked, holding her phone over the steering wheel. With one eye on the road, she steered with her wrists while she dialed the number.

He took his phone off mute. "You there, Sadie?"

"I'm here." Her voice was barely a whisper.

"Are you locked in the bathroom?"

"Uh-huh."

"And Davis is still in my office?"

"I think so. I'm not sure."

"That's okay. You just stay where you are." He wracked his brain trying to think what to do. He prayed none of the guests were involved. "Sadie, did Davis say what he wants?"

"He wants...to die."

Oh, dear Lord. Be with them. Please, God... "Is anyone else there at the inn? Any of the guests?"

"There was a couple out on the back porch earlier, but I don't think they heard us. Nobody else has checked in yet today."

"Okay. Okay, good. Did he say why he wants to die. Do you think he plans to...harm himself?"

"He has a gun," she whimpered.

"Are you sure?" The nausea came back with a vengeance.

"I didn't see it, but he said he did. Zach... He said he was going to shoot himself."

His breath left him and he fought to keep his voice steady. "Did he say why?"

"He said..." She dissolved into sobs. "He said he killed someone."

"Just now? At the inn?" His pulse ramped up.

"No. No, years ago. Two years ago, I think he said." He struggled to hear her over Liesl's conversation with a dispatcher.

"Did he say who he killed, Sadie? Or how he did it?" His mind swirled. What had made Davis decide to involve Sadie after all this time?

"I think he really did. Kill someone, I mean. Not on purpose. But I believe him."

"Okay. Well...let's stay calm, okay? Are you still safe?"

"I'm still locked in the bathroom. But I don't hear Davis."

"Don't worry about him right now. You just stay where you are. And stay away from the door. As much as you can." He didn't want to scare her, but he cringed, thinking how vulnerable she was in that room if the guy actually had a gun.

"We've called the sheriff and they're sending someone." He looked over at Liesl for confirmation.

She nodded, gripping the steering wheel tightly, but she quickly turned her attention back to her phone, apparently still on the line with the dispatcher.

He checked the time. Three o'clock. New guests could start checking in any time. "Sadie, are you still there?"

"Yes. I'm here." The girl sounded a little calmer.

"Did Davis say who he killed?"

A pause so long he thought for a minute she'd hung up. But finally, her answer came. "I...I can't say."

"What do you mean? He didn't say?"

"He said who, but...I can't tell you."

"Why? Did he threaten you, Sadie?"

"Kind of." She said something he couldn't make out. He checked and saw he only had one bar on his phone.

Liesl drove for an agonizing mile before they got into an area with reception again. "Are you still there, Sadie?"

"I'm here."

"Can you explain what you meant?"

Silence.

"Listen, this is important. You need to tell me everything."

Liesl held her phone out and whispered, "The dispatcher wants to talk to her. Can I put him on speaker phone?"

"Just a minute," he mouthed, holding up his casted hand. Pain seared through his wrist and he winced. "Pull over when you can so we don't lose reception again. We're not far from that patchy spot before you get to Sorrel Hollow."

She nodded and slowed the car.

"Sadie, the 911 dispatcher wants to talk to you. Is that okay? I'm going to put him on speaker phone, all right?"

"Okay." Her reply was no more than a squeak.

An exit appeared in the righthand lane, and Liesl slowed the car and descended the ramp. Near the bottom she pulled the car over and parked on the wide shoulder.

Good. Four bars. Zach nodded his approval. He could hear much better now. "Sadie, I'm going to put you on speaker now." He tapped the icon. "Can you hear me okay?"

"Uh-huh."

"I'm putting you on speaker," Liesl told the dispatcher.

"Hello? Is this Sadie?" the man spoke in a calming tone.

"Yes."

"Sadie, my name is John. I'm with the dispatchers' office and we're going to help you. Okay?"

"Okay? Is...is Zach there?"

He leaned close to the phone, holding it up, hoping for better reception. "I'm still here, Sadie. We have two phones on speaker so it might be a little hard to hear, but I'm here on the call with you. Please tell John everything you told me, okay?"

"Sadie?" The dispatcher spoke up and Liesl held her phone closer to Zach's. "Sadie, can you tell me your full name and the address where you are?"

"Sadie Jane Mitchell. I don't know the address... Zach? Oh, it's on Rosebud Lane. But I don't know the num—"

"Yes, 421 Rosebud Lane," Zach confirmed.

"And can you explain your emergency?"

Zach was proud of Sadie as she repeated what she'd already told him.

"Are you safe where you are now, Sadie?"

"I'm locked in a bathroom. I...I don't know where Davis is now. But I think he's still in Zach's office."

"The office on the premises at the inn? Does Davis have his phone with him? Can you give us his number?"

"I don't know. I think he had it." She rattled off the number.

Zach broke in, hoping he wasn't sabotaging some plan the dispatcher hadn't let him in on. "There's a landline phone in my office you could call if he doesn't answer his cell."

"Yes, good," John said.

Zach gave him the number.

The dispatcher talked to Sadie. Mostly small-talk. Zach assumed John was trying to gain her trust. He soon steered the conversation back to the urgent situation. "Are you sure Davis said he killed someone?" John asked.

"Yes."

"When was this? And *who* did he kill?"

"Um..." Her voice faltered. "Is Zach still there?"

Zach opened his mouth to answer, but something caused him to remain quiet.

"You can tell *me*, Sadie," John said. "I need to know so we can help him. Help both of you."

Zach waited, curious what she would say.

"He... Davis said he killed *Zach's wife*."

The air squeezed from his lungs.

Chapter Thirty-Seven

Zach turned to Liesl. She shook her head, feeling as baffled as he looked.

Cars flew by them where they were parked on the shoulder of the exit ramp. Zach was still on the phone with Sadie, but he kept silent, listening to her conversation with the dispatcher.

Liesl didn't dare get back on the Interstate for fear they'd lose the phone connection, but she was starting to feel a little unsafe as traffic increased, going considerably faster than the exit's forty-miles per-hour speed limit. And from the bits of conversation she'd heard, it sounded like there was an urgent need for Zach to get back to the inn.

The dispatcher had told them officers were en route to the inn, and Sadie seemed to have calmed down, but if Davis actually had a gun...

The dispatcher asked Zach to take Sadie off speaker phone because he was having trouble hearing. "Mr. Freylan, I'm going to ask you to hang up so I can call Sadie on her cell phone and use that direct line. We'll keep Ms. Bachman on the line there. Are you comfortable with that?"

Liesl could tell he wasn't, but he agreed anyway.

"Ms. Bachman, I'm going to put you on hold, but please don't hang up. Can you verify your number please, in case we get disconnected?"

She gave him the number. "I'm going to give Zach my phone now since I'm driving."

"Yes, that's good. Stay on the line and I'll keep you updated."

She handed the phone to Zach, but it went silent almost immediately.

She looked over at him, feeling the tension in the air. "How far are we from home now?"

"Probably thirty minutes." He raked a hand through his hair. "I'm going to give you permission to make use of that lead foot of yours."

She nodded and sped up to almost eighty. *Lord, please don't let us get pulled over.* Although, a police escort might not be a bad idea given the circumstances.

She drove in silence, peering over at her phone in Zach's hand every few miles. The dispatcher hadn't checked in since he put her on hold.

Finally she broke the silence. "What do you think it means... he killed your wife?"

He shook his head. "I don't know. But...I keep thinking about that day when I showed you the spot where Jenny's accident happened. And that car was there, remember? You thought it might have been Davis's car?"

"But you said Jenny died in the hospital a while after the accident."

"Yes, thirty six days later. I was with her when she died, so I know he didn't kill her. It must have something to do with the accident."

"You think he *caused* the wreck?"

He blew out a heavy breath. "It has to be something like that."

It felt like forever before they finally came to Willowtree's city limits and then turned onto Rosebud Lane. Before they'd gone a block, they could hear the sirens wailing and see the strobing lights on emergency vehicles in front of the inn. Two sheriff's cruisers and an ambulance were parked at angles in front of the inn.

Liesl drove around behind the house to where Zach usually parked his truck. Zach scrambled out of the vehicle, and she followed, leaving her purse and everything else behind. He motioned for her to follow him around to the basement entrance.

But before they reached the door, a woman in a county sheriff's uniform came running around the side of the house, her right hand poised over her holstered gun.

"Sir! Sir, you can't go in there."

Zach approached the officer while Liesl followed, staying just close enough to hear what they were saying.

"I'm Zach Freylan," he told the female officer. "I own the inn. Is everything okay? Is Sadie still inside?" He explained what they already knew about the incident.

"She's with two other officers in the hallway. She's safe. They're trying to talk the young man into coming out."

"Does he have a gun? Sadie said he might."

"We haven't been able to verify that. We're proceeding as if he does." The officer looked past Zach to Liesl and motioned her closer.

Zach put his good arm around her. "This is Liesl Bachman... my girlfriend. Liesl was the one talking to the dispatcher when I first got Sadie's call on our way back from Arkansas."

The woman gave a perfunctory nod. Liesl returned it.

Zach glanced toward the inn. "Can you explain why Davis said he killed my wife?"

She eyed him as if deciding how much to say. "He said he ran her off the road the night of her accident. He claims it was an accident. That he wasn't even sure what had happened until he saw it on the news the next day. But he's distraught. The girl said he was going to turn himself in, but then he backed out and became suicidal."

Zach frowned. "Is he still threatening to kill himself?"

"I haven't been inside for a while. I couldn't say."

"What about my guests? Is there anyone else inside right now?"

"No sir. We cleared the premises. I believe there were only three people here when we arrived, not counting the suspect and the girl."

"Okay. Thanks. Could I go in and talk to Davis? Try to get him off the ledge, so to speak?"

The woman seemed to consider it, then held up a hand. "Hang tight." She radioed someone and after a brief conversation, waved Zach toward the house.

A frisson of panic inched up Liesl's spine. "Be careful, Zach. Please?"

He pulled her close for a moment. "I will. Please pray God gives me the right words."

"I already am."

Watching him walk away, she'd never felt such love for anyone. Or such apprehension about what he was walking into.

ZACH CLIMBED the steps to the front porch and knocked softly. It felt strange to knock on his own door, but even though the officer had radioed that he was coming, he wasn't sure what was happening inside. Through the sheer curtains he could see shadowy figures moving around in the entryway.

Right now, he couldn't let himself think about what this whole thing might mean for the inn, but the question weighed heavy in the back of his mind. Even so, Davis Simmons's life was far more important.

A moment later, the door opened and a lanky, male deputy let him in.

Sadie saw him and almost knocked him over with an uncustomary hug. "I'm sorry. I never should have let him come over."

He held her at arm's length. "Are you okay?"

She nodded, not *looking* okay in the least. Her eyes were red and her hair hung in limp strands around her face.

The deputy motioned for him to follow and led him back to the kitchen. "I'll talk to you in a little bit, Sadie," he said over his shoulder.

The deputy closed the door between the kitchen and the hallway. "We're not getting anywhere with him. He's confessed to causing the accident that killed your wife. Says he didn't mean to. That it was raining that night and he didn't see her when he came around the curve until it was too late. He's remorseful but threatening to kill himself. Says he can't go to prison."

"Would he? Has anyone told him he wouldn't?"

"We can't guarantee that, and we're not going to make empty promises."

"It was two years ago. He would have only been sixteen when it happened. Maybe seventeen. He wouldn't be tried as an adult, would he?"

"You'd have to talk to an attorney about that."

"But if it was an accident..." Zach couldn't explain the lack of anger he felt. When he'd thought about this weeks ago when the insurance people had first brought up the possibility that there'd been a second car involved in the accident, he hadn't even wanted to think about the prospect of having to forgive someone for causing Jenny's death. But now that there was a face to the person responsible—a face he knew—now that a young man was actually considering ending his own life because of something that was an accident—or at worst, a case of teenage carelessness—he felt a strange peace envelope him. He could forgive. He'd been forgiven much himself.

He turned to the deputy. "I'd like to talk to him if I could."

"We need to find out for sure if he has a weapon."

"I understand. But maybe if everyone else goes...leaves me alone to talk to him, I might be able to calm him down."

The two deputies in the hallway conferred and set a few

ground rules. "At the first indication that he's going to use that weapon, you walk away. Understand? We'll have you covered. No heroics."

"What about Sadie?"

"The girl's mom is on her way. We'll have them wait outside."

Zach nodded, already praying.

The lanky deputy climbed the stairs that led to Liesl's suite. The other one went back to the kitchen where they'd taken Sadie.

Zach knocked on the door to his office. "Davis? It's Zach. Can I come in and talk to you? Please?"

He heard rustling behind the door. It sounded like his desk chair rolling across the hardwood. "No." The voice sounded weak, resigned.

"Please, Davis. I have something important to tell you." He waited a few seconds. "I'm alone. It's just you and me talking. Please open the door."

He was startled when the door creaked open. He waited for it to open farther, but when it finally did, he risked pushing it open a few more inches. "Can I come in?"

No response.

A few more inches. "Davis, I'm coming in."

His office was dark, the shades and curtains all pulled and only his desk lamp casting a pale glow in the center of the room. He closed the door behind him, but didn't latch it.

It took his eyes a while to adjust to the dim light and realize that Davis was slumped on the floor underneath the windows, his head in his hands, the hood of a dark sweatshirt hiding most of his features. His hands were tucked into the front pocket of the hoodie, but Zach couldn't tell whether the pocket hid a gun. Oddly, he felt no fear.

"They told me what happened. I'm sorry, Davis. I believe you —that it was an accident." He had to work to keep his voice even. "I wish you would have reported it. I'm sorry you've had this hanging over your head for all these years."

He waited, hoping for some kind of response. But nothing.

He moved to his desk in the middle of the room and leaned against it, half-sitting, trying to get as close as he dared to the young man on the floor. "You did the right thing to confess now. I...I don't know what this will mean for you. But if it was truly an accident, there should be a way for you to...make restitution."

He hoped he wasn't lying, but he had to offer at least a sliver of hope. And surely there was a way. There had to be. "You were young, Davis. And there are a million other people who've made the same kind of mistake but just didn't...have the same consequences."

A moan rose from the floor and Davis slumped lower, his head almost between his knees now.

"Listen, I want you to know I forgive you. And if I have anything to say about it, I won't press charges."

"I didn't mean for it to happen. You have to believe me."

"I do."

"It was raining. I could barely see the edge of the road. And then I came around that curve and out of nowhere the car was just there. Right in front of me. I...I thought it was stopped in the road, but maybe it was just driving slow."

He spoke so softly, Zach strained to hear.

"I slammed on the brakes but I couldn't stop. I tried to get over. But it was like our cars were locked together. I thought I was going to go off the road too. And then the car was just...gone."

Zach closed his eyes, an image of Jenny—frightened, panicked—so clear in his mind it took his breath away. "I'm sorry, Davis," he whispered. So much to be sorry about. But he needed to find words—true words—for this young man who had carried a crushing burden for too long. *Give me the words, Lord.*

And then, they were just there. No anger. No recrimination. No bitterness. "I'm sorry you've lived with this for so long. Please accept the forgiveness God is offering you...*I'm* offering you."

"It wouldn't bring her back anyway." He spat the words as if they were sour in his mouth.

"No. It wouldn't. But that wouldn't make you any less

forgiven. That's what forgiveness—God's forgiveness—is all about. It might not change what happened in the past, it might not change the consequences, but it completely changes what happens in the future." He waited, hoping for another response. "Do you believe me, Davis?"

"I want to!" The words came on a sob. "God knows I want to."

"Then just believe. Look at me." Taking care with his right arm, he slid slowly to the floor until he was sitting cross-legged in front of Davis. "You *can* believe. God has promised that if we confess our sins, he is faithful to forgive those sins. And that means you start with a clean slate."

"Tell that to the judge."

"I'm not saying there might not be consequences, Davis. I'm not a lawyer. I don't know about that. *I* won't press charges," he said again. A thought came to him suddenly and he felt like he was meant to share it. "Davis, nothing would have made my Jenny sadder than to think that her accident had caused someone else to lose their life. Please don't make what happened worse. Make it count."

"How? How can I possibly do that?" For the first time, Davis lifted his head and looked directly into Zach's eyes. And with the light that shone there, he felt the faintest promise of hope in the midst of such brokenness.

Chapter Thirty-Eight

Liesl checked her phone and shifted in the driver's seat, then peered out the windshield. The sheriff's officer had advised that she "go home." But when Liesl explained that she was staying at the inn, the woman suggested she wait in her car. So here she sat.

Almost an hour had passed since Zach had gone inside, and other than the officer pacing the premises, there hadn't been any activity. Lights burned in almost every room on the first floor except for Zach's office—where Sadie had said Davis was holed up.

She noticed that the lights that were on in a couple of neighboring houses when they'd pulled in were off now. No doubt those neighbors were watching through drawn curtains, wondering what on earth was going on at the inn.

Watching the minutes crawl by on her phone, Liesl rolled down the car windows so she could hear if something, *anything*, happened that might offer reassurance. But crickets. Literal crickets—or maybe they were cicadas?—chirping so loudly they drowned out any other sounds.

The night was warm and humid, but every so often, a breeze would sweep through the car.

The officer started another patrol of the property's perimeter, but halfway down the driveway, she stopped and seemed to be speaking to someone on her radio. She changed direction and walked swiftly around the side of the house before disappearing from sight.

A few minutes later, she reappeared with Sadie by her side. Sadie walked with her head down. They didn't seem to be talking, but it was hard to tell with the constant drone of cicadas.

It was all Liesl could do to not get out and talk to Sadie, but she knew better than to interfere. To her surprise, the officer led Sadie straight toward her car. Liesl got out slowly and closed the car door behind her. "Hi Sadie. Are you okay?"

The girl nodded, her face a mask of abject misery.

"Sadie wanted to talk to you." The officer looked apologetic. "If that's okay..."

"Of course." She put an arm around the girl and Sadie leaned in heavily.

"I'll be right over there if you need me." The woman pointed toward the inn. "We finally got hold of Sadie's mom. She's on the way to pick her up now."

"Is everything all right inside?" she whispered.

"They're still talking, but...things have de-escalated."

Liesl nodded and the officer walked away.

"I'm so sorry, Sadie. Are you sure you're okay?"

"I...I will be. I heard the deputy tell the other guy that Davis didn't really have a gun."

"I'm so glad." Relief surged through her and she pulled Sadie close. "He must have been feeling pretty desperate. You're sure he didn't hurt you?"

Sadie's lips formed a hard line. "Not...physically."

"I'm so sorry. If you want to talk, I'm here. You don't have to, of course," she added quickly, feeling guilty because she knew her offer was self-serving. She *needed* to hear some news.

"I was so afraid he was going to kill himself!" It came out on a sob.

"It sounds like he's okay now. Or he will be."

She nodded against Liesl's chest and the story poured out. "Davis ran Zach's wife off the road. He wasn't drinking or anything. It was totally an accident. He said he came around a curve and the car was just right there in front of him. He couldn't stop in time. He thought maybe the car had been abandoned on the road. It wasn't until he saw something about the accident in the news the next day that he knew someone was in the car. And he knocked it off the road."

"Oh, Sadie." What heavy news Davis had laid on her.

"His dad would have killed him if he knew. He's...not a nice guy. So Davis just kept quiet. But then after Jenny died, he knew he would be in a lot of trouble—maybe even get put in juvie—if anyone found out it was him. He didn't even know Zach then, but Davis said when he won that scholarship—and saw it was in Zach's wife's name—he kind of fell apart. Like it was some kind of cruel joke. He's lived with that for two years. He just finally had to tell someone."

"I'm sorry you had to carry this. It wasn't fair of him to put it on you, Sadie."

"It's okay. He had to tell somebody. He was going to turn himself in, but he decided instead to—" Realization came and her words turned to wracking sobs. "I thought he was going to kill himself. But I guess it was all just to scare me."

"He was...confused. It's going to be okay, Sadie. They'll get him the help he needs."

But Sadie's sobs made her wonder if maybe Davis *had* harmed himself. The officers wouldn't necessarily have told Sadie that. She looked to the driveway where the ambulance still sat, lights strobing.

Movement in front of the house caught her attention. The front door opened, and to her deep relief, Zach stepped onto the porch. Behind him, Davis emerged, an officer on either side of him. It was too dark to tell for sure, but she didn't think he was in handcuffs.

Sadie gasped and started to go to him, but Liesl held her back. "Maybe we should wait."

The girl didn't fight her, but put her hands over her mouth, watching, barely breathing.

Zach said something to the deputies, then went to Davis and put his left hand on the kid's shoulder. She would have given anything to hear what he was saying, to know what had happened inside during the past hour.

Everyone looked calm as Davis was led to a patrol car and helped into the back seat. But Liesl suspected the aftermath might be anything but calm. For now though, she whispered a prayer of deep gratitude and hugged Sadie closer.

A few minutes later, the ambulance driver turned off the lights and backed out of the driveway. The other emergency vehicles, except for a sheriff's cruiser cleared out one by one while Zach stood on the porch talking to the deputy in low tones.

Sadie's mom arrived and hurried over to Liesl's car where she and Sadie were still huddled together.

"Mom!" Sadie flew into her mother's arms.

"I came as soon as I could. Are you okay?" The woman embraced her and gave Liesl a questioning look over Sadie's head. "I'm Theresa. Is everything okay?"

"Hi, I'm Liesl. I think things are calm now."

Theresa looked over at the sheriff's cruiser. "The police are here? What happened?"

"I'll let Sadie tell you everything."

"Come on, honey. Let's get you home."

Sadie ran back to Liesl and gave her a hug. "Thank you."

"It'll be okay," she whispered, sending up a prayer that it truly would be.

The deputy followed Theresa out of the driveway, and Liesl looked up to see Zach crossing the lawn to her.

She ran to meet him and struggled not to collapse against him the way Sadie had fallen into her. "Are you okay?"

"I'm fine," he said, his voice gruff. "How are *you*? It looked like Sadie was really glad you were here."

She nodded. "She was pretty shook up. So was I until the deputy told me things had de-escalated in there. She said Davis didn't have a gun. Is that right?"

"He didn't. I think he was just desperate."

"And you're okay? You're sure?"

He wrapped his left arm tighter around her. "I'm more than okay. But my arm is killing me and I'm ready to drop. You must be too. What do you say we get in the house and get to bed. We can talk in the morning. And unpack the car then too. What do you need out of the rental car?"

"Just my one bag. Is my room still available or should I take a different one?"

"You can have any room you like. Apparently they found rooms for all my guests at a hotel in Sorrel Hollow. We'll sort it all out tomorrow. Okay?" He sounded exhausted.

"Sure. Give me the keys and I'll get my bag."

Without speaking, he pulled out the keys and started for the rental car. She followed.

Back inside, the only sign that tonight's drama had happened was the footprints and streaks of mud on the usually shiny wood floors.

Zach blew out a sigh and gave her a quick hug. "You need anything?"

She patted the bag that hung over her shoulder. "I'm good. I hope you can get some sleep."

He hugged her briefly. "You too. We'll talk in the morning. No need to get up too early either."

She nodded, knowing he must be completely exhausted, both physically and emotionally, and no doubt in pain, too. "Good night, Zach."

He gave a little wave over his shoulder, and she climbed the stairs to a room that felt more like coming home than anyplace she'd ever called home.

Chapter Thirty-Nine

Liesl awakened to the savory scent of bacon, but until she finally opened her eyes, she couldn't remember where she was. It all returned in a nightmarish rush, and she was thankful she'd fallen asleep almost the minute her head hit the pillow last night.

But now, scenes from last night played like a movie in her head. Things could have gone so very wrong.

But they didn't. Davis didn't have a gun. He hadn't harmed himself or anyone else. There would be consequences to pay, she was sure, but tragedy had been averted—at least for Zach and her. She prayed that was true for Sadie too. And even for Davis.

Zach must be up. She smelled coffee too, but she didn't think he'd been awake enough to program the coffeemaker last night.

She hurriedly showered and dressed in wrinkled clothes from her bag. At least they were clean.

She found him in the kitchen, stirring a skillet full of scrambled eggs—left-handed. A plate of crispy bacon waited on the counter beside the stove.

"Good morning, sleepyhead." His endearment and the smile that went with it made her heart swell.

"Did you sleep?"

"Like the dead."

"Oh." She frowned. "Can we come up with a better metaphor, please?"

He laughed. "Like a baby?"

"Better. And yes, me too. Thankfully. How's your arm this morning?"

"It's okay. I'll be glad to get this stupid thing off." He held up the purple cast.

"What a night, huh?"

"You got that right." He shook his head as if he still couldn't believe everything that had transpired.

"And not just last night...a lot has happened since we left here just a week ago."

"It seems like a lifetime." He dished up eggs. "You hungry? Why don't we eat out on the back porch, since we have the place all to ourselves?"

"Sounds perfect. And I'm starving." She took two mugs from the shelf over the coffee bar and poured them full.

They ate in a familiar, comfortable silence. But when Zach pushed his empty plate away, the floodgates opened. He told her every detail about what had happened with Davis last night. He spoke matter-of-factly, without much emotion—until he told her about forgiving Davis. His voice broke then. "It was almost supernatural. In the past, I've been so grateful I didn't have to forgive someone else's mistake for the accident. But when I said the words to him—*I forgive you*—it was just almost instantly true, and I realized I *did* forgive him. Completely."

"I'm so glad, Zach. That's a burden I wouldn't want you to carry."

"No. And Davis has carried a far worse burden for too long. I could see how relieved he felt when he finally realized I was sincere. And I truly was."

"Thank you, Lord," she whispered.

"Amen," he echoed. "And I'll admit, it's a lot easier when I remember how much God has forgiven me."

She nodded, understanding more in that moment than she ever had.

"So, what will happen to him?"

Zach shook his head. "I don't know. I'm not going to press charges, of course, but the sheriff's deputy who was here last night said that even though minors can't be held liable for damages, the state could still hold him accountable and prosecute him for involuntary manslaughter if they decide it was his recklessness that caused the accident. He thought it might help that Jenny didn't die at the scene. But I don't know. I hope and pray they won't prosecute him. But the deputy said it wasn't up to me. I just want to help him however I can...no matter what happens. I feel for the kid. And I don't think it's a coincidence that he won Jenny's scholarship." His voice broke again.

"No, I don't either. It's kind of amazing when you think about it. And the fact that he was dating Sadie. It was all kind of a full-circle miracle of coincidences."

"Did you think Sadie was doing okay when you saw her last night?"

"She was pretty shaken up, but I think she'll be okay. She really does seem to love him."

"Then he's blessed." He looked across the yard, seeming deep in thought. When he looked back at her, there was a glimmer in his eyes. "I'm blessed too. Thank you for being there yesterday. Even before everything blew up, it was really...comforting to have you with me in the car. But man, after Sadie called, I'm not sure how I would have handled it if you hadn't been there."

"You would have handled it just fine. I was scared to death."

"Me too. But we kept each other strong."

"You kept *me* strong. I don't know about vice versa."

"Well, I know." He rose and started gathering up their dishes. "I need another cup of coffee. Do you want one?"

"Sure." She rose and followed him to the kitchen with their mugs. She refilled their cups while he rinsed the dishes, but when she picked them up to carry them outside, he took them from her, one at a time, and set them deliberately back on the counter.

She gave him a questioning look.

"Do you know what today is?"

"What do you mean? It's Friday, right? All these days are running together."

He nodded. "Yes, it's Friday. June 23. The day you were supposed to check out."

She shrugged. "Well, technically, it's *still* the day I'm supposed to check out." Leaving here was the last thing she wanted to do.

"It's also the day you were supposed to be getting that kiss. Well, assuming we decided there was something here"—he motioned between them—"worth pursuing."

"We never finished that conversation, did we?"

The simmering look he gave her pretty much finished the conversation as far as she was concerned.

"You were asking me if I'd be willing to move. To make Willowtree my home base."

"Willowtree, yes. I was thinking more specifically of the inn. I know you have to travel to keep your deadlines, but at least I'd know you were coming back between books. You could have your room...until we're completely sure this is what God wants for us. We can figure out the rest as we—"

"One day at a time."

"What do you think?" The hope in his eyes stirred her deeply.

"I think you were supposed to be kissing me right about now."

"Is that a yes?"

She nodded. "It's a yes to the kiss. And it's oh-please-dear-God to a future with you. Do you think we can make that work?"

He grinned. "Let me see..." The kiss he gave her, sweet and deep, held all the promise she'd ever dared to dream of—and so much more.

Epilogue

One year later

L iesl was already awake when her alarm went off. Six a.m. She hit snooze and scooted to the center of the bed to curl up close to her husband. *My husband.* Even after two months, those two words still seemed like a dream. And filled her with joy.

Zach stirred and put an arm around her, pulling her closer. "What time is it?" he mumbled.

"Six," she whispered. "I'll start breakfast. You go back to sleep."

"Mmmm. You're the best." He nuzzled her neck and within seconds, he was snoring softly again.

Before her alarm could wake him again, she extricated herself from his arms and climbed out of bed. She dressed quickly and went to the little kitchenette of their basement apartment. The first light of morning was just slanting through the window, and she unlocked the door and stepped onto the patio, the flagstones cool beneath her bare feet.

The pots of petunias and geraniums she and Zach had planted were filling out nicely, though if the forecasted rain didn't come, she'd need to water this afternoon. This little patio was her happy place and early morning was her favorite time of day at the inn. She usually brought her coffee out here to watch the sunrise. But she couldn't linger this morning. They had special guests staying. She'd promised them her cinnamon streusel coffee cake and a savory breakfast casserole, and both took almost an hour to bake. To her delight, those two dishes had gotten several mentions by their guests in reviews on the app, one even saying they would stay here again for the breakfast alone.

She tiptoed upstairs and flipped on the lights in the kitchen. Her kitchen. At her request, they'd started serving breakfast at the inn again. It was often just a buffet with homemade muffins or scones, but on weekends, she liked to make the casserole or the signature coffee cake she'd perfected from Jenny's grandmother's recipe.

But this morning, she and Zach had invited their guests to a big sit-down breakfast on the back porch.

The rich aroma of ground coffee beans soon filled the kitchen, and she started the coffeemaker. While it brewed, she flicked on the table lamps in the entryway to provide light for anyone on the hunt for their morning caffeine. Smiling, she looked up the stairway that led to the little suite where she'd spent so many nights before their wedding.

Brad and Heather and baby Clari occupied the suite this week. Little Clari Marie had made her entrance into the world on the first day of December, three weeks early. She'd spent two weeks in the NICU, but now she was a chubby, happy girl who charmed them all with her toothless smiles. It had about undone Liesl the first time she saw Zach with the baby in his arms. They'd started to talk more and more about someday giving Clari a cousin to play with.

She padded barefoot down the hallway where their other guests were staying. Room #2 was where her parents slept. She and Zach had stayed up late with Mom and Dad the last three nights playing games, watching movies, and just talking.

She'd had some good conversations with Mom, too…healing conversations that made her realize that her parents were only human, and like most parents, they'd done the best they could at the time. She was truly thankful they seemed so happy together now.

A rim of light shone under the door across the hall in #3. Glory was an early riser, but she'd graciously deferred to Liesl where the kitchen and inn were concerned, only offering advice when asked and praising Zach and Liesl for the work they'd done on the inn. Given that Glory had grown up here, Liesl didn't take lightly what a gift that was. Getting to know Jenny's mom helped her understand how much Zach had lost, and he seemed pleased that she and Glory got along so well.

Rooms #4 and #5 at the end of the hall were empty, their doors open to air them out. After everyone left tomorrow, Sadie would come and help them get all the rooms ready for the onslaught of guests next week. The girl was almost like family now that she was working more hours at the inn.

After Davis Simmons had been sentenced to community service, Sadie decided to take a break from him until they both had time to heal. Thankfully, Davis was able to remain in school on the scholarship Jenny's life insurance provided. He had a lot to overcome, and she and Zach prayed for him often.

She walked back to the entryway and entered Zach's office—*their* office to check for any messages or reservations. There wasn't much to reply to since they'd blocked off the dates this week so they could enjoy their families without the distraction of other guests. They'd done the same in April when everyone came for their wedding. Liesl smiled again, remembering.

There was still some dispute about who'd proposed to whom and when, but following Zach's accident and the ordeal with Davis, they'd mutually decided it best to wait until the lease on her apartment had expired before setting a wedding date. She thought the waiting might kill her, but the summer had actually flown by while she finished the St. Charles, Missouri book. She'd gone back to visit Zach for a few days at the end of August and only fell more in love with him. But when she returned to Iowa, even though they FaceTimed almost daily, autumn seemed interminable.

She finally moved out of her Iowa apartment on New Year's Eve, and Zach reserved the suite for her through the end of March, "with an option to renew for the rest of your life." On St. Patrick's Day they picked out their rings from a custom jewelry maker on Willowtree's Main Street and started planning a simple wedding.

Zach kept saying, "Are you sure you don't want a big wedding?" And she kept assuring him she couldn't think of anything she'd love more than a simple ceremony here at the inn with just her family.

And their April wedding had been everything she'd dreamed of.

Well, except the part where Zach was in the thick of tax season and they'd had to defer their honeymoon. He'd picked up some seasonal work with an accountant in town. The timing wasn't great, but once he'd finished his clients' returns, they took a short weekend trip—to Hot Springs, of all places.

Zach bemoaned the fact that he'd been stuck in the hospital or hotel the whole time he was there before, so he'd never gotten to explore the little town's attractions. Turned out the joke was on him, since they'd spent most of their Hot Springs honeymoon in the hotel too. Although he hadn't complained one bit about that.

They would take a longer honeymoon to St. Simons and Jekyll Islands this fall. Zach chose the islands as their destination after reading Liesl's very first Best-Kept Secrets volume cover to cover and declaring the author "a marketing genius."

Liesl frowned at the reminder of a looming deadline. She'd spent the six weeks before their wedding in Summerville, South Carolina working on another Best-Kept Secrets volume and her edits were due at the end of the month. She'd make it, but it would be tight. After that, she wasn't sure where her writing career was going, but she was exploring locations much closer to home. Zach had suggested some places he'd like to travel with her, but right now she was perfectly happy to stay right here.

She quietly closed the doors to #4 and #5 and satisfied that everything was in order, returned to the kitchen.

The scent of brewing coffee greeted her, and after setting the oven to preheat, she laid out all the ingredients for the coffee cake. She'd made the breakfast casserole the night before so it only needed to be popped into the oven along with the cake.

She was spooning the batter into a Bundt pan and layering in the streusel filling when Zach appeared in the doorway, freshly showered and shaved. "What can I do?"

"Pour some coffee if you want. The cake is just about ready to go in the oven."

"It's looking good." He stuck a finger in the mixing bowl and licked off the dollop of batter. "Once that's in the oven, do you have time for a little break?"

"Sure, let me set a timer." She slid the cake in the oven and the casserole beside it. "What do you have in mind?"

"Come on, I'll show you. But you'll need to put some shoes on. I'll meet you on the patio."

"Okay." Her curiosity piqued, she ran downstairs and came back up with her shoes and a light jacket.

"Follow me." Zach led her down the alley behind the inn. The sun crested the trees as they walked, bathing the yard in its golden light. She walked beside him in silence.

At the far end of the yard, he crossed a weedy patch and pointed to a gnarled old tree at the edge of the alley. The branches were fully leafed out now and spring green leaves quivered in the breeze.

Planting one foot in the V between two branches, he hoisted himself up, then turned and offered his hand. His left hand, she noticed. It had been a long recovery from his broken wrist, and all these months later, he still sometimes favored his right hand.

Smiling, she grabbed on and he pulled her up behind him.

"Is this your tree? On your property, I mean?"

"*Our* property," he corrected. "I discovered something pretty amazing about this tree the other day when I had the ladder out to trim some branches. Come on up." He clambered higher in the tree, which seemed to be made for climbing.

She scrambled up behind him, careful to find secure footing. She glanced down through the branches once, and seeing the roof of the inn below them, decided not to do that again. "I think I'm getting a nosebleed," she teased. "How high are we going?"

"Almost there." He climbed up one more branch, then turned and crouched on a broad, sturdy limb. "Hang on right here." He showed her which branch to grab onto and helped her scoot out beside him on a natural platform created by two parallel limbs.

When she was settled safely in the crook of his arm, he sighed. "I think I'll build us a treehouse up here someday. A place where we can escape when things get too crazy down there."

"You think things have been crazy?"

He looked sheepish. "A little. I mean, I love our families, but I'm ready to have you all to myself again."

That earned him a kiss.

When they came up for air, he gave her a sidewise glance. "You do know what today is, don't you?"

"Today? It's Sunday."

"June 23. The anniversary of our first kiss."

She shot him a look. "That was *not* our first kiss."

He had the decency to look sheepish. "Well, it was *supposed* to be our first kiss."

She lifted her head for their thousandth kiss. And prayed there would be a million more.

"But hey... I didn't bring you up here for kissing." He leaned forward and lifted a branch above them that curtained the landscape. "*This* is what I wanted to show you. Just look at the view from our future treehouse."

She followed his gaze and her breath caught. Below them a

patchwork of roofs and church steeples and narrow, winding streets gave way to a distant rolling meadow that disappeared beneath a forest.

But the image that took her breath away was the mountains, layer upon layer, deep green fading to purple and then the hazy blue that gave the mountains their name. She could make out the Seven Sisters in the distance and it thrilled her that she knew their story. These Blue Ridge Mountains had wooed her into Zach's life at just the right time. But more importantly, they had brought her back to the God who'd created her.

"The God who touches the mountains," she whispered.

Zach nodded and kissed the top of her head, seeming to read her every thought.

God's fingerprints were all over their lives, and she would be forever grateful.

DEBORAH RANEY dreamed of writing a book since the summer she read Laura Ingalls Wilder's Little House books and discovered that a little Kansas farm girl could, indeed, grow up to be a writer. Her forty-plus books have garnered multiple industry awards including multiple ACFW Carol Awards, the RITA® Award, HOLT Medallion, and have three times been Christy Award finalists. Her first novel, *A Vow to Cherish*, shed light on the ravages of Alzheimer's disease and inspired the highly acclaimed World Wide Pictures film of the same title. *A Vow to Cherish* continues to be a tool for Alzheimer's families and caregivers. Deborah is on faculty for several national writers' conferences and served on the executive board of the 2500-member American Christian Fiction Writers organization for eighteen years. She is a recent transplant to Missouri with her husband, Ken Raney, having moved from their native Kansas. They love road trips in their camper van, Friday morning garage sale dates, breakfast on the screened porch overlooking their wooded backyard, and spending time with their kids and a baker's dozen (and counting!) of precious grandkids.

Visit Deb on the Web at www.deborahraney.com.

For other books
by Deborah Raney

To learn more, visit:
deborahraney.com